Sugar Revolution

Lyle Garford

Published by:
Lyle Garford
Vancouver, Canada
Contact: lyle@lylegarford.com

ISBN 978-0-9952078-0-6

Cover by designspectacle.ca

Book Design by Lyle Garford
lyle@lylegarford.com
www.lylegarford.com

First Edition 2016
Printed by Createspace, an Amazon.com Company.
Available on Kindle and other devices.

.

Dedication

This one is for absent friends.

Prologue
November 1786
London, England

The King's mood darkened as he turned his thoughts to the situation with his son. Prince William Henry, young third in line heir to the British throne, had grown adept at manipulating the people around him and using his position to maximum advantage before he was even a teenager. Dismayed, the King turned to the rigid discipline of the Royal Navy to provide a cure. Not expected to inherit the Crown, the young Prince was thus sent to sea at age thirteen as a midshipman. But a career in the Navy was not having the intended effect on the now twenty-one year old Prince and the King's pent up displeasure was clear in his meeting on the issue with the First Lord of the Admiralty.

"Dammit, Lord Howe. I don't understand why I continue to hear reports of unacceptable behaviour on the part of my son. Please tell me the Navy has not lost its sense of discipline." The King scowled to emphasize the point and was gratified to see the First Lord squirm in visible discomfort.

"Your Majesty, it has not. I confess to a certain frustration, too, as the reports you have are correct. The Prince has continued to display impulsive and headstrong behaviour. He is manipulative of those around him, regardless of whether they are above or below him in the command structure."

"And now I hear promoting him is your answer to this? How is that to solve anything?"

"Your Majesty, I felt the burden of command might give him opportunity to find maturity. A warship Captain has no one else to blame if things go wrong and even the smallest decisions have weight. I am posting him to Antigua, where he will be under the command of Captain Horatio Nelson. The Prince's First Officer is Lieutenant Isaac Schomberg, a capable and experienced officer. I can think of no better role models for the Prince."

The King grunted and paused a moment in remembrance. "Nelson, yes. That was rather presumptuous of him to write directly to me about the smuggling issue two years ago, but I cannot fault his achievements."

The King stared away into the distance in thought for several long moments before turning back. "Lord Howe, I approve of this strategy, but I desire one thing. When you next communicate to Captain Nelson please ensure he understands what we are trying to achieve here with my son. In particular, make it clear I have direct interest in his success in this matter."

"Consider it done, Your Majesty," replied the First Lord as he rose to leave, relief at having escaped further wrath obvious on his face. "I am confident the Prince will grow quickly in his new role, especially with the guidance of Captain Nelson."

Chapter One
December 1786 to June 1787
English Harbour, Antigua

Captain Horatio Nelson rubbed his chin as he sat deep in thought in the aft cabin of his warship, contemplating the new challenge before him. Royalty had arrived on the Caribbean island of Antigua in early December 1786, borne there by the Royal Navy frigate *HMS Pegasus* as replacement for one of Nelson's squadron returning home.

Prince William Henry, now Captain of the Pegasus, was the centre of attention from the moment he arrived on the scene. With a promotion to Lieutenant at age twenty and now confirmation as Post Captain of *Pegasus*, the Prince's spectacular rise to command past many other deserving officers was interpreted as a sign he was in high favour. In turn, everyone around him wanted to be in *his* favour.

Nelson had faced his share of problems during his tenure commanding the Northern Division of the Leeward Islands squadron and the Royal Navy Dockyard at English Harbour, and the Prince was rapidly becoming yet another to deal with. From the moment the Prince appeared on the scene he had set about acting as if he were already King, manipulating everyone about him at every opportunity.

Nelson felt torn and, in honesty, had succumbed more than he wanted to the Prince's manipulative ways. Nelson picked up the First Lord's letter from the desk and sighed as he read it again. What was expected of him was clear, but Nelson felt a deep conflict within. His role was to follow orders, but no one could claim to be more loyal to the Crown. The problem was Nelson felt an overriding desire to support royalty at all costs. How to remain true to his loyalty while finding a way to influence the young Prince was the challenge.

Nelson wasn't alone in succumbing, as everyone of consequence on the island had fallen under the Prince's spell. The rest of the Navy officers on the island were disgusted at the fawning displays of support shown for the Prince. Where only days before the plantation owners and businessmen on the island had been sullen and disgruntled, in open support of the new rebel American state, the Prince's appearance transformed all of them into staunch supporters of the Crown. Prior to his arrival invitations to Navy personnel to attend social events were as rare as cold weather on the island, but endless opportunities to attend balls and dinners for the Prince and his colleagues were now forthcoming. The Prince himself was only too happy to be the centre of attention. Making it clear he was a steadfast supporter of the need for slavery to continue unabated endeared him to their hearts.

Despite his dismay at some of the Prince's behaviours, Nelson's blind loyalty wasn't his only problem. Nelson had come to *like* the Prince in the short time they had known each other. Following the bond of genuine friendship with the Prince seemed the only path Nelson could follow and, feeling certain he could succeed, he resolved to use it to steer the Prince in the right direction.

Commander Evan Ross was in a reflective mood as he cleaned up his desk in the Dockyard at the end of the day, looking forward to the Christmas season and taking a little time off.

The past three years since he arrived on Antigua had been both challenging and frustrating. Evan, then a Lieutenant, and his companion James Wilton, a master's mate, first met Captain Horatio Nelson when he had arrived at Antigua to assume command of the squadron and the Royal Navy Dockyard. The two men were recovering from injuries suffered in a fight with smugglers. Evan had lost his left arm to a gunshot that shattered the bone and James had been shot in the thigh. Abandoned on Antigua by their former Captain, the two men were in deep despair for their future until Nelson found them.

While many saw only disabled, injured men with no future, Nelson saw opportunity. He soon had them working as spies, helping to stop rampant American smuggling in the area that was starving a treasury in dire need of customs duties. Frustrated by the extent of complicity displayed by rich local plantation owners and local officials bribed to look the other way, Nelson needed the help. Evan and James gathered enough intelligence of smuggling activity to enable Nelson and his squadron to stamp it out.

Evan and James had also uncovered a plot concocted by two spies to destabilize the British held islands. The French and American agents, working in partnership, encouraged the ongoing smuggling and tried to push already sympathetic local plantation owners to rebel against excessive taxation. Unknown to the owners, however, they were also in the process of arming runaway slaves to enflame the situation when Evan and James learned of the plot. In a series of desperate actions the two men helped Nelson put a stop to it all.

Evan and James were rewarded with promotions, but with no openings on warships anywhere courtesy of being at peace, the two men had to settle for a different assignment. Notice was taken of their success with covert activities, resulting in a longer assignment to serve as naval intelligence officers to British diplomats throughout the Caribbean. For this they reported to Captain Sir James Standish, based in Barbados. For cover the two men served as commanding officers in the Dockyard, ensuring its readiness to meet the needs of warships in need of repair.

As he left his office, Evan chanced to encounter Nelson and the Prince, also leaving for the day, and together the three men walked to the gate of the Dockyard. Alice, a beautiful, black former slave prostitute who had helped Evan build informant networks around the island, was waiting outside the Dockyard for him to appear. Despite their backgrounds, Alice and Evan had fallen in love with each other. Evan bought her from her owner, a man with one of the largest plantations on Antigua who also was her father, and set her free. Alice couldn't enter the Dockyard itself as women weren't allowed on the site, but it had become a ritual to meet Evan at the end of each day to walk back to the home they shared between the Dockyard and the small village of Falmouth Harbour.

Evan stopped to converse for a moment with the Dockyard Shipwright, who had waved him over at the gate to ask him a question before he could get away. Nelson and the young Prince continued out the gate and Nelson veered off to have their coach brought around for their departure. The Prince saw Alice standing to the side, wearing a fetching white dress Evan had bought for her, and detoured over to where she stood.

When Evan finished with the Shipwright moments later he saw the Prince talking to Alice and realized immediately there was trouble. Alice had never directed her fiery anger at him, but he had seen it before and he saw the evidence on her face now. Nelson could see her anger too, and both men converged quickly on Alice and the Prince. As they got there Alice spat out a heated response to something the Prince said.

"*No*, I think *not*," said Alice to the Prince, with a hiss that lashed him as if he had been whipped.

Evan stopped beside Alice and placed his hand on her shoulder as the Prince took a step back, a look of shock on his face.

"Anything I can help with here, my dear?" said Evan.

But Nelson intervened, having already read the situation and obviously desiring to separate them fast.

"Captain Henry," said Nelson, his tone of voice carrying enough edge to convey he would brook no arguments. "We must be on our way *now* or we shall be late for our engagement. Good day, Commander Ross."

Nelson turned to Alice and paused for the briefest of moments. Seeing Evan's protective hand still on her shoulder, he gave a small bow. "Good day, madam."

Evan watched with interest as Alice recovered herself enough to offer a civil nod to Nelson, but the fire of her anger still burned in her eyes. The look on the Prince's face had turned from shock to obvious affront, but before he could speak Nelson grabbed the

Prince's elbow, steering him to their coach and getting in. Puzzled, Evan turned to Alice once they were gone. "What was that all about?"

Still smoldering with obvious anger she glared in silence after the departing carriage. Relenting, she turned to face Evan. "So who was that bastard?"

Evan raised one eyebrow, unable to resist because of the irony, while he nodded his head in the direction of the departing coach.

"Well, that bastard, as you call him, is none other than Prince William Henry, third in line to the British throne. He also happens to be Captain of the *Pegasus*, the new frigate that has joined the squadron. And the other fellow pulling him away was the good Captain Nelson himself. My God, what did the Prince say to you?"

"Huh," said Alice, as she paused to scowl at the departing coach. "God help all of us if that's the kind of beast we've got lording it over everyone."

Taking Evan's arm she nodded in the direction of their home and they began walking. Evan acquiesced, but continued giving her sidelong glances in hope she would offer more.

Sensing his gaze, she finally relented. "Look, let's say I think he's another one of these animals that see nothing but opportunity to take advantage of black women so they can indulge in their sick fantasies. We're all just ignorant slaves anyway, right, so what does it matter? I—ah, enough."

Alice gave his arm a squeeze, making a visible effort to calm down, and looked up at Evan's concerned face.

"I'm all right. He made me mad. Thank God you aren't anything like him. You're the real prince around here and you're a better one than this monster could ever hope to be."

"Hmm, well, perhaps it would be best if you stopped meeting me outside the Dockyard as a precaution to ensure no further unpleasant encounters."

By the time the holidays were over Nelson's supreme confidence he could change the Prince was already being tested to the limits and he was once again back at his desk contemplating what he now knew. More important, the question was what to do about it.

Rumours of the Prince's frequent dalliances with an endless series of black slave women made available at his whim by willing plantation owners around the island had become so prevalent any attempt to deny them was impossible. By itself this could have been manageable, but Nelson had learned the Prince's relationship with his First Officer Lieutenant Isaac Schomberg was not. Nelson was dismayed to discover the two men had been at odds with each other from almost the moment they met.

The Lieutenant, a seasoned veteran of the American Revolutionary War and a skilled seaman, was thirteen years older than the young, inexperienced Prince. Nelson understood many would sympathize with the Lieutenant, as it must have been galling in the extreme to have the Prince promoted to Post Captain rank above him at so young an age. Although everyone knew Lieutenant Schomberg was a far more deserving officer, the situation could still have worked because the Lieutenant, despite whatever frustration he felt, was at the least a dedicated officer. The real issue was the Prince failed to see all he had to do was give his Lieutenant free rein to do his job. The Prince had never been a diligent student even at the best of times, which fast became clear to the professional men of the sea surrounding him, adding to the problem.

The first bad weather they encountered on the trip outbound from England had been the start of it. If the Prince's orders had been followed the ship would have been lost. Schomberg and the rest of the crew were forced to ignore his orders and do what was necessary to save their lives. From that point the Prince felt the need to reassert his authority by interfering in even minor decisions that everyone understood were the domain of the First Officer.

By the time *Pegasus* reached Antigua the situation had degenerated to the point of regular, sometimes public shouting matches between the two officers in full view of the rest of the crew. The disdain the two men felt for each other had already hardened into an unbreakable wall between them and the damage seemed irreparable. Reluctant as he was to call his royal friend to task, Nelson had no choice.

"Captain," said Nelson, feeling disconcerted at how far gone the situation was and struggling to find some way to resolve it. "It is your responsibility to manage your people appropriately. I am loath to interfere with how you handle the Lieutenant."

"I know Horatio, but the man is trying beyond all belief."

"My Lord, please be careful how you address me, especially when we are discussing Navy business," said Nelson, with a weary voice. "I know we have quickly come to consider each other very good friends, but you could slip when others are around and this would be inappropriate."

"You are right, Captain. Well, I shall continue to do my best with the man, sir."

But it had not gone well. An unbridled shouting match in late January of 1787 observed by several witnesses from the *Pegasus* and the Dockyard forced Nelson to act and, fearing the threat to authority, he came down hard on the Lieutenant, placing him under arrest and removing him from the Pegasus. But the problem was this was not a viable solution.

Placing an officer under arrest meant the officer had reason to expect a trial of sorts, with opportunity to explain and defend his actions. Someone would be a winner and someone a loser, and word of the details of what had happened would be public. On one hand potential public humiliation of a Prince of the realm was not to be countenanced, while public punishment and disgrace of an officer known by many to be excellent at his duties was not the level of support competent professionals of the Navy had reason to expect. The matter spiraled out of Nelson's control as word of the dispute soon went beyond the borders of the Dockyard and was all over the island almost from the moment it happened.

Nelson understood from the warning signs of people's reactions how the decision was being received and it was here he made his second mistake. He saw the predicament he was in, but chose to let the decision stand and remain firm in resolute support of the Prince.

When word eventually reached the Admiralty from other sources, the First Lord shook his head in disbelief and dashed off a letter to Nelson querying what was happening. By the time Lord Howe got the response yet another complaint about the Prince's behaviour had risen to his attention. In a fit of petulance upon arrival in Antigua the Prince had refused to provide the usual paperwork in support of his supply requirements.

This led, in the eyes of the First Lord, to Nelson's third mistake. Doing his best to ignore the matter as a petty detail may have seemed reasonable to Nelson, but the immutable rules of the Navy and its bureaucracy were not to be denied. The Dockyard was required to provide regular reports to the Victualing Board, which was prompt in expressing its bureaucratic outrage at the failure as loud as it could.

The First Lord was shaking his head once again as he considered what to do, when word came the King wanted to see him on the matter. Knowing he was in for another testy meeting, the First Lord gave a resigned sigh to himself as he reached for his hat and left to attend the palace.

"Lord Howe," said the King, the tone of his voice betraying his feelings enough to make the First Lord brace himself as he sat down." Please tell me you know what is going on in Antigua with this arrest of the Prince's First Officer. More to the point, please tell me you know what in God's name Nelson thinks he is doing! I thought I made it clear you were to communicate my expectations to him."

"Your Majesty, I have only recently found out myself and I agree, the last thing we need here is a public airing of this nonsense. I have no idea what Captain Nelson is thinking, but I assure you he was told how we expected the Prince to be handled. Leave it with me to resolve and be assured there will be no scandal about this."

"I should bloody well hope not!" growled the King, but he looked mollified enough. The First Lord gave an inner sigh of relief.

Returning to the Admiralty, the First Lord wrote terse orders to Nelson to wind up his affairs and return to England. They also specified the Prince and his ship the Pegasus, minus Isaac Schomberg, were to be detached and reassigned to the Jamaica station. The First Lord's final order was to release the Lieutenant from his arrest and with as little ceremony as possible have him returned to England.

The duty Marine guarding Nelson's cabin door came in with Evan close behind him. Stamping to attention, the Marine announced the visitor's arrival. "Commander Ross to see you, Captain."

Evan came to a stop in front of the desk as the Marine left. Nelson remained standing and staring out the wide stern windows of the aft cabin of *HMS Boreas*, a sleek frigate of the Royal Navy bearing twenty-eight guns and his command for the past three years.

"Reporting as ordered, Captain Nelson," said Evan, saluting as he spoke.

The Captain waved a hand vaguely in the direction of his desk without turning away from the view. "Thank you for coming Commander Ross. Have a seat. I was taking a little break. You can remove your uniform coat and make yourself comfortable. It is beastly hot out there again today."

"I agree and thank you, sir," said Evan as he shrugged out of his coat, grateful to be out of the sun and into the more bearable interior of the cabin. With the vent windows open what little breeze was present made enough of a difference to help cool the cabin.

The stifling heat pervasive in the month of June on Antigua was a harbinger of even hotter summer months to come. English Harbour was not the best place to be during these months unless you were looking for smothering heat. The well-sheltered harbour serving as excellent protection from the devastating hurricanes plaguing the Caribbean in late summer and early fall was also well known for having a large windless area courtesy of the same geography protecting it from storms.

Evan settled in, waiting for the Captain's attention. But Nelson remained where he was for several long moments more before he gave a deep sigh.

"I shall *not* miss this place, Mr. Ross." Turning, the Captain walked over to slump into the chair behind his desk and glare at the ever-present pile of correspondence and paperwork strewn about on its surface. The look of undisguised distaste mingled with weariness on his face surprised Evan by its intensity.

"I will be up half the night dealing with all of this, Mr. Ross. Well, it must be done if I am to sail for Nevis to say goodbye and then onward to home tomorrow. It has been a long three years on this station."

The tired, drawn features and almost disheveled appearance of the Captain worried Evan. Nelson had contracted malaria earlier in his career and like many others suffered from periodic recurrences of the disease. Even the Captain's boundless energy had been no match for the fever, vomiting, and devastating headaches of the recurrent malaria bout that started over six weeks ago. While he had recovered enough to resume his duties, everyone around him knew Nelson could have used more rest. But no one was surprised to find the Captain back on his feet as soon as he was able to struggle out of bed. Captain Horatio Nelson was not a man to remain lying around any longer than he had to.

"Lieutenant Wilton and I were both pleased to know you are recovered, sir. I confess we feel the opposite to know you are leaving us. Do you have any word of your replacement, Captain?"

"No, except it is likely he will not arrive until after the hurricane season ends and the regular meeting in Barbados of Captains on station is finished. I think both a new Admiral for the Leeward Islands and Barbados will appear at the same time as a new senior officer for Antigua. In the interim Captain George in *HMS Venture* will serve as senior here."

"Thank you, Captain. Do you have any final orders for us, sir?"

Nelson shook his head. "Nothing new and, so you know, I did ask. The response was a straightforward message you are both to carry on with your cover roles as commanding officers for the Dockyard and, of course, continue to take direction from Sir James Standish in covert matters you involve yourselves in. I will leave direct orders to this effect. I can only assume this means the various parties with interest in your work are pleased with what you have accomplished. Of course, you will continue to ensure the Dockyard repair facilities are expanded as we have planned while meeting ongoing needs as they arise."

Nelson paused a moment, offering a tiny shrug to Evan. "Yes, I know. Both you and the good Lieutenant still wish for a commission afloat, but this assignment remains as all there is on offer. I confess the current peace we are enjoying is lasting a lot longer than I had thought. I think the French have too many of their own problems to let their natural arrogance get them in trouble with us again at the moment, but mark my words, though. This will not last."

"Yes, Sir James has articulated much the same thinking to me, sir."

Nelson nodded. "I'm not surprised. He is astute and we are fortunate to have him. So Commander, the real purpose of this meeting is just to say goodbye and express my appreciation for your support these past three years that have been so trying."

"Captain, I speak for both Lieutenant Wilton and myself when I say it has been an incredible honour to serve with you. We had both thought our careers were over until you found us. Thanks to you both of us have been promoted and have assignments where we can continue to serve in a way that has value."

Evan paused a moment to allow a tiny smile to crease his face. "And who knows, maybe the frogs or the Dons will oblige and create enough problems that more ships and officers like us are needed at sea some day. But seriously, on our honour, sir, if there is ever any service we offer you, we are yours to command. We both agree it would be a dream come true to serve with you once again."

"Honour," said Nelson, as he leaned back in his chair and stared away into the distance for a moment. "Yes, a conversation about honour began our relationship, didn't it?" Nelson returned his gaze to Evan, unable to keep a sad, doleful look from his face. "Honour was in short supply back then, wasn't it? And I dare say it still is, sadly."

"Sir, I completely agree," said Evan, offering a careful nod in reply. Seeing an almost maudlin Nelson was a new and unsettling experience. But then, Nelson had reason to be unhappy, as having a wayward Prince of the blood on his hands had not been his only challenge during his time in Antigua.

For a time, complete success with achieving his orders seemed within reach despite the Prince. Smuggling had dropped to almost nonexistent levels by late 1785, but then the Swedes saw opportunity where others did not. The Navigation Acts covered direct trade between America and British islands, but they did not cover trade with other islands. Exploiting the loophole, they purchased the nearby island of St. Barts from the French and declared the capital Gustavia a free port. The Americans swarmed in and the Swedes began making tidy profits shipping cargo the Americans offloaded in Gustavia to all of the islands in the area.

Nelson did what he could by sailing into Gustavia with the full might of his squadron and all the bluster he could bring to bear. The Swedes stalled for time, knowing Nelson could not start a war on his own. Nelson continued pursuing American smugglers motivated to cut the Swedes out of the arrangement. Thinking the Navy may have moved on, a few risked trying once again dealing direct with buyers via the secluded beaches that were everywhere. Seizing their ships continued to be his best weapon to deter the smuggler's behaviour, as few owners could afford the risk of having a valuable ship condemned in a British prize court.

But the Captain's cares had only grown. In August of the previous summer Admiral Richard Hughes in Barbados hauled down his flag and sailed for home, leaving Nelson as the senior officer for the entire Leeward Islands squadron. No one mourned the Admiral's departure as he had displayed a singular lack of zeal to achieve anything of consequence and, in particular, was unsupportive of anything Nelson had done. But no replacement had yet been sent and the constant stack of paperwork sitting on Nelson's desk was enormous. Combined with the challenge of managing a willful Prince, the burden was heavy indeed.

Nelson shuffled some papers on his desk absentmindedly. "You know, Mr. Ross, I have always striven to conduct myself with honour in everything I do. I am a faithful servant of the Crown, and of *all* of its representatives, and my honour demands I do what I believe is right to show this support at all times. It's a pity not everyone can see that, but my conscience is clear on this. Well, enough said, I appreciate you have come to see me today."

"Captain, I couldn't imagine you doing anything without honour, ever," said Evan as he took the cue the meeting was over and rose to leave.

"Is Mrs. Nelson joining you on the *Boreas* for the journey home, sir?" said Evan, making conversation as he deftly pulled on his uniform coat once again. Years of practice doing it using only one arm had long since made the process unconscious.

"No, Mr. Ross," replied Nelson, a real smile brightening his face for the first time since Evan had arrived. "Finding someone to share my life has been the one positive development stemming from my time out here. It was unfortunate you weren't able to attend our wedding on Nevis this spring. It was everything I could have hoped for, especially with the Prince himself there to give away the bride. Anyway, I wouldn't subject her to the constraints of a long journey on a warship. She is to follow me soon on a much more comfortable merchant ship."

"Well, Captain, once again it has been a true honour to serve with you. Lieutenant Wilton and I wish you and Mrs. Nelson all the best for the future," said Evan.

"Thank you. Mr. Ross? Write to me periodically, both of you. I will not forget the service you and Mr. Wilton have done me. I shall do what I can to have an eye on your careers."

Evan paused a moment, too moved by the unexpected offer to speak.

"Captain. We shall be eternally grateful. We are yours to command, sir."

Saluting one final time, Evan turned and left the cabin. Walking back to his office in the Dockyard he couldn't help reflecting on the impossible situation Nelson had faced. That such a dedicated servant of the Crown should end up in circumstances where no matter what he did criticism of his actions would come from the royalty he was sworn to support was a supreme irony.

Slipping into his office chair in the Dockyard and eying the pile of paperwork that had grown on it in the short time he was gone, Evan shook his head in dismay over it all.

The next morning dawned with enough of a breeze to permit the *Boreas* to sail with care out of English Harbour instead of having to submit to the laborious, grueling process of being warped out of harbour to freedom.

Both Evan and James came to watch the *Boreas* depart. The two men stood to the side out of the way of the frenzied sailors bustling about loading a few final barrels of supplies and fresh water for the long journey home.

Evan used the time to fill James in on the details of his conversation with Nelson the day before. James grunted in response and was silent for a time, digesting what he heard. Without taking his eyes from the ship James gave a small sigh.

"This isn't what he wanted, is it?"

"No," said Evan. "But we did our best for him and he knows it."

"So where does this leave us now, Evan? Are we ever going to get out of here and onto a ship? God Almighty, there must be someone out there stupid enough to start a war somewhere. Let's face it, we're both bored out of our minds."

Evan shrugged. "Who knows? I guess we carry on and we see what the future brings is where it leaves us. I have a feeling we are not done with Captain Nelson, though. We may need his support some day down the road and he may need ours."

James sighed. "Yes. You may be right. God, let's hope so."

The bustle on the dock subsided as they spoke and the lines tethering the ship to shore were cast off. The ship itself was now a hive of activity as men swarmed aloft to unfurl the sails while others on deck went about their tasks. The quarterdeck was also alive with action as the First Officer shouted a stream of orders at everyone in sight.

But one figure stood apart from the rest on the quarterdeck. As the ship gained way and came about to head for the entrance to the harbour Nelson turned to face the Dockyard one last time.

Evan and James both stiffened in response and as one the two men saluted the lone figure. Nelson reached up to his hat and raised it in brief acknowledgement before turning away. The two men continued to stand watch as the ship laboured to tack out of the harbour.

As it stood out to sea, disappearing at last from their sight, Evan sighed and turned back to James.

"Well. Let's go see what the future holds."

Chapter Two
June 1787
Paris, France

The family had been astounded when Anton read the unexpected invitation to dinner aloud to them. The well-dressed messenger that had delivered it, waiting at the front entrance for a response, was perplexed when he was summoned inside to face a barrage of questions, but he had no knowledge of reasons for the invitation. The request itself held no clues. Left to stew in frenzied, fruitless speculation all they could do was command the messenger to report they would attend and focus their energy on preparation for the event. With the day now at hand, their eyes were lit with energy in anticipation of having the mystery solved.

"My God, we're here already," said Emilie, peering out the window as the carriage began slowing to a halt. Emilie's sister hesitated before giving in to lean forward for her own quick glance too, despite a clear struggle on her face to maintain an outward, dignified calm. Their destination was a mansion in the exclusive Le Marais district of Paris, home to a host of wealthy French aristocrats.

Anton wasn't surprised at the nervous anticipation of the women, given his own inner struggle to maintain the facade he wasn't affected. Invitations to dine at this particular residence would not normally be forthcoming to their family, despite their noble family lineage dating back more than a century. Both women made one final, anxious appraisal of their attire as they waited for the mansion's doorman to open the carriage door. The two had spent hours agonizing over what to wear, ending in a frantic, lavish spending spree on new dresses for the occasion. Anton was himself dressed with impeccable elegance and attention to detail.

Watching their agitation he couldn't help giving a small chuckle of amusement that caught their attention. "Relax, my dears. I guarantee you both look stunning. You are going to have every man in attendance tonight fawning over you all night long."

Emilie, the younger of the two women at age twenty, gave him an arch look of dismissal.

"You're our brother, Anton. You have to say that."

"Nonsense," said Marie, older of the two sisters at age twenty-two, as she gave Anton a brilliant smile. "He's right, we are stunning creatures. Follow my lead, dear sister."

The two other male occupants of the carriage both offered enthusiastic agreement. The Chevalier Jacques de Bellecourt, twin brother to sister Marie, was dressed to the same level of elegance, as was Baron Henri Durand, their twenty-three year old cousin. He focused a hopeful look on Emilie.

"Emilie, you look ravishing. I would be proud to be your escort anywhere."

Emilie sniffed and turned her head away. Anton knew, as did the rest of the family, the open secret of Henri's desire for his cousin, but the feeling was not reciprocated. Henri gave a tentative, rueful grin to Anton before giving his own attire a quick, surreptitious last check.

Twenty four year old Count Anton de Bellecourt gave them an indulgent look. Despite his young age he was used to being in charge, fostered by a paternal feeling for his family stemming from being the oldest sibling. Their parents had perished along with those of their cousin Henri at sea in a storm appearing from nowhere on a return voyage from Italy almost five years ago. Coming into their titles and wealth at a young age was a shock, but the surviving children adapted. The tragedy of losing both sets of parents at the same time drew all of them closer than they had ever been.

The carriage door opened and Anton nodded to the two women, knowing it was not as simple as merely telling them what they wanted to hear. They were in truth a vision of loveliness. Both wore pale white dresses fringed with plenty of lace, cut low enough to hint at well-formed, tempting breasts hidden from sight. Their mother's sparkling necklaces and earrings framed strong, but attractive features. Marie's long pale blonde hair and striking blue eyes contrasted with Emilie's dusky auburn blonde hair and deep brown eyes inherited from her father.

"Now, my lovely sisters, go forth and hold your heads high. Remember, we are nobles and we belong here too."

The women nodded and picked up the skirts of their dresses, careful to exit the carriage with dignity. One of several well-dressed doormen on hand to assist visitors offered them his hand down to ensure a smooth exit. As their coachman was dismissed another carriage came up, but the family as one had already turned their attention to the entrance before them. Anton gauged the subtle cues about the entrance that spoke of a degree of hidden elegance and wealth beyond where the doorman was now beckoning them. With a quick side glance he saw the rest of the family were assessing what lay before them too.

His intuition about what awaited proved correct, as the doorman ushered them into an interior with a degree of opulence beyond even his wildest expectations. An immense chandelier lit the wide expanse of an entrance hall lined with marble statuary and expensive, high quality portrait paintings of distinguished looking men in military uniforms and elegant, beautiful women in flowing ball gowns. A wide, curving staircase led to the upper floors.

With eyes wide they clustered together looking about the entrance hall. In hindsight, Anton realized he should have known the home of one of the leading citizens of France would be this lavish. But then, the mansion of Marie-Joseph Paul Yves Roch Gilbert du Motier de Lafayette, known simply by most people as the Marquis de Lafayette, could not have been otherwise.

"Good Lord," said Jacques, in a whisper low enough only his companions could hear. "And I thought *we* were rich."

"Ah, I was expecting something like this," replied Anton with a shrug that was belied by the look of awe on his face. "Our host comes from an old, very wealthy family. But we aren't exactly country peasants, you know. Remember, we have titles, too. Walk around like we own the place, as we do at home."

Another small crowd of well-dressed servants waited inside. One of the men stepped forward to greet them, accompanied by a female servant bearing a sterling silver platter covered with crystal flute glasses filled with bubbling champagne. As she offered drinks to each of them in turn Anton proffered his card to the male servant, who digested it for a moment before turning to bow to the group.

"Ladies, gentlemen, welcome to the home of the Marquis de Lafayette. He is in the main salon with some of the other guests that have already arrived. If you would follow me I shall announce you."

The room he led them to was even more lavish. As they were announced to the small crowd already inside the newcomers did their best not to appear as awed as they were. Expensive, well-crafted gold gilt work framed the entire room while the centrepiece was a huge crystal chandelier even larger than the one in the main entrance hall. An enormous table filled with an incredible array of hors d'oeuvres was set against one wall.

"Count de Bellecourt!" exclaimed the Marquis, as he strode across the room to greet them. The Marquis had chosen not to wear his military uniform this night, but he was dressed with faultless quality and taste that was impossible to ignore.

"Welcome to my home, all of you. And especially to these lovely ladies!"

Eyes shining, both women proffered their hands and the Marquis obliged with a slight bow, brushing their hands with a light kiss before giving Anton an impish look. Turning back to Emilie, whose hand he was still holding, he assumed a dance position and she pirouetted in response.

The Marquis grinned as he finally let go of her hand. "Had I known how lovely your sisters are I would have invited you to join me for dinner much sooner! Ladies, I insist upon a dance with each of you before the night ends."

They gave the Marquis polite laughter in response as the guests whose carriage had arrived right behind them were announced. The Marquis's face lit with recognition as he glanced at the entrance, but before he turned away he smiled once again at the group.

"Well, I have yet more guests to greet so I must leave you for a bit. Please help yourselves to some hors d'oeuvres and drinks and enjoy yourselves. I want you to know how glad I am you are all here tonight. We live in difficult times for our country and we must all consider what we can do to help. Yes, we shall talk much of the future tonight!"

"We have all been looking forward to this night, Marquis," said Anton. The Marquis responded with a polite nod and turned away.

"My *God*, he is so handsome and dashing," said Emilie, staring at the departing Marquis with naked desire in her eyes.

Anton had to agree with her. A few months short of his thirtieth birthday, the Marquis bore himself with an energy and enthusiasm that made him seem even younger. His aristocratic good looks combined with his fit, military bearing meant Emilie was not the first woman to view him with desire. His self-assured, commanding presence was also hard won. Everyone knew the Marquis had served with distinction in several major battles during the American Revolutionary War both before and after France entered the conflict. His reputation as a leader was well deserved.

"Well, my dear, in case you didn't know, you are several years too late to go about setting your sights on the Marquis. I believe he's been married for well over ten years. But not to worry, I'm sure there will be other dashing young men about tonight."

The crowd was indeed young, with no one present looking to be over the age of thirty. The trouble was every one of the young men in sight all had women as beautiful as Emilie and Marie already on their arms. Despite this the two women had several surreptitious side-glances sent their direction from some of the men, earning them disapproving frowns from their own companions.

Anton recognized a handful of the people present as young, titled aristocrats like themselves and surmised the rest of the crowd would also be wealthy people with inherited titles acquired at least two or more generations earlier. Even so, their host lived in a different world. As someone travelling in the highest circles of French society the Marquis was an eagle flying high above his guests.

This alone would have made him the real centre of attention, but his was a commanding presence dominating any conversation he joined. As servants roved through the crowd of now close to thirty people with trays of wine and dainty hors d'oeuvres, the Marquis was the magnet attracting everyone, including Anton. Some wanted to hear of his exploits during the American War while others probed for his views on the current situation in France. The Marquis was happy to oblige everyone.

"You were in several significant battles on the side of the Americans, Marquis," said one of the guests in the crowd around their host. "Which was the most challenging?"

"Yorktown, without a doubt. An animal is always going to fight the hardest when it is trapped, and the British certainly were. Our brothers in the Navy blocked theirs at the Chesapeake and their Army could not be supplied, whereas the support was there for our combined forces with the Americans.

But it was still a hard fought affair and there were many acts of valour to celebrate."

"The fight was that desperate, Marquis?" said Anton, who had gravitated closer through the crowd.

"Absolutely. Even with our success at sea the British were not cowed. But the Americans to a man were fighting for a great cause and would not be denied. Why, I think one of the bravest men of all fighting these battles was a slave, if you can believe it."

The faces of several of the people in the crowd around the Marquis crinkled with puzzled looks, making Lafayette smile.

"It's true. His name is James Armistead and he is both a black man and a slave. He petitioned his master to join the army and fortunately he ended up joining me. I immediately saw his potential not as a soldier, but as a spy!"

"As a spy?" said a young, well dressed man beside the Marquis. "Is this sort of thing really necessary, sir?"

"Oh yes," replied the Marquis, a small hint of amusement apparent in his voice at the naiveté of the question. "The objective in any conflict is to win, sir. Knowing how your enemy has deployed his forces and how he intends to prosecute the fight is invaluable in building a plan to counter them. It's even better if you can feed the enemy misinformation about what you plan to do. And the noble Mr. Armistead successfully did all of this for us."

"*Noble*?" said Anton, looking around to see others in the crowd looking bewildered and even uncomfortable. "That's the first time I've ever heard anyone use that word to describe a black man, let alone a slave. Truly noble, sir?"

"Absolutely," replied the Marquis, with a firm tone in his voice making his conviction on the subject crystal clear. "This man joined to fight for a great cause, liberty and freedom from tyranny, not for himself but for all of his fellow Americans. And he willingly took on extremely dangerous work. He infiltrated enemy lines and pretended to be an escaped slave wanting to help the British. They used him as a local guide and once he had their trust he was able to listen unfettered to the officers and their plans. He found ways to feed all of this information back to me and I, in turn, gave him misinformation about our plans that he was successful in subtly planting in the minds of our foes. My God, had they realized what was happening it doesn't bear thinking about what the British would have done to him."

"This is fascinating, Marquis," said Anton, wearing a thoughtful look on his face. "I have to confess I have little experience with black people. The common wisdom is they are little better than beasts, fit only to labour in the fields of my family's sugar plantations or perhaps to be servants at best. So to hear you describe this man as noble—well, it's a rather dramatic contrast, you understand."

"Yes, and thank you, Count de Bellecourt. You have given me opportunity to talk about why I have invited all of you here this night. Well, we shall talk more over dinner, but this is a good example of where reform in accordance with only the highest of principles is needed."

The crowd was taken aback at the sudden fire in the Marquis's eyes.

"Yes, France needs reform in so many ways! But as for Mr. Armistead, I assure you in my experience he is by no means an exception. These people are not simple beasts. I too was once ignorant of their capabilities, but no longer. See here, I have a question for you, my friends. If black people are willing to lay down their lives for the principle of freedom from tyranny and oppression, why should they not be free too?"

The crowd around the Marquis had by now grown even larger. The novelty of the idea had several turning to look with uncertainty at the reactions of the rest of the crowd. But most were focused on the Marquis.

"Marquis?" said Anton, deliberately allowing his curiosity to show. "So what happened to Mr. Armistead? Was he freed?"

To everyone's surprise the Marquis's face fell and he frowned, looking away for a moment to obviously collect his thoughts before responding.

"No," replied the Marquis with a sigh. "No, sadly, he and the other black soldiers I met have not been freed, at least not yet. I am hopeful this will change, though, and I am actively trying to influence my American friends on this matter. Actually, I've been thinking about putting a group of like-minded people together to keep the pressure on. Perhaps a society of influential people willing to speak up."

"Well, I have a confession, Marquis," said Anton. "The reason I asked about this was I have a memory of being told of something their ambassador to our country said a while back. Thomas Jefferson is his name, I believe. I heard he was advocating all slaves should be freed? So if this is the case, why would someone like your Mr. Armistead not have been set free for his valiant service?"

"An excellent question, Count, and yes, you are correct. I fear our American friends have a contradiction in their thinking on this matter still. But please don't misunderstand me. I have the utmost respect for Mr. Jefferson and Mr. Washington and all of their leaders. But I confess I was disappointed to learn Mr. Jefferson was promoting an end to slavery here in France while he was, and still is, telling them back in America the time is not right."

Anton deliberately let a puzzled look show on his face before responding to the Marquis. "Really? Why would this be, sir?"

"Well, what other reasons could there be, except the usual? Money and politics, sir."

The Marquis spread his arms wide, palms open, to appeal to his listeners and to express his frustration.

"You all must understand what is happening. America is a young country. Yes, they have won their freedom, but the cost has been staggering to their economy. Times are very hard there and it will take a long time to rebuild. So when Ambassador Jefferson tells us the time is now to let freedom from tyranny ring for everyone, including black slaves everywhere, he is speaking from his heart. When he tells the people *back home* the time is not right to end slavery, he is speaking with the economy in mind. There are many, many plantations and businesses in America depending on slave labour."

"Still, wouldn't it at least make sense to reward those who served?" said Anton.

"It certainly would, my dear Count. The problem I believe they fear is such a move could open a Pandora's box. More and more reasons to grant freedom would appear and in the end they simply don't know what the outcome would be. It's a fear of the unknown, really. They simply can't see how they would function without the slave labour to make it all work. Unfortunately, I think most plantation owners in America do not yet understand the potential of these people. Sadly, the common view held by most is black people are little more than beasts and this notion is still very much alive."

"But know this, Count de Bellecourt," added the Marquis, his passion burning in his eyes. "I still consider freedom from tyranny for everyone, including black people, the *greatest* cause of our time. Sir, this fight is not over and I welcome anyone to join our cause."

Anton felt his own mind was alight and on fire, lit by the Marquis's fervour, but before he could respond one of the servants signaled for the Marquis's attention from the fringe of the crowd.

"Ah, Andre? We are ready, are we? Excellent. Please make your announcement."

Nodding, the servant strode over to a set of large double doors at the end of the room and turned to the crowd. Holding a small bell he rang it with insistent purpose to catch everyone's attention.

"Ladies and gentlemen, your attention please!" he said, loud enough to be heard above the now dwindling buzz of conversation.

"We will be commencing the dinner service in twenty minutes and we ask you be seated by then. The seating has been prearranged and your name is on a place card at your seat. If anyone desires to attend to personal needs before dinner please ask any of the Marquis's servants for directions."

Turning about he opened both doors wide, revealing an enormous dining hall. A massive dining table big enough to accommodate over thirty people was set with expensive dinnerware. More huge paintings lined the walls and three crystal chandeliers lit the room. The servant strode to the far end of the dining hall and opened yet another set of doors, which was obviously a prearranged signal for the group of musicians in the next room to begin softly playing dinner music.

The main salon turned into a hive of activity as the conversation groups broke up. As the de Bellecourt family coalesced together once again Anton noticed their flushed faces and smiled.

"So, I lost you all in the crowd. Did you meet some interesting people?"

"We did," said Marie, smiling in return. "We wanted to know more about who we are sharing dinner with so we went to find out. Anton, there are people here from all over France, not just Paris!"

"Yes," said Henri. "These are all people with titles like us. There are some I know of and a few I have actually met before, but don't know well. It seems to be a diverse group, but what I noticed is everyone here is young."

"Hmm," said Anton. "None of this is a coincidence. The Marquis hinted he had a reason for asking us all here tonight. I suggest we take our places and find out more of what he is up to."

Once the crowd was seated the Marquis ensured their glasses were filled once again before he rose to speak.

"Ladies and gentlemen, my friends! Welcome to my home. We will talk much tonight, but first I must show you my hospitality. Let us begin with a toast. To our gracious King Louis!"

As the crowd lifted their glasses and echoed the toast starter dishes appeared and were consumed, only to have the table soon filled with a series of main dishes that kept coming. Twelve different dishes of beef were soon replaced by six dishes of pork, followed by a huge variety of chicken, duck, and seafood dishes all cooked in a flavoursome variety of herbs, spices and wine. As the main courses finally ended a vast array of desserts appeared. The diners washed it all down with an endless stream of excellent French wine.

The wine was making its effect felt as several conversations around the table were bubbling with loud laughter. Anton and the family were gratified to find themselves grouped near the head of the table close to the Marquis, who continued to dominate the conversation around him with an endless series of anecdotes from his experiences. Gradually the plates were cleared away and once again the efficient servant Andre appeared at the side of the Marquis, waiting to catch his attention.

The Marquis gave a brief nod when he saw him. The servant produced his little bell once again from a trolley beside him covered with crystal snifters and decanters filled with amber liquid. Conversations died away once again as the musical tinkling of the bell drew attention to the Marquis's servant.

"Ladies and gentlemen! The Marquis has some words for all of you now, but before he commences we will be coming around the table with cognac and other refreshments. For those who prefer wine we will bring fresh glasses and bottles."

As he finished the crowd of servants set about lining the centre of the long dining table with a series of decanters, bottles of wine, and steaming jugs of coffee. As they left the Marquis sat forward in his chair, elbows on the table and hands folded in front of him as he watched the crowd waiting in anticipation before him.

"Well, my friends, I hope you have enjoyed the bounty set before you this evening. I—"

"Hear! Hear!" called a boisterous attendee at the far end of the table in a loud voice. "A toast to the man who has provided us such a wonderful banquet this evening!" As the man raised his glass high to acknowledge their host, the rest of the crowd immediately followed suit.

The Marquis offered an indulgent smile and a languid nod of acknowledgement. "I thank you all," said the Marquis, as the smile drained away. "But I must confess I have invited you here for much more than a pleasant dinner. I am sorry if I have been mysterious with some of you, but I wanted opportunity to speak to all of you at the same time so you all hear the same message. My friends, I am troubled over the future of France. Deeply troubled."

The sudden silence his words brought as their import sunk in cast an immediate pall over the animated crowd farther down the table, puzzled looks appearing on their faces. Many of the rest of the people around the table raised eyebrows in mystified response too.

The Marquis laughed. "Oh, please, I seek not to destroy the pleasant evening we are enjoying. My friends, we and our families and the people coming before us have worked hard to gain the status and, let's be honest, the wealth we all enjoy. It is only right that we should all enjoy these fruits, so bring the smiles back to your faces. But I should be clearer in my meaning."

Anton saw the Marquis appeared gratified as the tense looks on the people lightened. He gave them an apologetic, small grin to encourage everyone before continuing.

"But yes, it is true I am troubled. Tonight we have people in the room here from all over our beloved country and this is no accident. The reason is I wanted all of you to hear what is going on not just in Paris or in your small region of the country. To start, I'm going to tell you what I think is happening and you all can tell me if I'm right."

"Here in Paris if you look outside your carriages as you drive through the streets you will find many beggars. Far more than there have ever been. People with nothing, absolutely nothing, but the clothes on their backs. Oh, not here or in the few richer districts of the city we all live in, because the police are paid well to keep it this way. There are also parts of the city not at all safe, and yes, I know this has always been the case, but these too are now far worse than they have ever been. People from the country have come to Paris to find work and there is none."

The Marquis paused a moment, and this time a despondent look appeared on his face.

"And in the countryside it all boils down to the harvest. We all know farms keep by far the vast majority of our people at work and if the harvest goes well we will stave off catastrophe for yet another year. A good harvest gives the peasants a little extra to spend on the goods our businesses produce. But the harvests have not been consistent and even now there are beggars in the streets of the small towns and villages throughout France. And there are far more brigands roaming the country than ever before. If you are traveling the roads, even in strength of numbers, you are well advised to keep your weapons close to hand. Beneath the surface the entire country is seething with unrest. So, my friends, is this description accurate?"

Anton watched several people peer at the Marquis, clearly considering what he had said, while others looked around to gauge the crowd's reaction. Seeing no one willing to take the lead Anton spoke up.

"Marquis, I believe you are correct, at least as it applies to the situation here in Paris. Our family has business interests in different parts of the city and I periodically visit with the managers in person. From what I've heard from them and what I've seen, your assessment is correct."

This prompted a man further down the table to speak up and agree the Marquis's description was true also, as far as it applied to his home region in the north of the country. Another man from the area around Marseille offered his agreement as others began nodding too.

"Marquis?" said Henri. "I too agree with your assessment. But is the sole cause problem harvests? I have heard people speak with frustration of this treaty the government has made with the English. They can sell their goods here now and, I must confess, the quality is better than what our businesses produce. I am told they are relying more on inventions making it so much easier to produce greater quantities faster and with quality as good as anything we can produce. I think in particular the clothing they are selling here is putting our own producers and the people working for them all out of work."

"Baron Durand, you are absolutely correct, and yes, I think it is more than problem harvests," replied the Marquis. "The goods they are producing are indeed better and this is a problem, too. We may not be at war with the English now, but this doesn't mean they are our friends. Far from it! But I cannot point to them and say it's their fault. They are merely doing what they have always done, aggressively trying to make money at the expense of others. No, we must look in the mirror, my friends."

The Marquis paused to take a deep breath, obviously weighing his words carefully. "To be clear, I'm not saying progress is bad. It's quite the opposite, really. I think we must reform our ways if we are to succeed. If we did so we could better manage the impact of things like this treaty, for example."

"So what do you see as the true problem, Marquis?" said another man, from further down the table.

"My friends, you must understand I agree with the philosopher Rousseau, at least in some respects. The institutions we have created are not serving us well and I think this is the real issue. My God, do I need to detail the excesses I know you have all seen on a daily basis? The worst sorts of liars surround our good King and they have nothing but their own interests at heart. They aren't even bothering to try and hide what they are doing. The government decides a new courthouse is needed somewhere? Guess who owns the land where it is to be sited and, what a surprise, the government pays a premium to get it."

The Marquis paused and, seeing nods of agreement, he continued.

"And this treaty with the English? Someone's pocket is fatter because it was done. The bureaucrats and courtiers are running amok expecting they are entitled to more and more for what little they do, while the King's ministers are finding new ways to try and squeeze more and more money from everyone with yet more taxes and duties. Everywhere you turn there are road tolls and yet more new taxes to burden us. Smuggling has become far more than a minor inconvenience, it is rampant everywhere. But who knows what the real financial situation is in this country? Please, may I have a show of hands to confirm? Is there anyone here who believes what the government is saying about this?"

Anton was not surprised no one raised a hand, and once again he took the initiative to respond.

"Marquis, I suspect no one here will disagree with anything you are saying. But what does this mean for everyone in this room?"

"It means we must change, my friends. See here, I think the country's finances are actually in very, very bad shape. And yes, some of this can be traced to our involvement in the War with our American friends. War is not cheap! But I regret nothing of what was spent and you should not either. We supported a truly noble cause that I think will gather strength and ultimately change the entire world. Think of it! We need freedom from the arbitrary decisions of tyrants seeking to line their pockets and nothing more. We need liberty for people enslaved in any form, whatever it may be. We need to rely on individuals everywhere willingly being guided by nothing but the highest of principles to effect change. France and America together could lead the world!"

"Marquis?" said another guest, unable to keep a hint of excitement from his voice. "I agree with you, and I expect the reason we are here is you seek our help. But how is it possible for the few in this room to bring into being change as profound as you suggest?"

"Don't underestimate yourselves, my friends. I believe the few here, if you choose to do so, can become leaders for the change our country so desperately needs."

"Marquis, I have to ask," said another man, his eyes almost bulging in wonder as he stared at the Marquis. The sharp edge in his voice immediately made everyone turn to hear him. "Are you suggesting a violent change like what happened in America? Good God, man, that would be insane. Please tell me that's not what you are talking about."

"Oh, no," said the Marquis, with a dismissive look. "What happened there was inevitable given the only principle the English live by is that greed is good. The English brought this upon themselves. We are French and we can do better. No, I seek a middle road, and I believe we can support our King and achieve major reforms by talking and by influencing those around us on the need for change. We do not need violence."

The Marquis continued when it was obvious the man was mollified. Animated with a light of burning passion shining on his face, he surveyed the crowd.

"So yes, I invited all of you tonight deliberately to try and win you to this cause! And yes, I intend to invite others and have this same conversation with them. This is not my cause. It is the cause of our beloved France. She needs your help! If you love your country then I submit you must stand up and do what you can to save her. You were invited because you are nobles, as am I. I ask you, who has the resources and influence to change the path our country is on, if not us? You have the education many do not and I think you understand the principles I am talking about. You are also all young and this is no coincidence. You have a stake in seeing a better future for both our King and country and even, dare I say it, the entire world!"

The resulting clamour from everyone trying to speak at once was such none could be understood. The Marquis could only hold his hands out palm downward to gesture for calm. As the uproar subsided Anton rose from his chair and looked around to catch everyone's attention, glass in hand.

"Friends, I propose a toast. Join me in raising your glass to a truly noble man, one our country so desperately needs. To an inspiration to us all, to the Marquis!"

The entire table rose to their feet as one with their glasses and echoed Anton's toast with gusto. As they settled down Anton again took the lead.

"Marquis, I can't speak for everyone here, but for myself at least, I am with you."

Anton paused as several people around the table nodded and shouted their agreement.

"But please, I think we still need your guidance. How do you see us proceeding in this?"

"My friends, there are so many different ways it would be impossible to list them all. In fact, I don't know what the end result of our movement will be, but I am certain the will of the people will bring about the best possible world for us all. If you see something clearly wrong happening, speak out. Look, each of you has contacts, people you know, business interests and connections throughout France and her colonies. If each of you commit to bring the cause of reform to the minds of others and if we influence enough people to demand change it will become an unstoppable force. Among other things I plan, I for one will continue to invite more people to dinner with me and to have this same conversation as often as necessary."

"Marquis?" said a man near Anton who till now had been silent. "My family has always maintained close ties with the judiciary and the legal profession through our financial dealings. I could perhaps seek out members of the legal community and promote this thinking with them. It might ultimately result in rulings more favourable to reform over time. Is this the kind of thing you have in mind?"

"Exactly! It will be an excellent start and I'm sure we would see benefits. Change will not come overnight, my friends, but it will happen."

"Marquis?" said Anton, feeling a deep, scorching inspiration surge through his body. "You were speaking earlier this evening of the black slaves working the plantations of America. You spoke of the slave you worked with as being noble and how liberty is deserved for all, but is still not a reality. There are many slaves working plantations in the sugar islands of the Caribbean too, and my family has extensive sugar plantation operations on St Lucia. Perhaps we could find a way to make our plantations more efficient and in so doing move to free our slaves and turn them into workers instead. We could promote this thinking widely to plantation owners, even to the British or the Americans, and serve as a model for them."

"My dear Count, I would welcome any effort to realize these goals. My friends, slavery is another form of tyranny being imposed on people and what he suggests is another example of how focusing on the highest of principles, freedom for all, can be turned into practical application. Count, you will find many men set in their ways on this and ready to resist you, even with violence. The British certainly will. But who knows, if you are persistent enough the light of freedom may finally end the darkness of slavery."

The Marquis paused a moment to give Anton a speculative look.

"Well, sir, I can see you have come to understand now. If you are truly set on this path do let me know and come see me. I may be able to help open some doors for you."

"What a wonderful evening!" said Emilie, as the family settled into their carriage for the ride home at the end of the night. "The Marquis is *such* an inspiration. But Anton, what do you intend to do?"

"I intend to act," said Anton with conviction in his voice, his mind still racing. "As you heard earlier we do indeed have extensive holdings on St. Lucia. I believe our sugar plantation is almost a thousand acres and has at least a couple hundred slaves or more. Henri, if memory serves our manager there looks after your holdings on St. Lucia, too?"

"Yes. Mine are not on the same scale as your side of the family I think, but it generates a tidy bit of income," shrugged Henri. "Georges deals with the manager there on my behalf."

"Yes, well, the Marquis *is* an inspiration," replied Anton. "I shall have to give more thought to the details when I haven't been drinking, but I am resolved on this. I'm going to St. Lucia because I would like to support the Marquis. Think of it! Finding a way to gain freedom for slaves everywhere. What a noble cause!"

"Excellent," said Henri, leaning forward with an intense look. "When do we leave?"

"I'm coming too," said Jacques.

"Hold on," said Anton. "I was thinking of this as a solo trip. Someone has to stay here and manage our affairs."

Marie's giggle of amusement was loud enough to turn everyone's attention to her. "Anton, if you think you're going to run off on an adventure to somewhere exotic like the sugar islands and leave us all behind to deal with boring lawyers and paperwork you are mad. Our solicitor Georges can be trusted and is more than capable of dealing with matters while we are gone."

"I agree, Anton," said Emilie. "I want to see more of the world. Paris is wonderful, but I want adventure too!"

"My God, do you realize what you are all talking about? It takes many weeks to travel to the Caribbean. There can be bad storms. Death from the diseases there is very, very possible."

"We are all young and strong," said Marie. "And we are all family, are we not?"

"My dear cousin," said Henri, leaning back in his seat with a grin. "They've got that look in their eyes again. I think you are going to lose this argument."

Anton paused a moment before throwing his hands in the air in mock exasperation. "Well. I would miss all of you badly anyway so I guess it's settled. But I must discuss this further with the Marquis and give it all more thought. I know he thinks we can bring about the change he wants by talking, but you all need to understand I'm not so sure about this."

"What do you mean?" said Henri, a wary tone in his voice.

Anton hesitated a moment before replying. "I'm not convinced he's right. Look, I'm the one dealing with local politicians and the men out there running our family businesses on our collective behalf. Let me assure you, their arrogance knows no bounds and I don't think their counterparts in the Caribbean will be any different. None of them, especially the British, will want to talk of anything threatening their power. This will require bold action. But see here, the question is do we all believe this is a worthy goal the Marquis has set before us?"

"Anton, I think we've all been inspired by what we heard tonight," replied Henri, the intensity apparent in both his voice and on his face. "And the truth is we've all been feeling a little adrift in our lives, haven't we? We all have enough money we don't have to work and we have time on our hands. So dedicating our time to this great cause seems a wonderful idea, at least to me. And I don't care what we have to do to further the cause. I believe."

Anton watched as Henri looked around and everyone gave firm nods of agreement. He also saw the same intense look of passion on the faces of the others.

Anton leaned forward wearing a conspiratorial look. "Excellent. I do too. The Marquis is a man of action and a real leader. He has challenged us to be leaders, too. For me, I'm ready for it. So if I am right and talk is not going to be enough, we may have to start a real fight for what we believe in, like the Americans did to free themselves. In our own way, mind you. Sometimes, people have to be *made* to change. I agree with the Marquis the British in particular will resist. So are you all still with me?"

Once again Henri looked for and saw nods of agreement, before smiling and turning back to Anton. "I'd say we are with you."

Anton smiled. " Good. We shall see what the future holds for us."

With that settled the two women began marveling yet again over the decor of the Marquis's home, leaving Anton's thoughts free to drift back over the evening. He doubted any of them truly understood just how hard the fist he intended to wield in pursuit of his goal would be, but he had plenty of time to educate them.

Chapter Three
December 1787
St. Lucia

The process of purchasing a suitable ship and fitting it out, together with finding a willing crew, took longer than Anton wanted. Despite the help of knowledgeable people engaged by his solicitor, he chafed at the slow pace until they explained the reason; no one with any sense was going to attempt a long journey into the Caribbean in the middle of hurricane season.

Still, Anton insisted on the fastest passage possible and spared no expense, eager to be about their mission. This resulted in acquisition of an almost new ship, a swift topsail schooner of a design growing in popularity with the Americans that a French shipyard had simply copied. This ship was built for speed and *L'Estalon* was indeed a fast stallion. The Captain he had hired, Giscard Dusourd, was one of the biggest rogues he had ever met, but it was clear the man knew how to ride this particular stallion. He also knew his way around the Caribbean, having served there during the American Revolutionary War.

Without being specific about what would be required, Anton soon satisfied himself Captain Dusourd had no scruples about anything he might expect of him. The crew the Captain hired were thugs cut from the same mould, making the journey from Marseille difficult for the women. Marie complained she felt she was inside a cage surrounded by a pack of starving wolves. Anton had been aware the journey outbound from Marseille in southern France would be long and tedious, and he hoped nothing untoward would happen. But he was wrong.

Toward the end of the voyage tedium gave way to tension when he and Henri caught one of the sailors, not realizing others had come on the scene, putting his arm around Emilie's waist. Their backs were to Anton and Henri, and Anton frowned at the realization Emilie didn't appear to be struggling to pull away.

"You! Get your hands off her, you pig!" shouted Henri as the two men strode up, with Henri pulling out his sword as he went. The commotion attracted others.

"Francois, what the hell do you think you're doing?" said Captain Dusourd, glaring daggers at the offender as he joined them seconds later.

"Nothing, Captain, I swear it! She wanted me to!"

"That's not true!" said Emilie, when the crowd turned as one to look at her. "I froze when he touched me because I didn't know what to do."

The sailor's jaw fell open and he turned to his Captain with a mixture of shock and surprise. "She's lying, the bitch. She's the one that rubbed her tits up against me without warning. I swear, I think she was even about to stick her hand in my crotch."

The response was swift. The Captain felled the man with a crushing punch, leaving him in a crumpled heap on the deck. After making sure the sailor wasn't going to put up a fight, the Captain gave the rest of his watching crew a dark scowl.

"The next bastard to touch one of these women is going to be food for the sharks. Is this clear, you fools? Leave the women alone! Now get back to work."

He stalked away accompanied by Emilie and Henri, while the sailor moaned and struggled to get to his feet. Anton lingered to watch as two of the sailor's mates helped him get up, unspoken questions in their eyes. The sailor rubbed his bruised face in response, then held out both hands palm up in mute incomprehension.

The others raised their eyebrows and looked in the direction Emilie had gone, before they turned back to their mate.

"Let's go, Francois. We all know women are trouble," said the older of the two sailors.

After this Anton and the other male family members made a point of ensuring the two women were never left alone. But having a pack of rogues for his Captain and crew was exactly what Anton wanted. To help offset the costs of the ship and its crew Anton had contracted to purchase and deliver a range of premium goods specifically requested by a local buyer their family already had connections with. The buyer would then contract the ship for short haul trips around the islands when not in use by the family for their own purposes. But not everything was going to be offloaded for sale.

The extra cargo hidden deep in the hold of *L'Estalon* was for other purposes. The Captain and crew were of necessity aware of it, but Anton had elected to keep his family in the dark. Anton accepted blood may have to be spilled to achieve his goal and that he had the personal resolve to see it through, but he wasn't so sure about the rest of the family. Time would tell.

Castries, the largest town and capital of the island of St. Lucia, was blessed with an excellent harbour.

Sailing into it went a long way to making everyone forget the tedium of the voyage.

"My God! This is so beautiful!" said Emilie, her eyes shining as she leaned out over the railing of the ship, her nose twitching at the exotic scents of the island. "Look at this! Smell this place, its wonderful!"

In truth, thought Anton, the scene before them was stunning. As their small schooner navigated the entrance into Castries harbour they tried their best to retain their dignity and not be awed by the scene before them, but they all failed miserably.

Once past the big headland at the narrow entrance the shoreline widened and wound around the smaller, picturesque bays of the larger harbour. A series of low, rolling hills dotted with buildings painted a riot of colours surrounded the harbour. Bright blues, greens, pinks and even yellows dominated. Lush green, tropical vegetation was everywhere. At the far end was Castries itself. The low, rolling hills carried on to the interior of the island, growing into much larger, towering peaks covered with even lusher, dark green vegetation.

The usual variety of shipping common to ports everywhere dotted the harbour, but two large French frigates dominated everything. One looked new, but the other was much older and appeared to have been converted for use as a troop ship. A few smaller warships were anchored nearby. Not far away was an American flagged schooner of the same, but much older design as *L'Estalon*.

"This really is a beautiful place, Anton," said Jacques. "Not too big, though. I hope we'll be able to find some kind of entertainment here."

"I have no doubt we will," replied Anton in a confident voice. "Well, we shall start by seeing what there is to entertain us on the plantation. Also, I don't think I told you, but I learned before we left we actually own a small manor house in town as well. Apparently father acquired it before he died. It's not suitable for all of us to live in for any extended length of time, but it will serve for short visits to town if we can't find entertainment elsewhere."

"Well, that's good to know. So, I was looking at the map, and if I read it correct the de Bellecourt Estate plantation is off in that direction toward— what was the town? Gros Islet?"

"I believe so," smiled Anton. "We shall leave the formalities to our Captain and be on our way soon enough I think. If it's as beautiful as this harbour I think we will like it here."

The riotous mélange of colour, sound, and bustle of Jeremie Street near the careenage in Castries where they had docked was a massive assault on the senses. Crowds of people, mostly black, scurried about their business in a scene that wouldn't have looked out of place in the nearest anthill. The buildings in town were all painted with the same wild assortment of bright colours as those on the hills surrounding it. A few combined the riot of blues, yellows, greens, and pinks all together on the same building with extra colours like red added in. Little shops selling all manner of food and goods lined the street. The tantalizing smell of fresh caught fish cooking on the open grills in use in several of the stalls drifted over it all.

But what seemed strange to Anton was the large number of beggars on the fringes of the crowd. Most were gap toothed, older black men and women with faces lined from age and fringes of white or grey hair. Some were much younger, suffering from missing limbs or other disabilities. Young children, wearing ragged scraps of clothing, ran to and fro throughout it all. Thin, scruffy dogs and cats prowled the edges looking for scraps. Few people were smiling.

Even stranger to see was a number of soldiers stationed on guard at regular intervals on the street, although most looked bored. A lucky few had found shady spots to sit while maintaining their guard and more than a few of these appeared to be dozing as they leaned against the wall.

As their belongings were offloaded, Anton found himself drawn into a conversation with Captain Dusourd and a local Customs official. Once he understood the reason Dusourd had appealed to him for help he was shocked.

"But these duties are outrageous, sir!" growled Anton to the Customs officer. "This is almost twice the rate I was told to expect. How are we supposed to make any profit?"

The Customs officer shrugged. "You will have to take the matter up with the Governor, sir. It's true the rates have recently gone up again."

"Again? What do you mean, again?"

"Well, this would be the third time in the last six months."

Anton and the Captain looked at each other, but all they could do was shake their heads in disbelief. As they finished dealing with the Customs officer a disheveled looking, middle-aged man with the obvious weathered look of a sailor sidled up to Captain Dusourd.

"Well, Giscard, it has been a long time, hasn't it?"

The Captain gave a start on hearing the man's voice, and quickly stepped back. Anton watched with open curiosity as the Captain's eyes narrowed for a moment before he mastered himself and offered his hand to the newcomer. Both men smiled, but the wariness of their greeting was obvious.

"Adam Jones. My God, yes, it has. Forgive my surprise, I wasn't expecting to see you here."

The man held his arms wide, palms out in response. "Well, imagine my surprise when you sailed right past me into the harbour."

With a quick glance back toward the harbour entrance and a nod of his head Dusourd indicated the nearby American sloop. "She's yours?"

"The *Beacon*. She's a decommissioned warship. I got her for a joint venture with my cousin."

"*Really*?" said Dusourd, his face a frozen mask. "And how is your cousin Nathan?"

"Fine. He is back in Boston, of course."

"And what brings you to St. Lucia? How long have you been here?"

The man shrugged. "Been here looking for business for a couple of months now. Times are hard and we have to find work wherever we can. If you need help with something I could be your man."

Anton was surprised to see Dusourd's eyes narrow once again, but he wanted to get going so he coughed to catch their attention before Dusourd could respond. The Captain took the hint.

"Count de Bellecourt, my apologies. As you can see Captain Jones and I know each other. We had, hmm, dealings with each other during the American War. Adam, let's meet for a drink this evening."

After arranging a time and place the American left. As they watched him walking away Anton turned to Dusourd with frank curiosity. The Captain wasn't smiling.

"What was that all about?"

"Hmm, you probably saw I was being careful with him. Count, this man is, ah—dangerous."

"Really? Well, perhaps he could be of use if the circumstances are right. You are meeting him tonight, so find out more and let's keep him in mind. Well, I think you have matters in hand so I will take leave now. I'll be in touch."

The Captain responded with a noncommittal, incoherent mumble, but Anton was already on his way back to where the family awaited his return. Anton saw Henri had already set about hiring transportation for the family for the journey to the de Bellecourt estate. As the family watched him finish, Henri turned back to where the rest of the family was waiting. A crowd of ragged children seized the moment to swarm forward and surround him, hands out in hope of a coin or two.

"No, I have nothing for you today, children," he said. Striving to back away from them he stumbled on a curb and almost fell, but the mass of small hands steadied him. Regaining his composure and his balance, he decided to relent and reached into his pocket for his coin purse at the same time as the crowd of children melted away in all different directions. Henri was puzzled as to why they would run, but he shrugged and went to join the others. As he walked over he was patting his pockets and wearing a frown.

"It's odd, I could have sworn I got my coin purse out this morning before we docked, but—oh my God!"

As the realization flashed across his face Henri rushed over to the nearest soldiers, with Anton following close behind. "Thieves! Those children stole my money!"

The two soldiers didn't move from where they were, leaning against a wall. Seeing Henri wasn't going to leave them alone one finally leaned forward and looked around before turning back to Henri. As Anton came closer the heady smell of strong rum surrounding the soldier almost overpowered him.

"What children are you talking about? Can you point them out?"

"Of course not! They ran off with my money. Aren't you going to do something?"

The soldier shrugged and leaned back against the wall again. "We are not police, sir. I suggest you report it to them. I'm sure they will do their best."

Henri stood glaring with open-mouthed shock at the two soldiers before shaking his head in disgust and marching with Anton back to the family. They stopped in at the police station on their way out of town, but Henri came stomping out within minutes of going inside.

"Incompetent fools! That was a waste of time. Thank God I didn't have much in my coin purse. We're going to have to watch ourselves here."

Once they left Castries, after paying what seemed an exorbitant road toll in two different spots, the serenity of the countryside was a welcome change. The plantation they found on arrival couldn't have provided a greater contrast to the bustle of Castries. The plantation was more than beautiful, mused Anton, it was staggering. Set in a broad valley between ranges of the rolling hills the simple tropical splendour of the place had all of them gaping in amazement.

"My God, Anton, I can't believe we own this. Coming here was worth being cooped up endlessly on the ship," said Marie as their hired coach pulled into a side road off the main route.

This lead to a large, two story stone building looming in the distance. Fields of ripe sugarcane waved in the gentle breeze on either side of the road. Glimpses of a series of one-story structures looking much more utilitarian could be seen off in a far corner of the estate, almost out of sight of the main mansion.

The coach pulled up to the front, followed close by the cart bearing their belongings piled high on it. A young woman with striking looks and light brown skin was sweeping the large verandah that ran the length of it with methodical strokes, but she stopped what she was doing and stared in open curiosity at the new arrivals.

"Can I help you, sir?" said the woman as Anton approached.

"Of course," replied Anton in a genial voice, looking her up and down with interest, realizing he liked what he saw. "You can go find some servants to carry our belongings inside."

"Sir? You're moving in?" replied the woman, her face crinkling in puzzlement. "Who are you?"

Anton raised one eyebrow in bemused response. "I am Anton de Bellecourt and my family and I own this place. Did no one tell you we were coming?"

A look of shock appeared on her face. "No, sir. My God, the mansion is not ready for you."

"Well, you're going to have to make it ready, aren't you? Now go find some help for us. Immediately, please."

As the woman ran off toward yet another small group of buildings tucked away behind a fringe of flowering trees Anton gave the coachmen some coins and told them to start unloading their belongings onto the verandah as the rest of the family mounted the steps to look at the view.

The mansion itself was built on the low, but steadily rising side of one of the hills lining the valley. Toward the interior of the island cane fields could be seen stretching off into the distance. Back in the direction they came from Anton saw the ocean glittering in the distance. Around the immediate grounds of the houses an amazing, colourful array of flowering bushes and trees framing a wide lawn. Flowers with red, yellow, and pink petals were everywhere. Dominating it all was an enormous tree with brilliant red flowers covering it.

"Anton?" said Marie, her voice muffled by the interior of the building. "They really are completely unprepared for us."

As the family filed in they all saw she was right. Sheets covered much of the furniture and a fine layer of dust was on everything.

Behind them a man coughed to draw their attention and they turned as one to find an older white man dressed in work clothes standing before them.

"Welcome, ladies and gentlemen. I am Gerard Montcalm, the operations overseer for the de Bellecourt Estate. I am led to believe one of you is Count Anton de Bellecourt?"

"That would be me," said Anton, frowning at the man as he stepped forward to meet him. "So why is the estate not ready for our arrival?"

"Count de Bellecourt, I am sorry. This is the first any of us have heard you were coming to St. Lucia. We will do our best to have the estate made fit for you. It may take us a day or two as we do not have the kind of stores in place you will need."

"I understand. Do your best. And where might I find the imbecile manager who has obviously failed us?"

"You mean the lawyer Moreau?" shrugged the overseer. "In his office in town, I imagine. We don't see him often."

Anton gave voice to his displeasure with a contemptuous sniff. "Well, we'll see about that. The fool is probably in bed with a whore. Given what we pay him I expected much better than this."

The rest of the day passed in a blur of activity. The mansion was made fit to live in as supplies were carried in, while a crowd of slaves cleaned the building from top to bottom. Before they began their leader came to introduce himself to Anton. He was a slave in his twenties with light, milky, coffee coloured skin, handsome and fit looking. Anton noticed he bore an aura of intelligence, and the rest of the slaves followed his orders without question. What was unusual was the obedient, quick response and outright deference on display to the man.

"Master de Bellecourt," he said, offering a bright smile as he introduced himself. "My name is Auyuba. We will soon have everything to your satisfaction. I am in charge of your house slaves and ensuring the needs of the family are met. I also have charge of your records and can answer any questions you may have."

Anton raised an eyebrow on hearing this, as it implied the man had a level of education few slaves would have attained. Sensing the intelligence behind the man's eyes Anton took a moment to appraise him before responding.

"Thank you. Hmm, yes, we shall have to talk. I think I would like to know more about you, but this can wait. For now we would like a tour of the estate. Tomorrow or perhaps the day after we shall journey to Baron Durand's estate on the other side of the island, so we would like transportation arranged for this. And please send a message to this fool Moreau I shall want to see him as soon as we return."

Auyuba gave him a broad smile and a brief bow in response. "It shall be done."

The lawyer Jean Moreau took four days to appear at the plantation. Anton struggled to contain his mounting frustration, but the days of waiting were fruitful, allowing him time to gain a much better sense of his surroundings. The family had journeyed to Henri's estate, which was nowhere near as extensive as theirs. Henri decided to stay at the de Bellecourt plantation rather than stay on his own away from the others.

As the lawyer bustled into the room Anton had established as his office with Auyuba in tow he did his best to give an appearance of energy and efficiency. Anton raised an eyebrow and offered a stony look in response, but the lawyer affected not to notice.

"Mr. Moreau. I am Anton de Bellecourt and this is Baron Henri Durand," said Anton, gesturing to

Henri sitting off to one side. "Baron Durand is here to observe. You will be dealing with him for his own plantation when you meet on site there."

"Count de Bellecourt, Baron Durand, it's good to finally meet you. I knew both of your fathers well. I apologize for the confusion over your arrival. I'm coming to realize the clerk I have managing my correspondence is an incompetent fool. The letter from your solicitor giving notice of your journey here was lost in a pile of paperwork on his desk. What can you do, eh? It's impossible to get good help out here."

Anton kept a stony look and didn't let it soften in response. The lawyer gave a tiny shrug of acknowledgment and tried one last time to mollify his obviously unhappy client.

"I must also apologize I could not attend to you sooner. I manage several different estates for owners back in France and I had some affairs on another estate that simply couldn't wait for me to attend to."

"Mr. Moreau," said Anton with a sniff. "I don't care if you were off seeing one of your whores on someone else's estate. You are paid handsomely to manage our affairs properly here and I shall expect better of you in future."

Anton was certain he saw a brief flash of annoyance in the lawyer's eyes, but the man smiled in outward apology. "Of course, sir. I shall do my best. Now, to business?"

Despite Anton's annoyance he had to admit the financial records of the estate were well kept and in order. Or they appeared to be. A sense it all seemed too good nagged the entire time. Anton grew certain someone was fiddling with the numbers, but couldn't put his finger on it. The profits seemed reasonable, but only just. Resolving to go over it all again in detail he nodded acceptance and congratulated the two men.

Anton was amazed to find Auyuba was the one deserving of the most praise. As they went over everything it became clear Auyuba really was the one actually maintaining the records, which confirmed he had a level of education astonishing for a slave. As they closed the books Anton had to ask about it.

"Auyuba? Oh, yes," said Moreau in response. "Indeed, he is the one who does most of the work here. My clerk and I taught him because it's much better to have someone on site keeping track of it all. It helps keep the fees I have to charge you reasonable! Yes, Auyuba learns fast and he's a bright fellow. Aren't you, Auyuba?"

Auyuba offered them a wide smile in return, but said nothing.

The lawyer turned back to Anton with his own smile. "Well, since you are conveniently here there is one other thing to discuss. Every year we review the status of your property and assess whether we need to add to it to meet your needs."

"Add to it? What do you mean?"

"I mean your slaves, Count de Bellecourt. Things change, sir. There are births, deaths, injuries, and runaways, this sort of thing. Auyuba, what is the tally this year?"

"Count de Bellecourt has 308 slaves, up a net gain of three for the year. The details are all here in this summary. Overseer Montcalm is requesting an additional fifteen slaves be purchased as most of our increases have come in mixed race births and our losses have been either blacks or mulattoes and sambos. There are seven of the latter groups he wishes to manumit as well. He has extra demands now with this little new field we have prepared for use."

"Mulattoes and sambos? What are they?" said Anton.

Moreau gave a startled look for a moment before responding. "Forgive me, I thought you knew the terms. Slaves coming from Africa are, of course, of pure black parentage. Over time here there has been, and continues to be, interbreeding with whites. A mulatto child is the product of one pure black parent and the other a pure white parent. A sambo is the product of a pure black and a mulatto parent."

"I see. But why is any of this relevant?"

Moreau was taken aback, raising his eyebrows once again. "Count de Bellecourt, this is very relevant. The value of any given slave depends on a number of factors such as their age, their skills, and supply in the local market. But their parentage is also important as it can determine what they are given to do."

Still puzzled, Anton glanced over at Henri to see if he was confused too. Henri shrugged and shook his head to show he wasn't getting the point either. Anton turned back to Moreau, not needing to say anything, as the question was clear on his face.

"Gentlemen," said Moreau, speaking slow as if talking to simpletons. "A slave with white blood in his or her background is always going to be more useful and therefore more valuable."

"Really?" said Henri. "Why?"

"Isn't it obvious? Pure blacks are capable of little more than hard labour in the fields. They are beasts, really. But add white blood to the mix? This changes everything. The more white blood the better.

These slaves will have far more intelligence and be capable of so much more as a result. Slaves such as this are not wasted doing field labour or menial work. These are always given tasks either as part of the household or are trained to do more complex tasks in the sugar refining process. Why, take Auyuba here. He is a valuable mustee slave with a much greater degree of white blood in his veins."

"A mustee? Some other combination of white and black parents I assume?"

"Exactly! You are beginning to understand. After mulattoes and sambos you have quadroons. These are slaves with mulatto and pure white parentage and are obviously much more valuable. Even better is a mustee, the product of a liaison between a white and a quadroon, so there is really very little black blood in the lineage. The most valuable is a musteefino, which is the offspring of a mustee and a white."

Anton turned to Henri, who raised one eyebrow, but returned his gaze in silence.

"Mr. Moreau," said Anton, turning back to the lawyer. "This seems rather—arbitrary, don't you think? I find it a little puzzling slaves with mostly black blood are incapable of learning new things."

The lawyer shrugged. "Count de Bellecourt, this is the system in use throughout the Caribbean, based on many decades of experience with slaves. In any case, you now have a bit of an imbalance that must be rectified. By my estimate you have three or perhaps four more household slaves than you need. These could be sold for profit to purchase more blacks. You should first familiarize yourself with your household to see which ones you want to keep.

You will of course want to take your personal needs into account as well."

"Personal needs?"

"Of course. Men have *needs*, yes? There may be one or more women you may wish to keep to service you."

A vision of the exotic looking house slave he had met on arrival waiting his pleasure brought a sudden wave of desire that conflicted with a nagging but vague unease over the idea of using a slave in that way. Moreau misread the conflicted look on Anton's face, so he continued before Anton could respond.

"Of course, there are a number of boys and young men in service around the household if you are so inclined. You need not concern yourself if so. We are all discreet and, after all, we are French and we understand."

"Baron Durand and I are inclined to women, thank you," said Anton, with a sharp edge to his voice. "Mr. Moreau, I confess I am surprised this is allowed."

A look of mild amusement played across the lawyer's face as he responded.

"But of course it is, my dear Count. Slaves are your property. Well, there is the Code Noir. It defines the conditions of their slavery and how they must be treated. This has been in place for over a hundred years, but really, you can do pretty much *whatever* you want with them. As long as you aren't outrageously excessive about it I guarantee no one will be hounding you. Look, if you aren't inclined to exercise your rights with them do let me know. I can recommend two or three discreet, high quality brothels in Castries if you so desire. They have some absolutely delicious women of all colours available. As I said, men have needs."

Anton and Henri both looked at each other and neither could resist a hesitant smile as the possibilities unfolded in their minds. Finding his voice now thick with desire, Anton cleared his throat and turned back to Moreau.

"Umm, yes, if you could leave us with this information it would be helpful. It was a rather long trip here."

"I understand," said Moreau with a smirk. Well, we can discuss selling some slaves again after you've had a chance to become fully acquainted with your household and have given it some thought. But the other issue to consider is overseer Montcalm's request to manumit seven slaves."

"This means they are to be freed, correct?" said Henri. "I've been wondering about this. Why would we free slaves only to have to replace them?"

"Oh, these would all be slaves too old and slow to work productively now."

"I see," said Anton. "So we are freeing them to a pleasant retirement after years of hard service for us?"

"Pleasant?" said Moreau, with a laugh and an incredulous look. "Count de Bellecourt, surely you saw all the beggars in the streets of Castries when you passed through town, did you not? Where do you think they all came from? When you manumit a slave you are both freeing them from slavery and freeing yourself of any obligation to feed and care for them."

"Good God, man!" exclaimed Anton, a look of shock on his face. "Are you serious?"

"Of course. This is normal business practice."

Anton couldn't resist a glance at Auyuba to see his reaction. The slave's face was a mask carved from petrified stone. After a quick glance at Henri, whose face wore the same shock Anton was feeling, Anton turned back to Moreau.

"We will be doing no such thing. We will free these slaves, but they can stay here and continue to have their needs met as before."

"My dear Count," said Moreau, an incredulous look creasing his face. "Do you have any idea what this decision will cost you? Maybe it isn't as bad in France as the rumours I've heard, but certainly the price of food and clothing locally has become very expensive. This will reduce your profits significantly over time and if you keep doing this eventually you will have so many mouths to feed there will be no profit at all. Doing this is unheard of. I cannot recommend you do it, sir."

Anton waved a hand in dismissal. "We have resources. And yes, I expect this may be unheard of, but I am resolved. The world is changing, Mr. Moreau. I am not afraid to try and do things differently. The more I think about it the more I find slavery distasteful. I will be looking closely at the entire way of doing business while I am here, because I think there has to be a better way."

This time it was Moreau's face that seemed carved from some hard substance.

"Really? Well, this is interesting," he replied after a few moments of contemplation and a small shrug. "It is your money to do with as you see fit, sir. And with this settled I shall now take my leave. Good day, sir."

"Mr. Moreau? There is one additional service you could perform for us. Do you know the Governor of St. Lucia?"

The lawyer was already halfway to the door, but he stopped and turned back to Anton with a questioning look.

"I do, sir. His offices in Castries are a little down the street from my own."

"Excellent. Please pass him a message I would appreciate a meeting with him to present my credentials as an envoy. Say in two or three days, at his convenience? I shall await word from him."

Moreau's eyes widened and his eyebrows went up a little, but he mastered his surprise.

"An *envoy*? I see. I shall ensure he receives your message. Good day, sir."

Moreau bustled out the door with Auyuba behind him. Auyuba and Anton looked at each other for the briefest of moments as the slave turned to close the door behind him. The look on the slave's face was still unreadable, but it seemed to Anton the slave gave him an almost imperceptible nod as he left.

Two days later Anton and Henri left to present themselves at the Governor's offices. The journey into town required payment yet again of two different road tolls in addition to passage through two separate roadblocks manned by soldiers. Although they were waved through without delay both men wondered at what was happening.

Castries itself was the same potpourri of beggars and people bustling about, with soldiers mingling in the crowds. As they entered the fringes of the main business district a sudden commotion made the horse pulling their carriage shy back. A small crowd of young black men burst from an alley between two buildings, separating to run scrambling in all different directions to get away from the soldiers hot on their tracks.

Two of the soldiers knelt to aim and fired at the fleeing men. Both shots hit home, screams of pain cut short as they flailed and clawed at the wounds in their backs before crashing face first into the dusty street.

Seeing the expensive looking carriage in his path the one coming their direction ran to the door and jerked it open. Anton and Henri were stunned to realize he had a long, vicious looking machete in his hands and was intent on boarding the carriage. But before either could act the soldiers caught up with the fugitive.

"No you don't!" shouted the closest soldier as he dropped his quarry with a savage blow to the head, the three foot long club he wielded landing with a sickening crunch.

A swarm of trailing soldiers grabbed the unconscious man and dragged him off. One paused to slam the door to the carriage closed before turning away.

Anton looked at Henri in shock. "My God, I think he was going to try and take us hostage or kill us."

Stunned it had all happened with no explanation Anton stuck his head out the window of the carriage to call after the soldier.

"I say, you there, what was all that about?"

The soldier stopped and turned to Anton in puzzlement. He regarded him with a disbelieving look for a moment before responding.

"Runaway slaves." Turning, he stalked off after the others.

The Governor's sturdy and large, stone walled office was the most well maintained building on the street. More and more soldiers were in evidence the closer they got. Once inside the pleasant, cool interior they didn't have to wait long before being ushered into the Governor's presence.

"Count de Bellecourt, Baron Durand, it is a pleasure to meet you. I am Governor Gilles Marchand," said the Governor, rising from his chair behind his desk to shake their hands. "This is my personal assistant Jules Caton. Welcome to St. Lucia."

Anton introduced both himself and Henri and as the Governor waved them into the chairs in front of his desk they sat down.

"Well, gentlemen, I must say it is refreshing to have more people of quality in St. Lucia. Higher society here is, to put it mildly, rather limited. Many of the plantation owners have long since left matters in the hands of local managers and returned home. But what local society we have will be ecstatic you are here. The women in particular are always starved for news from home. We must organize an event to present you."

"Absolutely, Governor. Actually, we had thought we would host a ball when we are ready for exactly this purpose. Perhaps your assistant could help with identifying who should be sent invitations?"

"Of course, Count! I am already looking forward to it," replied the Governor with a smile. "But I must confess, I am curious about what brings you and your family to St. Lucia. The lawyer Moreau said something about credentials as an envoy?"

"Indeed, Governor. Allow me to present this introduction from the Foreign Minister," said Anton, reaching into his coat pocket for a slim envelope he passed to the Governor.

The Governor opened it and scanned the contents. All that betrayed his reaction was the slight widening of his eyes, followed by a wrinkling of his entire face as he concentrated on what he was reading. After reading it through a second time he looked up from the paper he was holding to stare with renewed interest at the two men. Before he sat back in his chair he returned the letter to Anton.

"Well, Count de Bellecourt, I must say this is— umm, interesting. And it's very unique. You know, I've been a diplomat for almost thirty years and to be honest I've never seen anything quite like this. This is a rather lofty goal."

"Indeed, Governor. I consider myself privileged to have authority to carry out this important task. The times are changing, sir. I firmly believe France can lead the world to a better place by focusing on the highest of principles. Think of it sir, freedom for everyone, even slaves! Look, I know this must come as a surprise and change will not come easily. But we must start somewhere. So if I and my family can help by serving as envoys throughout the Caribbean islands, regardless of which country they are a colony of, to promote freedom from slavery and to find a better model for plantation businesses everywhere, well, we are proud to do so."

"Umm, yes, well, as I said these are lofty goals, gentlemen. I of course support anything our Minister wants to achieve, but I confess to thinking you will find this a difficult task. You will have enough of a challenge with our own community of plantation owners, let alone convincing the British and others of the need to do this. I am actually somewhat surprised, to be honest, as I know the Minister well and I've never heard him articulate a passion for high principles such as this."

"I confess he was undoubtedly influenced by my patron, the Marquis de Lafayette. It was he that approached the Minister to suggest this course of action. The Marquis is a strong supporter of reform, as you may know. And yes, we know the British will prove a challenge. But we intend to focus our efforts both here and on the British islands equally before we carry our message to the Americans or the Spanish. Slavery is quite widespread here in the islands, so where better to start?"

"Ah, the Marquis de Lafayette!" said the Governor, with a sudden look of understanding appearing before a mild, questioning frown replaced it. "Well, this explains much. Yes, I am aware of his thinking. Hmm, so what does this mean for me, sir? The Minister's letter does not provide direction to me, it merely introduces you and details your objective as an envoy."

"Why, nothing, really. Your good wishes and whatever support you believe reasonable to offer would be welcome. We have our own resources and expect nothing from anyone else."

The Governor relaxed, sitting back in his chair with a broad smile. "Well, then, this is straightforward enough. I offer you the best wishes for success in this noble effort. I confess I think you have a long road ahead of you, especially if you are thinking you can influence the British to change their ways, but if it turns out I can assist in some small way do let me know."

"Thank you, Governor, we shall keep this in mind. We shall await contact from your assistant and we promise our welcome ball shall be the social event of the year. Come Henri, let us leave the Governor to the rest of his busy day."

"Certainly," said Henri, as the two men rose to leave. "Governor, one question if I may, out of curiosity? We've noticed there seems to be rather a large presence of soldiers in the streets, which seems odd. We were also almost attacked on the way to see you as well. What is the local situation? Is there anything to be concerned about?"

"Attacked? What happened, please?"

Anton explained and the Governor frowned, but didn't seem surprised.

"Umm, well, lately there has been—unrest. Actually, it has been growing worse and worse for the last year. We've had several runaway slaves take to the hills, far more than normal. Having runaways is not unusual. It is the sheer numbers of them and more to the point, what they have been doing. Many have banded together to commit the most vicious acts of banditry and mayhem. But we have matters under control. Have you gentlemen established security for yourselves yet?"

"Security?"

"Yes, indeed, you should have a constant armed patrol guarding your household. You do not wish to be murdered in your beds like a few others have already been. Why, the British consul was even murdered down the street from here in front of your lawyer's office. Your man Auyuba found him. We still have no idea who did it. Well, we are doing what we can with the soldiers available to us, but as you can obviously see this island is rugged and has many places to hide."

"Good Lord," said Anton, a look of shock on his face. "We had no idea this was happening. What is behind all this, Governor?"

Governor Marchand regarded the two men with a speculative look for a moment before replying. "Times are difficult. Food prices are at their highest ever and with sugar profits declining, well, many owners have had their slaves on short rations. Actually, *everything* has become very expensive, not just food."

"As have the road tolls and customs duties, Governor," said Henri. "Could these not be eased to help the situation?"

The Governor raised one eyebrow at the question. "Sir, I don't think you understand how this works. What do you think pays for the soldiers guarding us all or for the overall administration of the colony? The only reason the troops are here is because I requested them and the colony is paying for them. I receive nothing from France. We must be self-sufficient. In fact, I get regular requests to make remittances to the treasury at home! I am constantly in battle with them over how much we get to keep."

Anton and Henri looked at each other before turning back to the Governor.

"Sir," said Anton. "It would seem we have much to learn. But if the situation is this desperate I think being successful with our task becomes critical. We must find a way to reform the system!"

"Well, as I said, I wish you success and if there is some way I can reasonably assist then do let me know."

"Thank you. Good day, sir."

Once assured the two men had left the office and were out of earshot, the Governor and his assistant turned as one to look at each other and both burst out laughing at the same time.

"My God, Governor, are those two serious?" said his assistant Jules.

The Governor was still chuckling as he motioned toward the cognac decanter. His assistant obliged and poured two snifters as Governor Marchand mastered himself.

"Yes, I believe they are, Jules. It became clear when they confessed the Marquis was behind it all." The Governor smacked his lips in appreciation of his first sip of the amber liquid and raised his glass for another taste.

"I confess I don't know much of him, sir. What is this really all about?"

The Governor eyed his glass of cognac with approval for a moment before replying. "Well, the good Marquis is a likable fellow in his own way, but he does not want to accept the truth real power in France rests with our friends in the palace surrounding and supporting our King. But this is how things work, always have and always will. Since he knows he cannot do anything directly about this he seeks other ways to batter down the walls our friends in the palace throw up. He seeks to shake up the established order in whatever way he can. The Foreign Minister was most careful in the letter not to commit him or us to anything in particular and is really humouring the Marquis. I have to say, I think the Marquis is becoming desperate if he's reduced to turning to naive fools like this."

"I see. So if they approach me for help on something, and you are not available to consult, I simply defer until you are?"

"Yes. You can help them with their invitation list for the ball as promised, but for anything else you can nod and smile and be vague. Well, if you know its truly something inconsequential then do help them out, but if not, or if they press you hard, you check with me."

The Governor smiled as he swirled the remaining cognac in his glass and then downed what remained.

"Yes, Jules, I think we can safely sit back and enjoy watching this unfold. This could prove the most amusing entertainment we've had around here for a long time!"

Chapter Four
December 1787 to January 1788
Antigua

Evan and James were both having difficulty keeping
their temper as they stood in the main storehouse of
Dockyard supplies, arguing with the two Lieutenants
tasked with running the administrative part of the
Dockyard operation. The two officers were part of the
civilian arm procuring and maintaining supplies for
the far-reaching needs of the Navy. In essence, they
were bureaucrats and both had proved unsupportive
to anyone's needs but their own. Evan and James
were suspicious the two men had attempted to subvert
the goals of their senior officers in past, but had no
proof. Still, the two Dockyard officers were
outranked and reported to Evan and James for orders.

"Lieutenant Burns," said Evan, with an edge
to his voice. "I don't care what this paperwork shit
says and whether or not it has my signature. I don't
recall signing it and besides, you know goddamn well
I would never have agreed to sell any of our supplies
to the bloody Yanks even if they were surplus, which
they were not. This is all nonsense and you need to
find an explanation and deal with this gap in our
critical supplies."

"Sir," said Lieutenant Long, the junior of the
two Dockyard officers, wearing an apologetic look.
"This does appear to be your signature."

"Yes, *appear* is the operative word, damn you.
This is a forgery and you two need to fix this or I
swear I will have both of you fools dismissed and
shipped out of here at the next opportunity."

"Let's get back to my office," said Evan as
they left the storehouse, leaving the two Lieutenants

behind. "The mail packet that came in this morning had a letter from Sir James I didn't have time to read. Let's hope it has something for us to do involving action instead of dealing with those two horse turds for a change."

"Evan?" said James, as he scanned their surroundings to ensure no one could hear them. "Is it my imagination or are those two bastards trying to set you up?"

"Of course they are. I guarantee you I did not sign the release order. I may have a lot on my mind sometimes, but I'm a long way from being this bloody senile. Those bastards have done something with those supplies and they are going to try and pin it on me. I need you to quietly check this out. See if any of your sources have wind of this. I'm going to look up the name of the Yankee ship in the Customs records and see if any of it tallies. The bastards may have bribed that idiotic Customs inspector. Come to think of it, see if those two have some explanation for how the goods were picked up given we stopped allowing foreign shipping into English Harbour months ago. You know what to do."

James grinned and nodded as they entered Evan's office. "It will be my pleasure. I think I'll try recruiting a couple of the workers in the Dockyard too, get them to sniff around a little. Maybe those two idiots have finally overstepped themselves and we really can get them shipped out. Think of the send off party we could have to celebrate!"

Evan snorted with mild amusement as he sat in his chair and tore open the sealed envelope. Having only one arm meant he had to use a small knife set into a vice attached to the side of his desk for exactly this purpose. He scanned the one page it contained quickly. He turned grim and he raised one eyebrow as he finished and passed it over to James.

"Well, it's about time," said Evan. "I was beginning to wonder if they were even going to keep this place going."

"Next week?" said James, putting the letter down after scanning it too. "In time for Christmas. God, I wonder what took so long."

"Well, with Sir James coming to visit us and the new commanding officer finally arriving on station I guess we'd better have the Dockyard is looking its best."

"So who is this Captain George Rand, Evan? Have you ever heard of him?"

"Yes, but I don't know much, nor do I know him personally. He's been a post Captain for at least three decades. Most of his service has been in the Mediterranean, I think. He's not seen much mention in the Gazette, at least that I'm aware of, so his career hasn't been distinguished. I guess we'll find out more from Captain Standish. If he doesn't know Captain Rand well he will likely get to know him better in the time it takes for the two of them to sail here from Barbados."

"Hmm, well, I think I'm more interested in why Captain Standish has given no hint as to the reason for his visit. He hasn't visited us since we were first assigned to work with him. This is unusual."

"I agree. Well, we shall find out. I think something is up, so let's hope he has something useful for us to do and even better, something involving action. God knows we haven't had any real action around here for two years now. Let's finish up and get out of here. I've had enough of this place for today and I've been looking forward to having an ale at the Dog all day."

An hour later they were sitting in the shade on the wide verandah of the Dockyard Dog Inn, with its panoramic view of the broad bay the little village of Falmouth Harbour was nestled beside. A wide variety of merchant shipping and local fishing boats dotted the bay.

"I like what they've done here, Evan," said James as a servant placed two brimming mugs in front of them. "I confess I wasn't sure about spending as much money as they have to fix this place up, especially given how everyone is always complaining about how no one has any money, but it looks to be paying off."

Evan nodded in agreement as he took an appreciative sip of his ale. Putting his mug down, he rubbed the small stump that remained of his left arm absentmindedly. Despite it being over three years since he had lost his left arm, phantom pain and feelings still bothered him on occasion. "I can't believe it's been almost two years now since they took this place over."

Much had slowly changed since Evan had bought Alice's freedom. Emma and Walton, former slaves operating the Flying Fish Inn on the harbourfront in St. John's, had combined resources with Alice to purchase the run down Falmouth Harbour Inn and rename it the Dockyard Dog Inn. Evan had been the architect of it all and, as he sipped his ale, was pleased with his handiwork.

Anyone returning to Falmouth Harbour wouldn't recognize anything about the old Inn except for the location and some of the old shape of the building still to be seen. Emma's husband Walton proved adept at construction and design. The building had undergone a significant expansion, with more rooms for travellers to stay in and sturdy, new stone walls added to help it withstand even the strongest hurricanes. New stables had been built out back. Open windows with hurricane shutters ready for when needed looked out from the main bar room onto the wide verandah with its own tables and chairs.

"I can't believe how busy this place has become," said James. "It seems to grow with every passing week."

Evan looked around the room and nodded. Even though this was a weekday and the usual dinner hour was still over an hour away, the bar was close to being full.

"Indeed. I had a feeling this would happen. The old Inn was always empty because it was such a dump no one wanted to be here. But even with times as hard as they are I figured there was enough of a population in this area they would support it. Why ride all the way to St. John's for a nice dinner or a drink if you don't have to? I knew word of Emma's cooking would get around too. And then there is the shipping. If the ship's masters need to deliver goods to plantations on this side of the island, why deliver them to St. John's? It's far better they can stay in a nice, reasonably priced place instead of cramped quarters on their ships."

"Yes, you called it right. And having all this shipping come here has made it a lot easier to quiz the merchant Captains about what they are finding on the French islands they visit. At least it gives us something to report on. It's no substitute for real action, though."

"No, it isn't," agreed Evan. "In fairness, though, given you and I were pretty much out of action with the yellow jack for so long I can understand why Captain Standish wouldn't have given us any tasks with substance to them."

Both men had succumbed to the fever in early spring of 1787 as a wave of the illness swept through the Dockyard workers and the sailors manning the ships in English Harbour. Once past the worst of it they had needed several weeks to regain their full energy and strength. But, at least they had survived. Several of those catching the virus had not, adding once again to the common wisdom the West Indies was not a healthy place to be.

"Yes, I think you're right," said James. "Then by the time we were back on our feet everything slowed down because of hurricane season. So you really think something is up? Our merchant Captains have hinted times are getting even harder out there, but we haven't heard anything about real unrest. God, some action would be good. We were given this assignment for three years and we've got less than half a year left. Let's face it, most of this has been tedious boredom."

Evan was about to respond when the soft touch of a woman's hand on his shoulder interrupted his train of thought, and as he focused on it Alice leaned around from his other side to give him a welcome kiss on the cheek. As she did one of her breasts slid with tantalizing slowness across his shoulder and even better, settled in place. Turning his head he found her low cut dress with the cleavage of her breasts leading to further depths of paradise direct in his line of vision. Across the table James wasn't hiding his appreciative grin.

"Hello, lover man," said Alice. "How was your day?"

"Getting better with every second," said Evan, still staring with enjoyment at her cleavage.

Alice laughed and straightened up, mock exasperation at the two men on her face.

"Is that all you two ever think about?"

Evan looked at James and both men laughed.

"Well, yes," said Evan with a shrug.

"As often as possible," offered James.

Alice groaned, but she smiled as she changed the subject. "Well, *my* day is going fine and I feel like celebrating tonight. The bastard that made my life hell from the day I was born is finally gone from our lives and if this isn't a reason to celebrate, I don't know what would be."

"What kind of celebration did you have in mind?" said Evan, his playful leer making it clear what the answer he wanted to hear was.

"Later," replied Alice, as she pulled closer to Evan again. "Mum is coming by too. Emma is cooking up something special for us all and I think they've talked some of the locals into coming by to play music. Hey, it's not every day the bastard causing us so much trouble packs up and leaves."

The bastard was none other than her father, John Roberts. Owner of the largest plantation on Antigua, he had been one of the local leaders directly involved with French and American agents plotting to destabilize the island over two years ago while evading payment of customs duties through extensive smuggling activity. Like many owners, Roberts felt free to use his female slaves to satisfy his lust and he had been more active than most. Alice had been one of his victims.

But now he had left Antigua, not expected to return, taking the only daughter he was prepared to acknowledge with him. Elizabeth was a little older than Alice, but except for the fact Elizabeth was white the two women could almost have been twins. Elizabeth had desired Evan and in honest moments with himself he had to admit he found it hard to resist. But all it took to dispel this was to see Alice and marvel that he had won her affections.

That Roberts was leaving was not a surprise to Evan. The reason put about was Elizabeth needed introduction into English society, and both he and his wife wanted to be there to supervise. In reality, Roberts was joining a steady parade of plantation owners returning to England, placing their properties in the hands of local lawyers and managers to oversee operations for them. With sugar prices fetching lower returns due to greater competition, as costs and taxes were going up, the incentive to put their full efforts into their operations was no longer there.

The only real surprise was it had taken this long for Roberts to finally leave. After selling Alice, Emma, and Walton, he had continued to sell other assets. The Flying Fish Inn that Emma and Walton had once run for him had been put on the market and sold along with three other businesses in town Roberts owned.

Seeing the pattern Evan put some of his own funds to use to make an offer through an intermediary to buy Alice's mother Anne for a reasonable price and set her free. Roberts had accepted and she came to live in a little nearby hut, earning Evan undying gratitude from both Alice and her mother. He couldn't help smiling at the memory.

"Well, you're right, my dear, this is a good reason to celebrate," said Evan, before turning to look at James. "And maybe we'll soon have other reasons to celebrate, too!"

"Sir James, it is good to see you again," said Evan, stepping forward to shake the hand of the distinguished looking, older man stepping ashore from the handsome 36-gun frigate *HMS Devonshire* delivering him to Antigua. As with the last time they had seen him the Captain was not in uniform.

"Thank you, Commander Ross," said Sir James, as he turned to greet James. "Lieutenant Wilton. It's good to see you both looking fit and healthy. I had a bout with yellow fever too, many years ago, so I know what you have both been through. Commander, is there anywhere local I can stay you could recommend? Somewhere I could hire transportation for myself too, hopefully?"

Evan gave a start, but he recovered quickly. "Why yes, Captain. I'm sorry if I seem startled, sir, I guess I assumed you would want to remain on board for the brief time you are here. There is indeed a new local Inn called the Dockyard Dog and I know you will find it most pleasant."

The Captain offered Evan a rueful smile before giving a quick glance over his shoulder at the frigate, a tense frown replacing the smile. As he did two sailors from the ship arrived carrying a small travelling case each.

"Hmm, yes, I understand why you would think this, but it would be best for a variety of reasons I decamp elsewhere. If you could give me a hand with my valises we can be on our way."

An hour later they were sitting on the verandah of the Dockyard Dog once again. The Captain declared satisfaction with his room as he joined them and eyed the fresh mug of ale Evan had ordered for him with obvious pleasure. Evan watched him scan his surroundings with practiced ease to ensure their conversation would be unheard, but Evan had already chosen the best possible location for this purpose.

Raising his mug the Captain drank deep before speaking. "I say, this is a lovely ale. Well, gentlemen, I shan't keep you in suspense any longer. I'm sure you're both wondering what brings me all the way to Antigua."

"Sir, we are. In fact, we are hoping you have something involving action for us."

Sir James chuckled. "Quite so, I thought this might be the case. Yes, I do have some tasks for you. I could have done all this by correspondence, but it has been far too long since I saw you both and sometimes it is better to have the kind of full conversation only possible in person. I needed to talk to Governor Shirley, too. So, I must first give you some sense of what is going on before we get to the jobs at hand. I know I've given you a sense in my letters the French are facing difficult times, right? Until now we have chosen to watch from afar and keep our activities fairly passive in nature, which has likely meant boredom for you two gentlemen. But the time has come to change the approach."

Sir James paused to sip at his ale once again. Holding out his mug he licked his lips in appreciation and smiled before putting it back on the table.

"Damn, this is good," said Sir James, before he turned to look at Evan and James.

To their shock his demeanor underwent a total change as Sir James looked around once more, obviously to be assured once again they could not be overheard. Evan was surprised to see Sir James shake his head and sigh, obvious worry and anxiety deepening the lines of his face.

"Right, what you need to know is we believe matters are getting worse for the French. God knows we have problems with our own economy, but all the signs are they are in far worse trouble than we are. And I think they know it. It's like they can see a storm coming they know will wreak havoc, but anyone with the power to do something about it is either being willfully blind or is so incompetent they can't even see it. Too many people caring only about themselves and damn everyone else."

"Sir James?" said James. "Pardon me for asking, but how do we know this? What signs are we talking about?"

"Don't be afraid to ask me questions, gentlemen. I need you both to understand what is going on. We know because we have sources in France keeping us informed, of course. Some are actual spies we sent, but others are merchants doing business. Diplomats too. We aren't choosy about where we get information. We even read the newspapers and read between the lines to get past the official story. And as to what signs, I'll give you a couple of examples. The price of bread in France has risen to insane levels once again and there have been several incidents of unrest. The army has had to be called in to back up local police on more than one occasion. And speaking of the army, it's not widely known, but the French are having problems *paying* them."

Sir James gave them both a meaningful look and paused to let the significance of it sink in as he helped himself to more of his ale. Evan and James turned as one to each other, grim looks on their faces.

"Good God, Sir James. This is indeed a concern," said Evan.

"Needless to say, we are extremely nervous about what may come of this. If the French army gets restive anything is possible. Politicians and diplomats like things to be predictable, at least as much as this can be achieved. Until now we thought it likely they would get this under control, but we have become far less optimistic. The real concern is someone may get the bright idea to find an external threat to paint as the villain and cause of everyone's problems, and who better than us? They know our economy isn't exactly humming either, so find some excuse and rally their military around the flag to come after us, right?"

"Is this a general threat or something specific to the Caribbean, Sir James?"

"Bear in mind we have no specific intelligence definitively saying this is what is going to happen," he replied. "Having hard, specific intelligence is a luxury we rarely enjoy. Rather, this is a case of doing a realistic assessment of the situation, coming up with realistic possible scenarios that could unfold, and then making sure the worst of these possible outcomes simply doesn't happen."

"So what this means, gentlemen, is the French have many possible ways to make a serious nuisance of themselves to us in many different places if this is where it all goes. However, our possessions in the Caribbean would certainly be high on their list if they were casting about for options. Everyone knows how important the sugar trade is to our economy. Find a way to impact this and we are suddenly in a lot of trouble."

"What about the other players in all of this, Sir James?" said James.

"Hmm, good question. For the moment, at least, we think everyone else has other matters on their minds. The Spanish have been relatively quiescent and look to stay this way. They are happy to keep the money coming in from their colonies so they can go back to drinking wine in the sunshine. The Dutch have their hands full with their own possessions, too. They would love to see our traders taken down a notch so they could rule the trade lanes, but they simply don't have the military resources to do it."

Sir James finished his ale and signaled for more, waiting till it had been delivered and they were alone again before continuing.

"And then there are the bloody Yanks. They are the wild card in all of this. Their economy is tenuous at best and realistically it should take them a generation or more to build it to a point where they could even think of challenging us, but they seem to be holding their own and have been far more tenacious about getting their house in order than the French. They seem to be increasingly preoccupied in dealing with the Indians in the Northwest Territories and have expansion in that direction on their minds. We have been expanding west from Canada too, in order to keep the Yanks in check, but overall we think they will be preoccupied with all of this for some time to come. Notice I said we *think*. Expansion never seems to be far from their minds and they have not lost interest in the Caribbean."

"So overall this means the French are the primary concern, Sir James? Do you fear the unrest in France will spill over here?" said Evan.

"Exactly, Commander, and we believe it already has. I know you have picked up the hints of unrest from the merchant Captains you talk to, but I have other sources to tap into and henceforth you will be provided with their intelligence on a regular basis. There have been uprisings on a few of the French islands with varying degrees of violence. Food prices and taxes have gone crazy, too, just like in France. St. Lucia appears to have been hit the hardest, but Martinique, Guadeloupe, and St. Martin have all had problems. The real concern is it seems the uprisings and the violence have been bad enough a naval force along with a substantial number of French army regulars have appeared at St. Lucia to deal with it."

"A *naval force*?" said Evan, as both he and James started in surprise and leaned closer to Sir James across the table. "My God, do you know the size and its composition?"

"This is an unknown, unfortunately. The problem with St. Lucia is we currently have a lack of informants with the requisite experience to properly assess this at the moment. The rumour is there are perhaps as many as five ships, but what they are we don't know. We have heard an unknown number of soldiers are now patrolling the streets of Castries and other major communities on the island. At any rate, the possible size of this force is catching everyone's attention. Needless to say, the new senior in command of this station has been tasked with keeping a weather eye on their activities above all."

"Is there anything we should know about Captain Rand, Sir James?" said Evan. "I confess we know little of him, but it is helpful to know what manner of officer he is if we are to work with him in future on whatever tasks you set us."

"Hmm, yes," said Sir James, sitting back in his chair and taking a moment to sip at his ale once again. When he began again Evan felt certain the Captain was choosing his words with care.

"Well, how shall I put this? I know Captain Rand from many years ago, when we were both much younger and shared a berth as midshipmen. Let's say we have had our disagreements over the years and things haven't changed much. But we get along when we need to. Captain Rand is a competent enough officer, but he can be rather slow to act. He is also attuned to political sensitivities, if you follow me. I don't think he will interfere in anything you are doing, but if he does to a point where it is impacting your ability to perform the tasks I have for you then do let me know and I will address it. My commission as a Captain does date from earlier than his."

"Thank you, Sir James. This is helpful to know. So, if St. Lucia is where things are happening and our sources there are not meeting our needs, is this where you need our help?" said Evan.

"It is. I've managed a couple of sources on Martinique, but they can be unreliable. On Guadeloupe I have a couple of sources, but they can be the same. The one I had on St. Lucia, usually most reliable, has mysteriously gone silent, and I don't like it. Meanwhile, I am swamped with a steady stream of correspondence from diplomats around the Caribbean asking for advice. Remember, there is no one doing a comparable service as we do elsewhere in the Western Caribbean. And, I've been doing my best to have an eye on the Dutch in Curacao and the bloody

Dons on the Spanish Main. Gentlemen, I need help and you are it."

"Sir? Do we not have a consul in Castries who could report on this?" said James.

A troubled look came over the Captain's face. "Well, yes, but he was my main source there and we have not heard from him for almost three months now. Letters to him have gone unanswered. John Andrews is his name and he is a friend of mine from many years back. It may be nothing or may be something. During the war he was involved with covert activities I had no part of, but aside from standard reports to me since then his work has been confined to the diplomatic realm. I will give you contact information for him and a letter of introduction."

"So our task is to make contact with him, sir?"

"Yes, but it is far beyond just that. We need more than what our consul and merchants who stop in there can see. St. Lucia is a vitally important island to the French and we need to know what they are up to. Thus, your first job is to find John and get his report. While you are there I want you to assess the French military forces, both navy and army, and to provide a full report on what you see and what you think they are up to. Captain Rand will be patrolling to see what he can find, but be assured he will be clamoring for your report the second you return. Most of all, I want a stable supply of information sources on that island. If something of consequence happens there in future, I want us to be the first people not on the island to know about it."

"So as of now this is your primary task, gentlemen. I cannot emphasize enough how important this is. There may or may not be some devious French plot underway and if there is, we'd better sort out soon what is going on. I have some additional discretionary funds you can use for, umm, friends willing to help us. I will have to provide you with some sort of orders to explain your presence to any who challenge you, but your cover as Dockyard officials will remain intact. I assume the operation is running in such a way your absence will not be a problem?"

"We may need to work on this a bit before we leave, sir," said Evan. "So our cover story should there be questions is we have just come to find our consul?"

"How you achieve your orders is your domain, gentlemen. I suggest you do everything possible to keep whatever story you use simple. In my experience simple is always the best strategy."

"Hmm," said Evan. "So if I were to travel to St. Lucia looking and behaving as a diplomat, much as you do, as opposed to in uniform, it would likely attract less attention. Lieutenant Wilton here, who has no profile as an officer, could dress and act as my manservant. This would free him to scout out some of the local haunts for sources. Does this sound like it would work?"

"Excellent, Commander. Your story could be you have been asked by local diplomats here on Antigua to find out what is happening to our consul. Yes, that could work. I can ask Governor Shirley to provide an introduction letter to this effect. If you run into anyone who knows you are in fact an officer you could plead you are on a diplomatic mission."

"Sir James?" said Evan. "How do you see us getting to and from St. Lucia? I don't know how long we need to be there. If we are forced to wait for merchant shipping or mail packets to get us around it could keep critical information out of your hands for far too long."

The Captain sighed and stared into his now half empty mug of ale. "You are right. I have had this problem over the years, too. I've made do with exactly what you suggest, but matters do seem to be heating up and timely information will be critical. Hmm, let me see what I can do about this. I fear I will have to deal with Captain Rand on it. Perhaps I can talk him into detaching a small sloop for you. It would still be a Royal Navy ship, but if your cover is as a diplomat I don't see why this wouldn't work. Yes, let me see what I can do. Well, gentlemen, if I stay and drink any more of this I'll be useless for the rest of the day. We shall talk again after I've had a chance to speak with the Governor and with Captain Rand."

Sir James rose and, after making arrangements to meet again in a few days, left for his room. Evan and James kept their faces straight until they were certain he was gone. Huge smiles broke out as they turned to look at each other.

"Oh my God, Evan," said James, reaching over to shake Evan's hand. "Well done! A ship!"

Evan grinned in return, but a note of caution sounded in his voice. "Let's not get our hopes up too much here. He didn't guarantee he could do it. But by God, it would be *good* to get a ship for us!"

Sir James proved correct in his assessment Captain Rand was slow to act. Every time an opportunity to meet with him was suggested his schedule was booked. The holiday season around Christmas meant an endless series of balls and diplomatic meetings enabling him to meet society on the island. After no less than four appointments to meet had been scheduled and then cancelled, Evan's frustration had become a constant sore.

But Sir James couldn't be ignored forever and the meeting took place in mid January in Evan's office in the Dockyard. The harsh, rhythmic impacts of the lash on human flesh sounding in the yard had finally ended and the meeting was scheduled for right after punishment had been rendered. Evan shook his head in dismay at the sounds. No less than eleven sailors had been tied to the grating one after the other to pay the price for drunkenness and fighting. By now no one was surprised at the large number facing punishment, as Captain Rand clearly had no qualms about using the lash. Evan understood the need for discipline, but his distaste for the lash remained as the punishment often seemed excessive for the crime.

Evan appraised the man as he walked in, glaring about the room and acting as if he owned it. Captain Rand turned out to be older looking than Captain Standish, although Evan had already learned they were both much the same age. Where Captain Standish was fit and distinguished looking, Captain Rand was not. The last time this man climbed a mast had to have been decades earlier, given how plump he was.

"Well, Sir James, I'm here," said Captain Rand. "You've been nagging me to meet so what is it you want? And who the hell are these two?"

Captain Standish nodded towards Evan and James as he introduced them. Captain Rand's eyes bulged at the mention James's rank.

"God Almighty, a Negro officer? What the Christ were they thinking?" said Captain Rand as he scowled at James, before the look turned to a disapproving frown. "And where the hell is your uniform?"

"Sir," said James, his face a blank mask. "My assignment is to remain covert and not to advertise my capacity as a naval officer."

"Covert?" Captain Rand groaned and rolled his eyes as he turned away to look at Captain Standish. "My God, Sir James. You *know* how much I detest this bloody *covert* nonsense. Is it really necessary to involve me in whatever horseshit you are mucking about in?"

"George," replied Captain Standish, a look of weary patience on his face. "We've had this conversation before, haven't we? So let's dispense with this and get down to business. You know I wouldn't bother you unless it was necessary."

Captain Rand scowled again, looking as if an unpleasant smell had permeated the room, but he shrugged and waved at Captain Standish to proceed.

"Actually, George, the horseshit I am mucking about in is the same horseshit of interest to you. Well, to clarify, I propose these two gentlemen here do the mucking about. You have orders to keep a weather eye on whatever these French ships in St. Lucia are up to and to check them if they start doing things contrary to our interests, right? The problem is you can't just sail into Castries and bully them into an explanation. You'd be buried in a heap of shit if you tried this and you know it."

Captain Standish paused, his expression daring Captain Rand to challenge the point. But once again Captain Rand shrugged his acknowledgement after a moment's pause. Captain Standish smiled and explained the assignment he had given the two officers and their need for a ship.

Captain Rand took a few long seconds to digest it all before turning to Evan. "You will provide me a copy of your report the instant you return to Antigua, of course."

"Of course, sir," replied Evan with a nod. "Captain Standish has already made this order clear."

"So George, as you can see your interests dovetail with ours. But we do need your support. If you have a small ship at your disposal these men could assume command of, it would be helpful. We both know things are getting tense out there and we need the information they can provide us as fast as possible. If they are sitting around waiting for transport with vital information not getting to us then our needs are not being met. And George, I am thinking one trip to St. Lucia is not going to be the only one in the cards."

Captain Rand couldn't help snorting with amusement. "God Almighty, James. I don't have any spare ships needing command officers and you know it. Why don't you make a case to the Admiralty, for God's sake?"

"In hindsight I should have done this sooner, but then things are moving rapidly. I will make a case and get it off. But we don't have the luxury of two months to get a reply to sort this out, do we?"

"All right, I understand that. But like I said, I don't have any ships they can walk into and assume command of. And you are asking much for me to detach one of the few I have and put it at their beck and call."

Captain Standish replied by holding his hands up with palms open wide.

Captain Rand mumbled something incoherently in frustration, but relented. "Fine. As it happens, I have a small sloop of war at my disposal due in tomorrow from Barbados to join us. I had other plans for it, but I will instruct Lieutenant Kent of *HMS Alice* to place himself and his ship at the disposal of these officers until we get an answer from London. At least this will give me the benefit of another set of eyes on those frog bastards in St. Lucia in addition to whatever your *covert* people come up with. So don't dawdle on getting the case off, James."

"And you, sir," said Captain Rand, as he turned to glare at Evan again. "Get me some answers, fast."

"We will not fail, sir."

"Right. Is there anything else we need to discuss?" said Captain Rand, rising from his chair.

As Captain Standish shook his head Evan spoke up. "Sir? It may be helpful to know that besides assisting the Captain here with covert activities we have an overt role as officers in charge of the Dockyard. If you have any concerns or needs not being met please address them to me for action. Also, Lieutenant Wilton and I worked closely with your predecessor Captain Nelson on the issue of local smuggling to circumvent customs duties. We have maintained our local intelligence sources to a limited degree and can continue to provide you with reports on possible smuggling activity."

"Nelson?" said Captain Rand, a look of distaste on his face. "Yes, I've heard about this bloody upstart. Thinks he knows better than people with a lot more experience than he. Can't imagine why anyone pays attention to him. Spending all his time chasing after smugglers, I ask you. That's the job of Customs, for God's sake. You needn't bother sending me reports on any of that, because the Royal Navy won't be wasting its time chasing smugglers while I'm in charge around here."

Captain Rand put his hat back on his head and, opening the door to leave, he paused and looked hard at Evan.

"Lieutenant Kent will have his orders shortly and will be in touch. Get me the goddamn report and do it fast."

Chapter Five
January to February 1788
St. Lucia

Anton couldn't bear it any longer.

On a business trip to Castries with Henri he was secretly pleased when Henri wanted to split up, pleading business with the lawyer Moreau over the sale of some slaves. Agreeing to meet again a few hours later Anton loitered a short while and then headed straight for one of the brothels Moreau had told them about during their first meeting.

The well-dressed thug answering the door scrutinized the man before him with care, but with it obvious Anton was a man of quality he ushered him straight into the parlour without question. The name Moreau brought an immediate smile to the madam who appeared and it broadened even more when Anton pulled out a heavy coin purse to pay the negotiated fee.

"Do you have a preference in your women, sir?"

"Umm, preference?"

"You know, colour, or their age, or other qualities?"

"Just bring me a range of choices and I shall make a decision," said Anton, his voice tight with anticipation.

She returned soon enough, ushering in five women all wearing flimsy, sheer nightgowns leaving little to the imagination.

"I'll leave you a minute to make a choice," said the madam. "We have another gentleman has arrived looking for our service so he will be coming in shortly to make a choice too."

Anton waved acknowledgement without even looking at her, intent more on sizing up the bounty standing before him. The five women stared back, appraising him in return. Seeing the quality of his attire they all began flirting with him in anticipation of a generous tip.

Anton soon realized his choice would be between two of them. One was a lithe, sultry woman with small, but pert breasts, dark straight hair and light brown skin. The other had much darker skin, larger breasts, and a full figure on the opposite end of the scale from the other woman. The large, dark areolas of her nipples were easy to see under the light gown she wore and Anton found his gaze kept wandering back to them. She gave him a wanton smile in return, as if she could read his mind. He was about to call her over when the door to the parlour opened once again.

"Anton?"

Shocked to hear his name, Anton looked over to find Henri standing in the doorway, wearing the same look of surprise Anton knew would be on his own face. Both men burst out laughing as everyone else in the room looked at them as if they were mad.

"Finished business early, did you?" said Anton with a grin. "Well, join the party."

Three hours later the two men did their best to look inconspicuous as they left the brothel, although it mattered little. No one took any notice as they returned to the inn where they had stabled their horse and buggy.

"Well, this is better," said Henri. "I get rather wound up if I haven't been with a woman for too long. So tell me, how was yours?"

Anton had stuck with his choice of the darker woman with the large breasts. "Yes, I know what you mean. And yes, I confess I rather enjoyed this. First time I've had a black woman."

Henri had gone for the other woman Anton had not chosen. "Indeed. I think I may try the one you had next time. I like the thought of juggling those tits of hers. We must tell Jacques about this place."

Anton didn't reply as his thoughts were still on the last few hours he had spent. He had relished the taste of a woman so different from what he had known before, and he wanted more. The problem was his thoughts kept drifting back to the exotic looking young slave woman they had met the first day they arrived on their plantation.

Her name was Elise and he wanted her now more than ever. She seemed much like the house slave Auyuba, a sense of intelligence behind her eyes masked by dumb servitude. Every time they chanced to encounter a quiver of energy seemed to pass between them. But his determination to be an enlightened slave owner drove a frustrating spike into the idea of simply taking her. He understood as an owner he could do as he pleased, but the standard he had set for himself kept coming to mind every time he watched her move about the mansion. A trip to the brothel became an absolute necessity.

Still mulling on his dilemma Anton was forced to attend to his surroundings on the way back to the plantation. A road crossing their path was blocked as a large gang of slaves was being shepherded across, impeding their path. A small group of four bored looking soldiers followed. The overseers prowled the fringes of the group, lashing the stumbling wretches with indiscriminate, random strokes from short whips while others used long canes to beat their victims. One of the slaves stumbled and fell, gashed by a sharp rock as she landed. Still bleeding, she was manhandled to her feet and beaten back into place in the gang. Anton and Henri were shocked at the degree of violence being used and both men looked at each other with dismay.

"Anton, do they use this kind of harsh treatment on our plantations? I confess I haven't seen anything like this, but then I haven't been looking for it."

"I don't know. I haven't paid much attention either, but I've been meaning to. I will have to look into this. I wonder why they have soldiers with them?"

The answer came fast. As the soldiers passed by a thick patch of brush near the road a dozen angry looking black men waving machetes and clubs burst from their cover into the open. With inarticulate screams they fell on the startled soldiers in an unstoppable rush. Two soldiers were hacked down with vicious, bloody swipes of the machetes before they even had opportunity to draw their weapons.

Everyone else was frozen for a second by the attack, but the scene quickly dissolved into chaos. The remaining two soldiers found themselves in a desperate fight against double their number. With no time to bring their muskets into play they were forced to use them as clubs to parry the machetes. The rest of the attackers went for the gang overseers and more desperate individual battles commenced. Some of the younger and bigger male slaves joined the attackers, clawing at their overseers with their bare hands.

The bonus for the attackers was Anton and Henri. Seeing they were well dressed white men two of the attackers realized they would be owners and sheered off from the main group to focus on them.

Reading the situation fast Anton realized he had to act. With no time to bring the now skittish horse under control he shoved Henri out of the buggy and followed right behind him.

"Henri! Draw your sword now! Back to back!"

They weren't a moment too soon. The attackers could do little but prowl out of range of the swords with the two men covering each other. Seeing hesitation in the man facing him, Anton went to the attack.

Anton's years of training in fencing and swordplay paid off as the look on the face of his attacker turned to fear. The best the man could do was to fend off Anton's slashing cuts with increasing desperation. Realizing the man was about to turn and run Anton pushed forward with a driving thrust to the chest. The man dropped to the ground, screaming and arching away in pain.

Anton had never killed a man before. As he stood panting from the exertion, with the adrenalin rush still coursing through him, a searing range of emotions froze him. What astonished him most was the fierce, intense rush of victory, of having defeated an opponent bent on murder. And he realized he liked the taste of his triumph.

From where the main fight was still ongoing came a powerful bellow in a language Anton didn't recognize. Then he heard Henri give his own howl of rage from behind Anton.

"Bastard!"

Anton whipped about as the young black man who had been Henri's opponent ran past and joined the attackers now running hard back into the safety of the heavy underbrush. The sharp crack of a soldier's musket told of at least one soldier still in action, but as Anton looked at the retreating group he saw the shot had missed.

Henri limped over to Anton, covered in scuffs and dust from the road and holding a hand to his left leg. A slow trickle of blood seeped between his fingers.

"Good God, Henri! What did he do to you?"

Henri grimaced. "I stumbled and fell, but I managed to drop him by kicking his knee. He pulled a knife on me and managed this before he ran off. I think it's a flesh wound."

"Are you two gentlemen all right?" said a voice from behind them.

They turned to find one of the overseers had joined them, still holding his now bloody club in a vice like grip while scanning the area to ensure the attackers really were gone. The man had not escaped unscathed, as a vicious looking welt on the side of his face was already swelling and turning purple from burst blood vessels.

After introductions Henri showed the overseer his wound and the man winced. "You'd better come with us. We have someone at the plantation good with this sort of thing. Those bastards may not have left the area either. I'm surprised you gentlemen don't have guards. You really should."

The overseer pointed over to the crossroad where the chaos of the fight was still being cleared. The men could see a few bodies were stretched in disarray on the ground.

"This kind of thing is becoming a far too regular occurrence. It's almost as if these ignorant animals were organized."

Three of the four soldiers had been killed along with two of the overseers. Anton's attacker was one of three killed. Several of the survivors among both the slaves and the overseers were nursing vicious bruises and even some broken arms.

"We have only recently arrived," said Anton. "But it's becoming clear I really am going to have to find some guards."

An hour later Henri looked much better. The cut was indeed a flesh wound, but it had bled a lot. Now cleaned and bandaged, with the pain dulled by several glasses of rum, he told Anton he was ready to resume their journey.

Their host was Christophe Charbonneau, owner of the plantation. He smiled at the two men as they rose to leave. "Well, if you are certain I cannot offer you dinner then perhaps another time, gentlemen? It's so good to have some fresh faces here."

Anton liked the man right from the start. "You have done much already and we thank you for your kind offer, but I think we should be on our way. We shall be hosting a ball in the near future to acquaint ourselves with everyone on the island and you will have the first invitation, sir."

Christophe's face brightened. "Wonderful, sir. My wife will be in a frenzy to meet your family and hear news from home."

"Sir, I fear my family and I have much to learn about this island and how things work here. I would be obliged if I could spend some time with you to this end."

"Of course, sir! In fact, my overseer has noted you gentlemen have no guards. This is the first thing you should remedy because the roads truly are not safe. I shall lend you some of my men to see you home safely tonight."

"Auyuba. Elise. Thank you both for coming. Please shut the door and have a seat," said Anton.

As they complied a hint of something Anton couldn't identify crossed the young slave Auyuba's face, but he masked it well.

"So, you have heard what happened yesterday?"

"We have, master," said Auyuba.

"Please just call me sir. Look, I am interested in understanding what is happening here on the island and I think both of you can help with this. I'll be honest with you, my family and I have interest in seeing changes to the established order."

Auyuba, with his face still an impassive mask, stared back at Anton for a few moments before he replied. "Sir. I am a house slave. I know nothing."

Elise shook her head. "I know nothing of this, sir."

"I understand. You have no reason to trust me, but I hope to change this. See here, my family and I have been inspired by someone you wouldn't know to seek an end to slavery everywhere! Yes, I know you must think I'm mad, but it's true. I really do mean everywhere. We are committed to the noble cause of freedom for all. But this can't be done overnight and we need assistance. The man inspiring us taught me to first understand my enemy and his ways. Without this I cannot hope to defeat him. And for this, I need help."

Anton leaned forward across his desk and searched Auyuba's face. The slave retained his impassive demeanour, but his eyes betrayed an intense concentration.

"And I think, Auyuba, you are someone that can do this for me. Both of you can help. I don't believe for a second either of you are some dumb house slaves. I can sense you are both intelligent and I think you too have the desire in your souls to aid a truly noble goal. But even a big change has to start small and grow. I need your support. Please."

The two slaves continued gazing at Anton with unreadable intent, before turning toward each other as one. An unspoken agreement passed between them as Elise gave an almost imperceptible nod. Auyuba turned back to Anton, the impassive look back on his face as he responded.

"What do you want from us, master?"

"First, thank you both for your trust. I will do my utmost to keep it. For now, I want to understand if the slave population is indeed collectively trying to gain freedom. If so, I may at some point want to meet the leaders to see if we can work together to change all of this. I seek a way to turn slaves into workers, people paid to freely do what is now done only because they will be whipped if they don't. There has to be a better way!"

Anton paused a moment, concern on his face. "I am coming to understand violence is being seen by the slaves here as the only way forward. I would prefer we bring about change without violence on St. Lucia and any other French possession. We are French and we have a better understanding of the value of life. Yes, I would prefer something better, something—I don't know."

Anton paused a moment, struggling to find the words, before an inspiration came to him. "Yes, I want something like—a sugar revolution, if you will. Real change, but not something violent or unpleasant, at least not on our own islands. But if it takes violent revolt elsewhere then so be it, and I can help with this. The people in charge of British and Spanish held islands will not be easily swayed and I have no qualms about what may happen to them. So what do you think?"

The two slaves stared back at him for a few moments once again, before Auyuba spoke. "Sir, as we said, we really are just simple house slaves. But I think we both appreciate you are a good man and want to help. I confess we have heard rumours of anger and talk of change, but we do not know any leaders. There are many from plantations on the island that have run and are making lives for themselves in the mountains. I suspect if there really are leaders that is where they would be found."

"Do you think you could discreetly ask around and find out more?"

"We can, but this could be dangerous. I'm sure you can understand they would find it hard to trust any man that is a plantation owner."

"Well, I will have to find a way to earn their trust. Look, please do what you can and we will talk again. If you need time away from your duties for this let me know."

"Sir. We will do what we can. It may not amount to much."

"This is all I can ask of you. I will find a way to reward you for your efforts."

The two slaves nodded and rose, leaving the room.

As soon as they were out of sight Auyuba motioned for Elise to follow him to the rear of the mansion and into the kitchen pantry where they could talk in private without fear of being overheard.

Closing the door Auyuba turned to look at Elise, his face a frozen mask.

"Do you think this fool suspects?"

"No. And I think he really is an imbecile. I know he believes what he is saying because I've overheard him and the other pig called Henri talking like this before when they did not know I was near enough to hear them."

Auyuba chuckled. "We will have to be careful about this, but maybe we can use him. He hints at maybe providing weapons. My brother Asante on Antigua could use all the help he can get. I will give this some thought. You realize this French pig desires you?"

"Of course," she replied. She searched his face with a question in her eyes for a few long moments before sighing. "You want me to offer myself to manipulate him, don't you? I will do what I must, if necessary. But I tire of this, Auyuba. I slept with that animal Moreau for you and what has this gained us? Very little."

Auyuba reached up to stroke her face. "I know it seems like this, but I have his confidence. And I swear the day will come when I cut the balls off every one of these animals that has ever touched you."

"And what of this young white bitch, Auyuba? She desires *you*. I saw her brushing up against you yesterday."

"Perhaps I will manipulate her," smiled Auyuba, as he pulled her close in a crushing embrace and kissed her hard, melding his body to hers.

"We must go, Auyuba," said Elise, in a distant voice as she pulled away to catch her breath.

"I know, my love," said Auyuba, sensing her frustration.

As they left the pantry Auyuba vowed yet again to redouble his efforts and find a way to lead his people to freedom. Auyuba, distant descendant of hereditary princes of the Ashanti people of West Africa, knew he could do it.

The warmth of a February evening in the tropics was perfect for hosting a ball. All of the women in attendance were wearing their finest gowns and Anton was certain they were thankful they weren't sweating enough for the stains to show through. The Governor and his wife were in attendance, along with several officers from the warships and the contingent of solders they had brought to St. Lucia. Marie was in her element as hostess while Emilie was flirting with every male present.

Standing apart for a moment as a house slave refreshed his drink, Anton surveyed the crowd while the loud buzz of conversation swirled around him. The people were already growing animated, fed by buffet tables covered with a wide array of food. Seafood dominated, with plates of tantalizing fresh grilled fish as one of the main courses. Cold lobster salad proved equally popular, while a tender pork dish cooked with local spices also had a lineup of people waiting to try it. Anton had also spared no expense to bring the wares of the best dessert chef on the island to finish the meal. Several servants stood ready to replenish the dishes as needed. Another table held glasses and several bottles of French wine of excellent vintage, many of which were already depleted. Despite this, a sense of unease permeated it all. Every one of the guests showed up with several guards, all of them bristling with weapons.

"Count de Bellecourt, your hospitality is a refreshing change!" said Christophe Charbonneau as he came over to recharge his own glass. Anton offered a civil smile in return and nodded as they clinked glasses together.

"Yes, my wife is enjoying this immensely. I think everyone is, actually. We haven't had anything like this for some time. Too many troubles on our minds, I guess. But Count, I got here a bit late and in talking with some of the others here I've heard some interesting things about you and your family. You are indeed an envoy?"

Anton offered him a rueful smile. "I am, sir. I don't know what you've heard, but I suspect there are more than a few people here who think I am mad. Some even told me Negroes are slaves by their inner nature, so trying to change this is like trying to stop a hurricane."

"I confess a few of my fellow owners mentioned this," said Christophe with a cheerful laugh, clapping Anton on the shoulder. "But really, Count, you shouldn't pay much heed to them. I for one have no problem with what you want to achieve, as long as whatever you accomplish is done without ruining me financially!"

"Call me Anton, please. And thank you. I confess yours are the first encouraging words I've heard all evening."

"Well, I guess I'm not surprised. And do call me Christophe."

Reactions to Anton's pitch for support had indeed been mixed, ranging from sudden, frosty looks of incredulity to outright laughter at the idea of freeing slaves. But Anton had persisted and had grudgingly won commitment from many to consider whatever solution he came up with when the time came. Several had insisted he find a way to get the British to commit to change first.

"Christophe?" said Anton, as he surveyed the crowd once again. "Something I've noticed is there doesn't seem to be many actual owners present. I've been told many have left. Why is this? Is it all the violence?"

Christophe shrugged. "Many reasons for this. The risk of being murdered in your sleep is certainly part of it. A lot of the owners that came out here in 1783 when we got this island back from the British soon discovered they couldn't stand the heat here in the summer. Bad diseases you find only in the tropics can get you without warning. All this and it's getting much harder to make the same profits with prices and taxes being what they are. My God, smuggling is practically an art around here now."

"Is it like this everywhere, even on the British islands?"

"This is what I hear, but I don't know it for certain. We hear rumours of slave revolts being put down periodically on many of the islands, particularly Jamaica. I don't think the British economy is much better than ours. The return on investment is less even though demand is still high because there is so much sugar available now. And with the taxes we face these days? Well."

"So why are you still here?"

Christophe grinned and shrugged again. "I'm stubborn? Seriously, I've stuck it out because I actually like it here. Winters in France, I ask you. And the goddamn thieving lawyers you have to leave in charge if you're not here rob you blind!"

"Yes, I'm suspicious of this lawyer Moreau I've had in charge of our estate. Everything *looks* good, but it's too good. I am going to dig into the books when I get some time."

"The shark Moreau? Good God, I didn't know he was your man. I guarantee he has found many ways to cheat you out of your money."

He paused to offer Anton a rueful grin and sip his wine. "Anyway, it is unfortunate, but I think the time may be coming when I will have to join the crowd and leave. I don't like what is happening around here and it is going downhill faster every day."

"Seriously?"

"Seriously. Look at all the soldiers they had to bring in. I have no proof, but I think someone with a brain is at work behind all these attacks, a real leader. We've made a point over the years to bring in slaves from different parts of Africa to counter the possibility of slaves working together, of course. If they speak different languages and are from different tribes they'll find it hard to communicate with each other. They'll probably hate or, at the least, mistrust each other too. But something is going on. I'm worried there may be elements of the Akan who have ended up here."

"The Akan? Who are they?"

"One of the peoples of West Africa. It turns out they are warlike in the extreme. The Ashanti tribe in particular likes to be in charge. They've actually captured many people from other tribes and sold them into slavery."

Anton could only shake his head. "At least with the army here the situation should stabilize, don't you think?"

Christophe chuckled with bleak laughter. "That would be doubtful. Take a closer look at them the next chance you get. Oh, the officers are all decent enough fellows, but I pity them having the scum they have to lead. Most of the soldiers are drunk or on the way to being drunk, all of the time. And if they aren't drunk they're getting into fights. No, I'll rely on my own well paid guards, thank you."

"I see. Hmm, I appreciate you filling me in on all of this. I still have much to learn, I think. See here, if I'm going to find a solution to all of this I need to learn more about the whole business of sugar. I've been meaning to spend time with my overseer to learn the whole process, but I think your perspective would be so much more helpful. May I come over some day and see your operation?"

"But of course! I would love to return your hospitality. You must bring the whole family over for a day to visit and to stay for dinner. Yes, let's do it. I insist!"

"You've picked a good time to see the operation, Anton. I don't know if anyone has told you, but we harvest cane in the dry months from January to June," said Christophe as he led Anton, Jacques, and Henri on the horses he lent them off to a distant part of his plantation a week later. The women had no interest in learning about how sugar processing worked, so they were touring the extensive flower garden Christophe and his wife maintained.

Ahead the men could see a windmill towering above the trees. In the fields they passed gangs of slaves cutting and stacking cane onto carts, while in others the now harvested fields were being cleared of debris and trenches were being dug to plant new crops. The stench of manure being added as the new cane was planted was overpowering.

Entering a large clearing surrounding the windmill they found several small buildings, some of which were little more than a roof held up by four corner posts. Numerous slaves, most of whom were male, bustled about performing various tasks while being watched by white overseers carrying weapons. Christophe brought them to a halt far enough away they wouldn't interfere with the operation, but close enough they could see everything happening.

"I imagine you've seen your own operation by now and had some explanation of how it works?"

"Well, we've seen it and have had a basic explanation, but I would like to hear what you have to tell me," replied Anton.

"Certainly. I think this isn't going to be much different from your operation, except maybe for the windmill that I don't believe you have. The raw cane is fed into the crushing mill, those three vertical rollers over there. This squeezes the juice from the raw cane, which flows from the mill via those troughs into the boiling house."

"Christophe?" said Jacques. "I've heard processing cane can be dangerous. Is this true?"

"It certainly is, sir. Why, last week I lost a man because of it. He was feeding cane into the crushing mill when he somehow lost his balance. His hand got caught and he was pulled into it. Christ, what a gruesome mess it was. That would be the only drawback to using a windmill. It takes time to stop one of these things, as opposed to a mill powered by oxen."

Anton gave a start, seeing the possibilities offered. "Hmm, you don't have to feed and care for a windmill, do you?"

"Exactly, my dear Count."

"I wonder if there are other inventions that could be used to do this without relying on slaves? I shall have to give this more thought."

"Perhaps," replied Christophe. "If you come up with something please let me know. If it can decrease my costs while keeping my production levels the same or higher, I am all for it."

Turning back to the scene before them he pointed to another nearby open structure. "So over here is where the real action happens. The raw juice flows through sieves to get any leftover bits of cane out and ends up in the big storage cauldron you see on the one end. We start by adding juice to the clarifier, which is the first big open kettle at the end of the masonry structure you see over there. This whole structure actually houses a series of kettles with a furnace underneath each one. We add lime and boil the juice to get the impurities out. The boiler men skim it when ready and then ladle it to the next kettle."

"My God," said Henri. "Look at the heat radiating from those kettles. It must be hot as blazes standing beside one of those. And these children I see mixed in have the task of feeding the fires, correct?"

"Yes, and it is indeed extremely hot. This is why the boiler men are all stripped down to wearing a loincloth. I—"

A scream of agony turned everyone's head to find the source. One of the boiler men had bumped into a child and was now howling in pain as he danced about trying to brush away the scalding hot liquid spilled down his bare leg due to the collision. Bedlam ensued as he bumped the arm of another boiler man hard, splashing the contents of the full ladle of steaming hot, taffy like molasses he was holding in an arc wide enough to splatter two more men on their torsos. Their screams added to the chaos as several overseers converged to drag them all away from further harm and sort out the situation.

"Shit," swore Christophe. "Not again, goddamn it."

"Again?" said Anton.

"Oh, God, yes," said Christophe, shaking his head. "As you said, Jacques, this is a dangerous process. This happens all the time. Damn, those slaves aren't going to be much use to me for a while. Anyway, the final step in the process is the building over there called the curing house. The sugar is packed into moulds and left to drain off the molasses to get our end product. And this is really all there is to it."

"Christophe?" said Anton in an excited tone, as an inspiration seized him. "Why is this all being done at the same time? Couldn't you maybe use fewer slaves if you simply cut all the cane first and then had your field slaves come and do the processing?"

"The problem with that idea is the heat. The cut cane starts to rot fast. No, one has to get it all done as quick as possible."

121

"Huh," said Anton, feeling a little crestfallen his idea wouldn't work and no other obvious solutions were coming to mind. "Well, this has given us much to think about. If we come up with any ideas you will be the first to know."

Returning to their estate in the evening Anton poured three snifters of cognac, and with Henri and Jacques in tow the three men went to sit on the verandah. With a steady breeze to keep the mosquitoes at bay the men settled to enjoy the end of a pleasant evening. Anton swirled his cognac in his glass as Henri spoke up.

"So Anton, we've been here close to two months now. We've learned a lot, but I confess I am feeling a little daunted here. These owners seem pretty set in their ways and I don't see any obvious solutions to offer them that might change their thinking. And if we can't convince our own people then how can we possibly convince anyone else, let alone the goddamn British? So what do you think of this place and our mission now?"

Anton stared into his glass for a moment before downing another sip. "I think we have only begun. We must be patient, my brothers. Change is never easy. I haven't told you this, but I confess I am not surprised at the reception we've received. Perhaps I am more cynical than our friend the Marquis, but I didn't really think simply talking about it would get us anywhere. Too many other greedy, cynical people in the world I guess."

Both men chuckled with amusement as Anton gave them a wry smile.

"Anton," said Jacques. "I agree with you, and I think Henri does too, but neither of us know where we go from here. If talking isn't going to get us anywhere, what are we going to do? I remember when we first gave thought to this you suggested action would be needed."

"Action is absolutely what we need, but all in good time. Well, perhaps the time has come to fill you both in about the cargo we brought with us."

"Cargo?" said Henri. "What does this have to do with anything? Captain Dusourd has already sold it all, I thought."

"Ah, that would be the official cargo," said Anton with a smile. "I'm referring to the crates of muskets and pistols with ammunition we brought with us. We also have a quantity of knives and small swords I thought prudent to bring along."

"Good God, Anton!" said Henri, after recovering from his surprise. "When were you going to tell us this?"

"Well, now, actually. Look, like I said, I brought it as I was not at all convinced diplomacy would get the job done. There was no point getting all of you concerned about it if talking to people was going to do the job. And given it's becoming clear discussing it could take forever, now is the time to decide whether we want to actually put our unofficial cargo to use. I confess I think we should, but make no mistake this will be dangerous. I am willing to go it alone on this if need be. Or, if it bothers you both too much, I am willing to drop this whole idea."

"Anton?" said Jacques. "What does *dangerous* mean?"

Anton shrugged. "I think it means providing incentive to owners to find a better way to run their operations. If runaway slaves with proper weapons are constantly disrupting operations something will have to change. If plantations become unsustainable to run with slaves, maybe people will invent better tools to do the work. Like using windmills."

"Christ, Anton," said Henri. "You realize you are talking about arming the very people that could turn around and murder all of us in our sleep?"

"No, no. First of all, I am not suggesting we provide enough arms for anyone to defeat an army. We only brought a hundred or so assorted weapons plus the various blades. Rather, I suggest we reserve most if not all of what we have for the British islands. Look, let's face it. If the owners here aren't interested it is likely the British will be even less so. What we do is continue our attempts to convince people with talk and goodwill, while we make contacts in secret with locals and provide weapons. It's time we took our message to other islands. I don't really care what kind of mayhem results on British islands. On French islands we do the same, but provide only a few weapons and we encourage the locals to damage only equipment. Oh, maybe a few overseers will pay for making enemies, but I'm not concerned about this."

Henri grunted. "Hmm, I guess I like this approach. So when the havoc starts we point to it and turn up the heat on our efforts to convince people to change. But how do we get the weapons to the right people?"

"Well, I'm going to have another conversation with Auyuba and Elise. I planted a few thoughts in their heads a while back, so we'll see if they bear fruit. I'm hoping they can give me some contacts. I'm going to suggest we start with Antigua, St. Kitts, and Guadeloupe to keep some distance between whatever happens and us. Then we see how it goes. We can also maybe add to the fire a bit here on St. Lucia. But I don't know if I can do all this on my own."

"You need us, Anton. You need someone to actually make contact with the runaways," said Jacques.

"He is right," said Henri. "You are the public face of this. You should focus on doing the talking and being the brains behind all this. Let Jacques and me stay in the shadows and do the dirty work."

Anton sighed. "I confess I didn't want to drag you two into it, but the more I think about it I have to agree. Are you both certain you want this? I don't even want to think about the repercussions if we are caught."

"We talked about this, remember? We all agree this is a noble cause and besides, we all want some adventure, don't we? Besides, so what if our involvement leaks out? We are nobles and we have resources to buy whomever we need to buy. So count me in, Anton."

"Me too," said Jacques.

Anton smiled as he raised his glass in toast. "My brothers, to success!"

The three men touched their glasses and as one they downed the remnants of their cognac. "All right," said Anton, as the three men rose to go to their beds. "I shall talk to Auyuba first thing in the morning."

And in the darkness of the room closest to where the three men had been sitting, close enough to hear every word through the shutters of the window, Auyuba smiled.

As Anton finished explaining his plans to Auyuba and Elise he gave them a tentative smile. "So I am hoping you both understand what I am trying to achieve here and have decided to help. I am taking you into my confidence to prove I want to help you and your people. But I do need your confidence too if this is to succeed."

"Yes, master," said Anton. "We have given this thought and we want to help. I have contacted my brother Asante on Antigua, as I know he can help you with both that island and St. Kitts. I already knew he has had some prior involvement with runaway slaves, you see. As for here and Guadeloupe, I have already made contacts that will help further your goals on both islands. All I need to know is your schedule so I can arrange meetings."

Anton raised an eyebrow. "This was quick. I had expected this would take more time."

Auyuba gave him a cryptic look in reply. "I made up my mind after our first conversation and took the liberty of making contacts in anticipation. For Antigua I am merely taking advantage of an existing way I've used in past to communicate with my brother. Every island has fishing boats going out every day, you see. Sometimes they happen to stop and talk to each other. As for here and Guadeloupe, I was fortunate to find someone who assures me we can communicate with the right people quickly."

"Excellent. I want to start with Antigua and work my way back to St. Lucia. We will begin making arrangements to leave immediately and you will have our schedule soon."

Chapter Six
February 1788
Antigua and St. Lucia

Evan regarded the young midshipman standing before
him with an appraising eye. Timothy Cooke was tall
and still lanky, having turned eighteen years old a
scant two months prior. His uniform was a little worn
and he had already almost outgrown it. Whatever fat
he may have carried had been burned off by the bout
of fever he was recovering from, leaving mostly skin
and bones, but enough muscle remained in his broad
shoulders to prove he had spent much of his time aloft
in the rigging of whatever warships he had served on.
Evan smiled, knowing if the young man bore even a
hint of intelligence he would serve.

"Mr. Cooke. Thank you for coming to see me.
This fellow over here is my second in command
Lieutenant Wilton. He isn't in uniform for reasons
you don't need to know. If you greet him outside the
Dockyard you are not to acknowledge he is an officer.
Right, so you feel fully recovered, do you?"

"Sir, I do."

"Good. I had my own bout with the fever and
I know how long it takes to feel whole again. So, your
Captain has left you here and returned to England."
Evan raised an eyebrow to indicate this was a
question and not a statement.

"Sir. My Captain inherited me from his
predecessor. My uncle took sick and had to resign his
commission. The Captain replacing him had his own
preferences."

"I thought this might be the case. Believe me,
I know all too well how it can happen. So you are
hoping for a new posting with someone. I have

spoken with Captain Rand, the new senior in command here in Antigua. He confirms your availability and he has no room on any of the ships under his command for any more midshipmen. The only choice would normally be to send you home at the next opportunity, but as it happens I have need of assistance at the moment. This will be a shore-based assignment here in the Dockyard itself. Lieutenant Wilton and I anticipate being absent on other islands on occasion in future and I need someone to be in charge here while I am gone."

"Sir? I appreciate whatever opportunity I have to continue to serve. I must confess I know little of the workings of a Dockyard, though."

"That's all right, I was in the same position once too. The Dockyard Shipwright has charge of all the technical aspects of repairs and is competent in his role. Your job is not to interfere with him. Rather, you need to make sure he has the support he needs to get his job done. This means a lot of administrative oversight, making sure supplies are on hand and so forth. Of course, discipline has to be maintained. Frankly, the Dockyard workers aren't much different than sailors." Evan paused to grin. "They like rum too!"

Timothy laughed. "So treat them like sailors and I'll be fine. I can do that, sir."

"Look, here's the thing I want to be sure of. I suspect you don't want to be on the beach any more than I do. I could simply order you to do this, but I would much prefer you be willing to do it. If you don't, I will understand and we will send you home to take your chances. If you do stay you will at least have opportunity to gain knowledge of ship construction and repair. It may some day serve you well. I have authority from Captain Rand to offer this assignment to you for a one-year period. If an opportunity to get you on a ship comes up I won't hold you back. So what do you say?"

The young midshipman showed no hesitation. "Sir, you are correct I would like to be back at sea, but I appreciate the opportunity to serve with you. I willingly accept."

Evan smiled and stood to shake his hand. "Welcome to the Royal Navy Antigua Dockyard, sir. Now please wait outside for a bit. Mr. Wilton and I need to chat and then he will take you on a tour of the facility. He will be able to answer any questions you may have."

As the door closed behind him Evan and James turned to look at each other as one.

"Well, what do you think?" said Evan.

James shrugged. "I got the sense there could be a brain at work in there, which is more than could be said for a lot of mids. We'll soon find out, but I think he'll do."

"I do too. Thank God the pieces are starting to fall in place. I'd like to be at sea by this time next week, James."

"I'll get the basics of what he needs to know into his head by then, Evan. Should be right about the time we're waving goodbye to those two arseholes he's replacing."

"Yes, thank God. It took us a while to get the goods on them, but stealing as much from the Dockyard as Lieutenants Burns and Long did was going to get them caught sooner or later."

"Captain Rand sure didn't waste time, did he? I thought Captain Standish said he was slow to act."

"Hmm, I rather think the possibility of being associated with taint of any sort is all the motivation he needs to get going. Mind you, it isn't too big a step to temporarily withdraw their commissions and send them away on the next ship home. It'll be the Admiralty that will sort them out."

"Huh. Were it up to me I'd throw the buggers in chains for the trip. Well, I'd better get going on training this mid to cover for us."

As he rose to leave he paused and looked at Evan. "Say, have you decided what you're going to do about Alice yet?"

"No," said Evan, emphasizing his indecision with a shrug. "I am still of two minds. I am going to talk to her more about this. I don't think she appreciates the potential for danger."

"Maybe she needs a little action and excitement in her life just like we do, Evan."

Evan eyed James with a raised eyebrow, but he relented with a laugh. "You agree with her, don't you?"

James smiled. "Yeah, it took me a while to come around to her way of thinking, but I do agree with her. She could be of use to us. You know, it's your own fault for attaching yourself to a smart woman, Evan."

Evan laughed again.

In the evening Evan sat on the verandah of the Dockyard Dog across from Alice, once again watching the sunset. He smiled as he thought back to the day he and James told her they would be going to St. Lucia on a mission.

"Excellent! When do we leave?" she had said, her eyes lit with excitement. James hadn't helped by bursting out laughing at the dumbfounded chagrin Evan realized must have been all over his face.

Toying with his glass of wine as he turned to look at Alice, Evan had to make a decision. "So my love, are you still set on joining us in St. Lucia?"

Alice looked at him and shrugged as she reached out to grasp his hand once he put down his glass. "I know you want to protect me and this could be dangerous, Evan. But I'm fine with this. I still think I can help you and James gather information and maybe even find some sources for you. I promise at the first hint of any danger I will pull back. And besides, I'd like to see more of the world than just this island."

"I understand, Alice. But I need to be sure you realize if you are accused of spying there would be little if anything to be done to save you. I'll be travelling on a diplomatic mission and will have protection, but really, both you and James will be at risk. He is different because he is an officer and is willingly accepting his orders. He might be exchanged or deported if caught, but you? As a civilian you have no protection."

"Okay, so give me a position of some sort if this is what it takes. Make me an aide or something similar with a fancy title."

"Well, that's—" said Evan, before pausing with his mouth hanging open as he thought it through.

Several moments later Alice interrupted his thinking. "Evan, your mouth is still open."

He realized all he could do was laugh. "You know what, I think making you a consular aide could work. I could even do the same for James and this way we can maybe keep his status as an officer secret for even longer. Hmm, I will talk to Governor Shirley about the idea."

"So I can come with you?"

Evan smiled.

HMS Alice proved to be a two-year-old brig sloop of war almost a hundred feet in length. With one six-pound cannon fore and another aft together with fourteen more in total on the sides she packed a heavy punch. Two of the heavy calibre, short-range carronades rounded out her armament. Although she would need her speed to get close enough to an enemy to use them, the carronades were a devastating weapon.

As Alice stepped on the deck of a warship for the first time in her life she appeared to struggle not to gawk in open-mouthed awe at the bewildering maze of rigging aloft. Evan allowed himself a tiny smile as he watched her, knowing the perspective from on deck was vastly different than seeing it from afar.

As the young officer in command who looked to be about the same age as Evan stepped forward, Evan nodded to acknowledge his salute. Evan could see he looked a little puzzled, as Evan, James, and Alice were all dressed in civilian clothes.

"Commander Ross, I presume? Welcome aboard, sir. I am Lieutenant Kent, in command of *HMS Alice*."

"Thank you Lieutenant. I am indeed Commander Ross, although for the purpose of this mission I would prefer you refer to me simply as Mr. Ross, as I am on a diplomatic mission. These are my, um, diplomatic aides. This fellow here is James Wilton and this is Alice Roberts."

As Alice stepped forward to acknowledge the Lieutenant with a radiant smile, allowing him to take her hand and perform a brief bow, Evan struggled not to laugh. He knew from experience what an impact a beautiful woman could have on a warship filled with over a hundred young officers and sailors, and from the look on the faces of the waiting men Alice already had them all in her thrall. Her first conquest was the young Lieutenant himself.

"Alice, is it?" said Lieutenant Kent, doing a bad job of hiding how awestruck he was. "Forgive me if I am being forward, but I am absolutely certain they were thinking of you when they named this ship."

Alice gave him a radiant smile in return. "Your flattery is very kind, Lieutenant. This is my first time on a ship. I hope the *Alice* will be kind to me too."

"I guarantee you are in good hands, madam," said the Lieutenant as he forced himself to tear his eyes away and turn to Evan. "Sir, we are ready for sea and can depart as soon as the last of your belongings are brought aboard."

"Please do. We know to stay out of everyone's way, sir."

An hour later they were under full sail and in open seas cruising at a pleasant six knots in the light swells. Alice took to the experience like an old hand, with no hint of seasickness. Evan came up behind her as she stood by the railing, watching the flying fish scared up by the ship burst in swarms fanning out in all directions to sail over the water for amazing distances. Seeing no one was watching Evan put his arm around her.

"Well, what do you think, Alice? Fancy life as a sailor?"

As she turned to him Evan was surprised to see tears falling from one eye that she brushed away as she pulled him tight to her. She snuffled a moment as he drew back a little to look at her with concern.

"Are you all right? What's wrong, my love?"

"Nothing. It's the opposite, you wonderful man. This is so beautiful out here. I had no idea the ocean is so huge! I am so grateful you have brought me along to see this and be here. I don't think I've ever felt more alive. God, I don't know what I did to deserve you."

"Well, wait till we get to St. Lucia. You'll like it. I was there once before when I was a midshipman and can tell you it's very different from Antigua."

"How so?"

"You'll see."

With the last rounds of the salute still echoing around the hills Alice turned to Evan, her eyes shining as they navigated the harbour entrance and sailed into Castries. "Evan, this is beautiful. I don't have words for it."

"It is, isn't it? Forgive me, Alice, but I must ignore you for a while. Those French warships over there need my attention."

"Evan?" said James, focusing intently on the ships docked in the port. "This older frigate has to be sailing en flute. It's riding too high in the water to have armament. I think they've converted it to carry troops."

"Yes. It's too old and shabby to be doing anything else. The other frigate is definitely not shabby, though. Minerve class? It would have more than thirty-two guns, wouldn't it?"

"I'd say so, probably closer to forty guns. Those three over there look like older schooners. Nothing we couldn't deal with, but that frigate would make short work of us."

"Well, they seem as interested in us as we are in them," said Evan, gesturing to the French sailors lining the rails to watch them as word was passed of their arrival. "By the way, before I forget about this again, please don't give away the fact I speak French. Pretending otherwise may come in handy down the road."

Almost as soon as they docked a Customs official came on board and began haranguing Lieutenant Kent, whom it turned out also spoke French. Evan had to turn away to hide a smile as the minutes passed and the drawn out conversation got heated.

James turned away too and muttered in Evan's ear. "What's happening?"

"This Frenchman is being a pompous pain in the arse, but I'm beginning to like our good Lieutenant. He is dishing it right back at this fool and I think they have it sorted out now. We are being released rather grudgingly and freed to get on with our business."

Soon enough Evan, James, and Alice were all standing on the dock. Alice was in awe watching the bustle of the port, but to Evan's relief she seemed unafraid.

"Christ, look at all these soldiers they've got standing on guard everywhere, Evan," said James. "I think we're right, the old frigate has to be a troop ship."

"I agree. All right, you two know what to do? Your cover story is you're looking for supplies for me. Hopefully that will suffice for now. Alice, at least until you get your bearings please stay close to James. I may see you two about town, depending on how soon I can get in to see the Governor to present my credentials. I'll be trying to find our consul John Andrews too. So we meet back at the ship by sundown, right?"

"Don't worry, Evan," said James. "We'll be fine. I've been here before too. There are a couple of places I want to check out, but there's one in particular called The Thirsty Sailor I'll be looking into. If the same owner is still there he could be a good source for us. If you get time see if you can find it as we might be there. If not we'll meet you at the ship. Come on Alice, let's go."

As the three of them parted ways the two men watching them from a distance stepped out from the shadows they had rushed into in their haste to remain hidden. The older of the two men pointed to Evan as he spoke.

"I'm sorry for the haste and the mystery to rush you into civilian clothes, Durant. I wasn't sure when they sailed past, but I am now. I know this man, and he is both a British Navy officer and a spy. Because he knows me I would rather not be the one to follow him, so you must. Do not reveal yourself to him. I want to know where he goes and whom he sees. These other two I do not know, so I will follow them. Report back to me tonight at the ship."

The young midshipman nodded and left to catch up with Evan. The older man turned to look for his targets and saw he was in danger of losing James and Alice in the crowds, so he walked as fast as he could without drawing attention to catch up. As he did the need to know what his foe was doing here burned almost as much as his desire to repay Evan Ross for the defeat suffered at his hands. Over two years ago Evan had foiled his attempt to destabilize the British sugar islands and sent him packing in ignominy.

Marcel Deschamps, Captain of the French Royal Navy frigate *Marie-Anne*, wanted a reckoning with Evan Ross. The Captain couldn't lose sight of his other role as a spy, though. Keeping a wary, covert eye on whoever was in his domain that could prove a threat was of utmost importance. When *L'Estalon* had appeared Deschamps had taken even more precautions than usual to keep a low profile in order to watch the new arrival. Knowing of Giscard Dusourd from the American War, Captain Deschamps knew well that if anything nefarious was in progress, Giscard Dusourd would be certain to have a hand in it. Deschamps had until now contented himself with keeping a surreptitious eye on the man. The arrival on scene of Evan Ross ratcheted up his suspicions a hundred fold that something was afoot.

"This posting is getting more interesting every day," said Deschamps under his breath as he reached a point close enough to his quarries he could stay undetected without losing them.

"Governor Marchand, I appreciate you have made time to see me," said Evan. The Governor smiled as he passed Evan's credentials back to him and waved a languid acknowledgment, so Evan explained the reason for his visit. The Governor's smile melted away when he heard Evan's explanation.

"Ah, I have been expecting someone would come. I did send word to Barbados of what happened, but I sense you do not know? I have been busy with affairs here on St. Lucia, so perhaps I was a little slow getting my letter off. Your consul John Andrews is dead, Mr. Ross."

"Dead, you say? Good Lord, what happened?" said Evan, his dismay clear.

"Bad business, sir. He was murdered with a knife in the street outside his office one evening. We questioned everyone we reasonably could, but nothing came of it. He had no known enemies and there appears no motive for the murder."

"Was he robbed?"

"No, which is odd. Perhaps the killer was scared off by the approach of the man who found him."

"Who was this, Governor? I'd like to speak to him if possible."

"A house slave named Auyuba. He runs the house affairs for the de Bellecourt family, but he also does work for a lawyer named Moreau here in town. The slave is well known and, as far as I know, beyond reproach. He would have no motive for doing something like this, but I'm sure the lawyer Moreau can arrange a meeting. His office is a little down the street from here. I have the key to your consul's office for you." Reaching into his desk drawer he pulled out a small ring with a key on it and passed it across the desk to Evan.

"I see. Well, thank you, Governor. I will ensure word gets through to those who need to know to begin a search for a new consul. Hmm, I think we will be here a few days while I go through his office. I may pick up some supplies for myself while I am here too, perhaps some wine and cognac. Hard to get on Antigua, unless you are prepared to deal with smugglers, of course."

The Governor smiled. "Of course. You are a man of discerning taste, I see. If there is anything my office can assist you with do let me know. Good day, sir."

When Evan explained what he wanted to the lawyer Moreau the man tried to assure Evan meeting Auyuba would gain him nothing, but Evan was insistent. As he left he asked for directions to The Thirsty Sailor and learned it wasn't far. Evan continued on to the dead consul's office, which was tiny and stuffy from being closed up since his death. Evan spent the rest of the afternoon skimming over his papers, but could see the man was not involved in anything sensitive enough to warrant being murdered for.

What did interest were the man's financial records. The dead consul had deposit records showing he was financially well off, enough to make Evan sit forward with a start. The sums reflected were far more than what the salary of a diplomatic consul would command. Evan made a mental note to ask Captain Standish about the consul's background, knowing the explanation for the large amount of money could be innocent enough.

With tired eyes Evan paused as he walked into the bright sunlight, shading them as he stepped outside. From the corner of his eye he saw a nondescript young man lounging in the shade of a tree give a start, look away in haste from Evan, and slip away into the shadows of a nearby building. With senses now on full alert, Evan made a show of disinterest, rubbing his eyes, and looking away before sauntering down the street. After walking almost two blocks away he feigned interest in a food stall he had passed and turned on his heels, scanning the ground he had covered from the corner of his eye once again. The same young man was about fifty feet behind and he ducked into the shadows when Evan turned.

Deciding the time had come to turn the tables, Evan walked out of sight around a corner and increased his pace as fast as he could without attracting attention. Ducking in and out of the crowds he found a shop open to the street selling clothing with a convenient pillar he could lurk beside as he pretended to examine the merchandise. Soon enough the now distraught young man rushed by, head swiveling in all directions as he tried to find his missing quarry.

Once he was certain the young man was well past Evan slipped out of the doorway and began to follow him. After ten minutes of fruitless searching the now dejected looking young man struck off toward the docks of the harbour. Evan stared, deep in thought, as he watched him board the *Marie-Anne* and salute the officer of the watch before disappearing below.

Now much more on his guard Evan retraced his steps and decided to see if he could find The Thirsty Sailor. Tucked away on a little offshoot from Peynier Street, The Thirsty Sailor was an unexceptional looking building on the exterior, but inside it seemed clean and well maintained. James was seated in a corner table away from the few other customers and in earnest discussion with a grizzled, older man. As Evan joined them at the table he realized the man was missing his left leg from the knee down.

"Evan, good timing on your part. I was having a conversation about our situation and needs. This is Paddy Shannon. He knows who you are and what we want."

"Pleased to meet you, sir," said Paddy, eyeing Evan carefully as they shook hands.

"Paddy here is ex-Navy, Evan. He was the purser on my first ship, but he is now the owner of this establishment."

"I see we have a lack of limbs in common, sir," said Evan.

The man gave Evan a doleful grimace. "Got into a toe to toe fight with a much bigger frog warship during the war and for a change they actually shot low instead of going for our rigging. Wrong place at the wrong time, I guess."

"So Paddy here believes he can help us, Evan. Paddy, why don't you fill him in and tell him a little about yourself?"

"Well, when I got this I decided I'd had enough. Can't afford to lose any more body parts. I'd done all right with prize money and my, um, earnings as a purser, so I resigned and settled here." He paused to smirk when both Evan and James grinned at the mention of his earnings, as pursers were well known throughout the Navy for being opportunistic when it came to handling the Crown's money. "Couldn't bear the thought of going back to grey skies and rain. But there was also Ella to consider."

As Evan raised an eyebrow James spoke up. "You two have more in common than missing body parts, Evan. Ella used to be a slave, but now she's his wife."

"Well, she *was* my wife, James. She passed away last year. I met her years ago and bought her freedom, set her up here for the day I could retire. But now all I have is my daughter, Manon." As he spoke a lithe young black woman of about eighteen years old came toward the table with a fresh pitcher of ale for the three men. James gave a start and sat forward, staring with open appreciation. She gave him a wary eye, but lingered to smile for a long heartbeat before giving a demure nod to her father and returning to the kitchen.

"You be nice to her, James," warned the old man. "I know what you're thinking and I haven't forgotten how you operate, you rogue. Don't think for a moment I'm too old and feeble to cut your balls off."

James laughed and spread his arms wide with mock innocence. "I'm always nice to the ladies, Paddy."

The old man grunted. "You know what I mean. So yes, I wasn't happy when those fools gave this island back to the frogs, but what can you do? I'm settled here now, and I've acquired a taste for cognac anyway. Look, I understand you need information about who is doing what on this island, right? Well, you can look no further. I know every tavern and innkeeper on this island and if I don't know someone or something, I guarantee I know someone else who will. Actually, Manon is the one who will make the connections with the others. We have a deal with innkeepers around the island to go in together on purchasing supplies, see? Saves plenty if you do it this way. I'm not too mobile obviously, so she does all the travelling. Of course, this will cost you. A little extra gold will go a long way to keep me happy as I get older and can only help Manon, so there you have it."

"What are these French warships and all the troops doing here, Paddy?" said Evan.

The old man shrugged. "Most of the troops are getting as drunk as possible on the cheapest wine or rum they can find. The ships haven't stirred since they showed up here over two months ago. But there is rumour some of them are going to be shipped to other French islands. The only thing of consequence they've managed is to bring the violence a bit more under control."

"Violence?"

"Sure. The runaway slaves. It seems like more run every day, and they've been downright vicious about attacking whites. There's always been deliberate destruction of equipment and general mischief, of course. The thing is, though, it used to be rare someone would be physically attacked, but not anymore."

Evan's brow furrowed as he digested what the old man said. "Hmm. It seems likely then that all these troops and ships are just to keep a lid on things. Correct?"

"For now," said the old man. "But I'm happy to keep an eye on them for you, for the right price. And we use fishing boats to pass messages, as I discussed with James here."

Evan nodded and after some haggling they settled on a fair amount. Evan was sliding a small bag of coins across the table to the old man and getting up to leave when the door to the inn opened and Alice walked in. As she joined them and was introduced, Paddy smiled in open admiration.

"My God, you remind me of my wife when she was younger. She was the prettiest woman on the island back then, and I'd say you've taken over the role."

Alice gave him an indulgent smile and they rose to leave, assuring Paddy they would be back to talk further before returning to Antigua. Walking back to the ship they had to pause as two well-dressed, good looking young women came out of a shop followed by a tall, handsome black man and a beautiful young black woman.

As the older of the two white women entered the waiting carriage she paused for a brief instant to let her gaze linger with open interest on Evan. Once inside the carriage she made a point of sitting near the window where she could look at him further. While the others were waiting their turn, the younger woman and the two blacks Evan surmised were slaves stared with frank appraisal at the three people waiting for them to get out of the way. The remaining white woman turned her nose up at Alice, lingered for a few moments on Evan, but locked eyes with James and left them there. James gave her a polite smile in return as she finally turned away and got into the carriage too.

The black male slave saved his attention for James too. James stared impassively back, matching the ice in the stranger's dark eyes. Alice, meanwhile, had seen where the older white woman's attention was and was now engaged in a similar, invisible struggle with her. The man gave a tiny nod of acknowledgement before he too got in, followed closely by the black woman. The armed guard, bristling with weapons and doubling as a coachman, soon had the carriage on its way.

As they resumed walking Evan turned to James. "Hmm, I wonder who they were? Sure seemed interested in you for some reason."

James grunted. "Ever have the feeling the second you meet someone they're a mortal enemy? Doesn't happen too often, but when it does I pay attention. I don't know who he is, but he'll bear watching if we meet again."

Alice gave Evan a sidelong glance. "Well, all I know is if I cross paths again with the white bitch in the carriage making eyes at you, there's going to be trouble."

Evan grinned with amusement as he resumed walking, filling them in on his day and what he had learned as he went. That he had been followed elicited concern, making both Alice and James swivel their heads about to scan the crowds.

"Relax," said Evan. "I've been keeping a weather eye ever since we left the shop. I haven't seen the guy and, as near as I can tell, we aren't being followed right now. We're going to have to be wary, though."

"I agree," said James. "I dropped into almost every tavern in town and asked lots of questions. I didn't get anything much more than what Paddy gave us, though. I talked to a few of the sailors off the ships in the harbour, too. Got some real suspicious looks from one group of them. A nasty bunch off that schooner, the *L'Estalon*."

Evan eyed him speculatively. "That bad? If you find out anything about who they are or what they are up to let me know."

"Well, I had a nice day," said Alice. "I think I was in almost every shop in town and I talked to so many people in them its almost a blur now. But I think I know about the ship you're talking about. It belongs to a family of aristocrats from France. They own plantations here. The head of the family is an envoy. Apparently he's trying to convince the locals to end slavery, and he will be visiting other islands to do the same there too. This includes Antigua. The locals here all think he's mad, of course."

Alice paused, as both Evan and James had turned to look at her and stopped in their tracks. Looking puzzled, she stopped too and stared back at both men before putting both hands on her hips. "What?"

The two men looked at each other and laughed, before Evan replied. "It's all right, my dear. I think we are both pleasantly surprised you are already producing nuggets of information for us."

Alice raised an eyebrow as she turned up the corner of her mouth. "I don't know why you're surprised. If you talk to people nicely most of them are only too happy to tell you what they know. Makes a boring day in a shop go faster. Anyway, I also found a couple of places we can buy wine if you want. Cognac and brandy too, but I hope you brought lots of money. Everything is *really* expensive here, worse than on Antigua. All that most of them talked about is how bad the economy is. And all these soldiers here? They were brought in to protect the people, but one of the reasons everything is so expensive here is the people are having to pay for their upkeep."

Evan replied as they resumed walking. "This is good to know, too. Well done, both of you. We shall see what tomorrow brings."

The sun was almost below the horizon as they reached the ship and walked up the gangplank. As they disappeared on board Marcel Deschamps stepped out from the deep shadows he had been hiding from sight in and rubbed his chin, before turning away to head for his own ship.

Moreau could see his two visitors appeared surprised when Auyuba walked into the office and was introduced. The one in charge named Ross seemed to recover fast. He asked a series of probing questions of Auyuba to elicit more details from him about what happened, but got nothing.

"I am sorry I have so little to offer. I knew master Andrews, of course. I take care of household matters for my owner and help master Moreau here, too. Because I am in town frequently I often stay overnight with Mr. Moreau. This is a small island and most of us involved in business matters know each other. Master Andrews was a nice man, but I have no idea who would murder him. All I know is I stumbled over his body right outside his office after leaving Mr. Moreau's office late at night. His body was still warm, but I knew the knife wound in his back was fatal. I must have scared off whoever did it. I called the watch, but they found nothing."

"I see," said Evan, rising to leave. "Well, thank you for meeting us. Good day, sirs."

As the door closed behind them Moreau and Auyuba looked at each other for a moment, before the lawyer rose to open another door at the rear of the room. "Come in, gentlemen."

As Giscard Dusourd and Adam Jones walked in and sat down both wore wary looks. Adam Jones spoke first. "Well?"

Moreau shrugged. "They got nothing and they have no clue. How could they? They wouldn't know the lying, double-crossing pig Andrews is rotting in hell because he deserves to be, after robbing us like he did. He must have thought he'd gotten away with it after all these years. If your cousin Nathan hadn't found out how little he actually paid out in bribes to get people to look the other way while we smuggled arms to our rebel American friends and paid him outrageous sums to make it happen, we would still be as in the dark as those fools that just left here. And I still think those rumours someone sold information about our plans to the British weren't mere rumours. It all points to him playing all sides to his own advantage and I hope he's in the deepest, nastiest part of hell because of it. Anyway, there was nothing in their questions leading me to think they are interested in his past from so long ago. I think there is nothing to worry about."

"I disagree, Jean," said Dusourd. "One of the two coming to see you was a black, right? My men tell me a black fellow off that British ship was asking questions all over town. He seemed interested in my ship and what we are doing. And what about Andrew's office? The Governor told you he'd handed the keys over to them. Who knows what records the bastard may have left?"

"Giscard, you're here on legitimate business so there is nothing to hide. And why would Andrews be stupid enough to leave a record?"

Dusourd shrugged in frustration, but Adam Jones spoke up. "Well, since it was Auyuba distracting Andrews while I put a knife in his back I don't know why the rest of you are sweating about this. But I have to agree I don't like the thought they were nosing around to that degree. And so you all know, I got word that same bastard was asking questions about my ship. You know, maybe another knife in the back would make this problem go away."

"I agree," said Auyuba, joining the conversation for the first time. "Those two had a woman with them and I've learned she was asking questions all over town, too. I don't like the way he was looking at me when I saw him yesterday and today, so why don't you leave this black sailor to me? Maybe the others will get the message and leave."

The others around the table all smiled.

James had always known the possibility of running across someone objecting to his questions was real every time he trawled for information, so he was always careful to sip his drinks far slower than everyone around him. Even so, after a full evening the effects of the alcohol always caught up with him to a degree. On his way back to the ship with little new information to show for his efforts he was glad he was only a little inebriated when a hand reached out as he passed a building, grabbing his collar and yanking him off his feet into the darkened alley beside it.

Being a little fuddled from the alcohol was what saved him, as his assailant misjudged how easy James was pulled off his feet. The knife intended for his heart only scratched his shoulder, wringing a gasp of pain from James. The attacker lost his grasp as James fell face first into a reeking pile of garbage strewn against one wall of the building. As James rolled to face his assailant he saw the dark outline of the man bending to strike again. With no time to think James threw a handful of garbage hard at what he hoped was his attacker's face. He was rewarded by an angry outburst in a language he didn't recognize.

Kicking hard at where he thought the man's knees were he connected with some part of his body, this time eliciting a sharp gasp of pain.

James struggled to his feet in time to grab his assailant's arms before he could strike again with the knife. The two men struggled hard against each other for several moments, each trying to find an advantage, but to no avail. Both were matched in strength.

His attacker changed tactics, pulling James backwards and to the side to slam him into the wall of the building. Stunned for a moment, his grip loosened enough for the assailant to pull away. Instead of pressing the attack, however, he ran. By the time James realized what was happening the man had disappeared. Angered, James ran in search of him in the direction he thought the man had gone, but his quarry had disappeared.

"Bastard," muttered James as he resumed his course back to the ship.

Evan was aghast at the picture James presented. Blood from the scratch on James's arm streaked down his side.

"I'm okay, Evan," said James, reassuring Evan. "This cut is nothing and this shit all over me is just garbage."

As James explained what happened Evan's brow furrowed. "So what do you think, was this a robbery attempt?"

"No. Well, I can't be certain, because he didn't have a chance to get that far with me. I also can't be sure, but I think I recognized his voice, if not his language. It was far too dark to see him, but I'm almost positive it was the black slave Auyuba we interviewed the other day."

Evan stood frozen for a moment, considering the implications. "Why the hell would he be attacking you?"

"This would be the question. I know I told you he was an enemy, but I wasn't expecting it would prove to be true this quick."

"Hmm. I don't like this, but I don't know what we can do about it. Confronting him tomorrow isn't going to get us anywhere. Well, I don't like leaving this an open question, but I think we should stick to our plan to leave tomorrow. We've accomplished our mission. I went through our dead consul's office again today and got nothing new for my efforts. Alice has managed to recruit two women in the shops and another two household servants as sources, and thanks to you we have Paddy and his daughter to serve as a conduit for it along with whatever they get so we have our network. I'm inclined to report on it all, including this little incident, and see what Sir James has to say. We can always make some excuse to come back and dig more."

"Well, if it was this bastard Auyuba I'd like a shot at getting up close and personal with him, Evan."

"You may get your wish, but not now. We sail tomorrow."

Chapter Seven
March 1788
Antigua

As they sailed into St. Johns harbour Marie and
Emilie stood by the railings enjoying the sight. Off to
one side enjoying the vista too were Auyuba and
Elise, brought along to see to the families personal
needs while they were gone.

"It's so different from St. Lucia, Marie! The
hills are much smaller and it looks so dry."

"Yes," said Anton, who had come over to join
them. "Captain Dusourd says this particular island is
quite dry most of the time. It does seem strange after
seeing how lush St. Lucia is. Apparently every island
is different."

"So what are we doing first, Anton?" said
Marie.

"I don't want to stay on the ship the whole
time we are here, so we find accommodation, then I
go see the Governor. I expect we will be here a
while."

When the Customs official greeting them
learned who they were and their purpose he
scrambled to find his superior, who was fawning in
his willingness to help. He suggested the family take
temporary rooms at a local Inn called The Flying
Fish, the best accommodation to be had in the area.
Anton agreed at once, as the Flying Fish was one of
the locations Auyuba had told them contacts with the
locals could be made. Henri and Jacques checked it
out and deeming it basic, but acceptable, the family
moved in. Word was sent to the Governor that Anton
desired an audience. The day after their arrival Anton,

Henri, and Jacques all presented themselves to the Governor.

Governor Thomas Shirley let nothing betray his thoughts as he read through the document the French Foreign Minister had provided Anton, taking his time to read it through a second time before passing it back.

"Well, Count de Bellecourt, this is interesting. I have to say I'm a little surprised at this initiative as I wasn't aware ideas of reform were a priority for the current French administration. I have heard times are difficult in France and I would have thought dealing with that would be more the focus."

"Indeed, Governor, there are challenges everywhere and many are rising up to address them. My family and I are a part of a larger initiative by our patron the Marquis de Lafayette."

"Ah, yes, I know of the Marquis. Well, this explains much. In any event, welcome to Antigua. We don't often get a visit from French nobility of your stature. There are many here who will be pleased to meet people of quality, if nothing else. I shall organize a ball as soon as possible to present you and your family, and you can make your case directly to everyone present. I will send word when I have details. Where are you staying?"

The Governor's eyes widened when they told him. "Good Lord, you'll not stay another night in that place while I'm in charge around here. I have another residence here in town I use for visiting dignitaries. It's on one of the hillsides overlooking St. John's, so it gets a pleasant breeze and has a wonderful view of the harbour. You shall have it for the remainder of your visit. My staff will organize moving you there at once. If you have need of servants we can arrange for this too."

Anton thanked him and explained all they would need were kitchen slaves to cook meals, so the Governor promised these would be provided too. As they left the Governor's office and gained the street Anton turned to the others. "Well, this was a good start, I think. We need to get the other part of our plan into action, now."

"It's already underway, Anton," said Henri with a smile. "I talked to the black fellow running the bar at our Inn and I'm sure he was the contact Auyuba gave us. He was suspicious, but I think I allayed his fears. He said he would get word out, but it would take time."

"Excellent. We're going to be here for a while so it won't be a problem."

The ball was set for three days later at the manor house of Randall Johnson, owner of one of the biggest plantations on the island. Evan finished pulling on his best dress uniform coat to attend, helped by Alice and watched by James.

"So these French diplomats are the same ones we heard about on St. Lucia, Evan?"

"Have to be. I'm interested to hear what they have to say. I'm also interested in their ship and what else they might be up to around here. I think you two should start nosing around a little and get some of our friends to have an eye on them."

"James and I already have plans, Evan. Since you are leaving me to my own devices tonight he and I are going to St. John's. The Flying Fish has new people running it, but I think we still have some friends there."

"Excellent. I'm still surprised at how interested Sir James was when we told him about this ship's Captain. All he could tell me was he knows John Andrews had mentioned dealings with this Captain Dusourd, but this is all he knew and there is obviously some murky history there. That our dead consul had all that money was a surprise to him too, and it's obvious he is suspicious there is a connection. He said he was going to do some digging on his end into this fellow's background and would let us know."

"Well, his orders were to have an eye on this guy, so we will, Evan. Do you think we'll get orders to go back to St. Lucia?"

"Not anytime soon. This latest letter from Sir James that arrived this morning confirmed that. He seems to want to play a wait and see game. See what intelligence Paddy and our friends come up with. Captain Rand is still interested, but given all the signs are those French warships aren't going anywhere soon he seemed less on edge about it. So we wait."

As Alice pinned Evan's empty sleeve up and stepped back to admire her handiwork, she grinned and ran her hand over his chest. "You know, there's something about a handsome man in a uniform that is irresistible. So have fun at the ball tonight, but don't forget where to find the best looking woman on this island."

Evan laughed. "Yes, I have a pretty good idea of where that may be. In my bedroom."

Still smiling, Alice came close enough to brush her breasts against his chest as she whispered in his ear. "I'll be waiting to help you out of that uniform."

Despite the growing stream of plantation owners leaving their operations in the hands of local managers and returning to England, there were still plenty of people clamouring for an invitation to the Johnson plantation ball, which soon became a major social event attracting a wide range of people from all over the island.

Although the Captains of all of the ships on station together with a Lieutenant from each were invited, Captain Rand left everyone including Evan to their own devices to get to and from the event. Evan caught a ride with Lieutenant Kent from *HMS Alice*, but they were relegated to leaving their buggy some distance from the plantation manor and forced to walk all the way up the dusty road to the entrance.

Before going inside they brushed the dust from their clothes, but no one paid them attention anyway. Evan and the Lieutenant acquired glasses of cool champagne from a passing servant and after a first tentative sip he smiled in appreciation.

"I say, this is excellent quality," said Evan, holding the glass out to admire the contents. "I wonder where Johnson got this stuff? The smugglers are back at it again, I think."

An older man, one of the local plantation owners reaching for his own glass, heard Evan and laughed. "Actually, sir, you can stand down this time. For a change it's been acquired legitimately. The pompous frog this ball is being held in honour of graciously decided to offer a couple of cases he brought with him for this purpose. He must figure we'll be more receptive to the nonsense he's spouting if we're all too drunk to do anything other than listen to him."

Both Evan and Lieutenant Kent chuckled in response and Evan looked around the room. "So where is our honoured guest, anyway?"

"Well, there are actually a few of them. They're in the main ballroom over there," he said, indicating the direction with a nod of his head. "If you can stand listening to these fools you'll at least get to enjoy looking at the two women."

This got Lieutenant Kent's attention. "That good?"

The owner laughed. "I wouldn't get your hopes up, young man. In addition to being extremely good-looking I suspect they both have rather expensive tastes. But who knows? Maybe one of them will be your ticket to riches untold. I bid you both good hunting, sirs."

Evan and the Lieutenant went in the direction he indicated and soon found a large crowd formed around a young, well dressed man who was holding court with the crowd and deep in conversation with a couple of plantation owners on Antigua. Having attended several balls on the island because of his elevation to the position of Commander of the Naval Dockyard Evan was now familiar with most of Antiguan society. He picked out the faces of the visiting aristocrats with ease and smiled to realize the women were indeed the same two he had seen on the street in Castries over a month ago.

The one with the long, pale blond hair that appeared a little older was looking bored and paying more attention to the crowd than the conversation everyone was listening to. She saw him come in and they locked eyes, her face lighting with unconcealed interest. Evan decided the businessman was right, as both women were indeed ravishing. To Evan's eye the older woman was more striking due to her classic beauty. Evan gave her a small smile at her interest, but to his mind Alice was still the most beautiful woman on the island and he turned away to focus on the conversation dominating most everyone else's attention.

A spirited debate on the topic of slavery was underway. Evan leaned close to a planter standing next to him to catch the man's attention. "I assume this fellow is the guest of honour?"

"You are correct, sir," replied the planter, his voice low so as not to disrupt the conversation. "This young Frenchman is Count Anton de Bellecourt. He's fighting a losing battle, but I give him credit for trying hard. The two delectable creatures with him are his sisters. Marie is the older pale blond creature and Emilie is the youngest. Those other two puffed up dandies with him are Baron Henri Durand and Chevalier Jacques de Bellecourt."

Nodding his thanks, Evan focused on the conversation. The Count was pressing hard on some point, while the brows of the two planters he was debating were both furrowed as if he was speaking some unintelligible language from the far side of the earth.

"Really, gentlemen," said Anton, spreading his arms wide. "Your own scholars are telling you the facts don't support maintaining slavery as a way of doing business. Why, there's this young fellow at your school in Cambridge to consider. Thomas Clarkson is his name, I believe? I understand he has done a lengthy study and published his findings that slavery is both a poor business model and morally not supportable as Christian behaviour. His findings validate the work your scholar Adam Smith brought forth over ten years ago now."

"Good God," moaned one of the planters. "Yes, we've heard of these academic ninnies. How can some fool too young to know what he's about have reasonable people paying attention to this tripe? The man has never spent any amount of time on an actual plantation, for God's sake."

"Well, I'm young too, but I have made the time to read his work, gentlemen, and I am impressed. I think he did a good job of researching his topic. He has plenty of statistics to support his case. Why, the numbers of British seamen involved in the capture and transport of slaves dying from violence or disease is staggering. The same applies to the slaves you purchase. All of these factors are costs that in the end must be paid by the people that buy your sugar. I suggest this is too high a premium for our societies to pay. It is money that would be better spent to improve conditions for workers and on actual pay for them. If they had money they in turn could buy your sugar too, thus increasing your profits even more. I submit that, even if you ignore the moral issues, the man is right about the economics of this."

This time the other planter spoke up. "My dear Count. We respect you have your thinking here, but you really must leave things like this to men of business who know what they are about. A few sailors involved in the trade and perishing is simply a cost of doing business. This is a dangerous profession in a dangerous world. It's the same for the slaves. This is no different than running a cattle or a sheep operation, you see? Some of them will die, despite your best efforts. There are dangerous elements of running a sugar plantation, too. And your notion that we should pay them to do the work? Count, I can't believe you are serious. Most slaves really are just beasts, you know. Yes, a few of them have shown they can be educated, but this simply doesn't apply to the vast majority. They wouldn't know what to do with money even if they had it. Look, for the most part we treat them reasonably well, to my mind. We give them Sundays off. We feed them well enough and they have opportunity to grow a little extra in the gardens we provide. What more could they want?"

"Well, freedom might be a start," replied Anton, his voice oozing with deliberate sarcasm. "I can see we will agree to disagree on this gentlemen, but I really think you should consider my message. The world is changing and this is why I am here. Yes, France is in need of some changes and I think you have need too. From what I understand there is a large movement growing in your own country to do exactly what I propose. It's called The Society for Effecting the Abolition of the Slave Trade, is it not? And it has some prominent people involved. One of your Members of Parliament, a William Wilberforce, is thinking of signing on as a champion. I hear there is even talk of a boycott of sugar itself because of this."

Both planters scowled in response as several people in the crowd grumbled at the mention of the name Wilberforce. "Yes, we've heard of this boycott nonsense and this pack of woolly headed fools. A boycott of sugar? They have no idea what this would do. Sir, the sugar trade is vital to more than the British economy, it is vital to the world. Your economy would crumble too if this silly boycott moves beyond our borders. And from what I hear your economy is already starting to crumble as it is.

You are having many problems with your harvests and this is bad news."

"Crumble?" replied Anton, a look of disdain on his face. "I don't know what your sources are, sir, but I'd say you are stretching the point considerably. Oh, we face difficulties like everyone else, but we are a resourceful people, much like our friends in America. You must agree with me on this, at least?"

"Well, I *do* agree with you about the Americans. And they have been friends to us here in the Caribbean, unlike our own government," replied the first planter, scowling in the direction of a group of Navy officers standing nearby. "But I think you said part of your mission is to carry this thinking to the Americans eventually too? Well, I hope you have a bottomless source of wealth to carry the message, because it's going to take a long time for the idea to be accepted."

"Perhaps. But one must start somewhere, sir. For example, I am keen to experiment and explore new ideas to improve processing methods. Think of it as finding a solution that would maybe improve your profit margin at the same time as freeing these people from slavery."

"Hmm, I like your thinking if it involves making me more money, sir, but I fear you have not thought through the consequences of what you are saying. Who exactly would clothe and feed the Negroes if they weren't slaves? Good God, man, they would go back to living in the forest like the beasts they once were. Working for us we can at least afford to have them baptized and give them a basic Christian education. You don't want them to step backwards into the bestial state they were once in, do you?"

Evan was so intent on the ebb and flow of the debate he didn't notice her until she was close enough the rich scent of her perfume enveloped him. Turning, he realized the older of the two French women was now standing beside him and smiling. Recovering himself, he put his glass down on a nearby table and reached to take her hand, offering a brief bow acknowledging her presence.

"Madam. Welcome to Antigua. I am Commander Evan Ross."

"Commander, it is nice to meet you. I am Marie de Bellecourt. But this is not the first time we've met, is it? It was you I saw on the street in Castries a while back, wasn't it?"

"It was. Yes, I recognized you, too. It would be hard not to," he added, a wry grin on his face. "I think you and your sister have the attention of every male in attendance tonight. They will all be jealous I have yours."

Marie laughed. "Well, it's their own fault for spending their time discussing boring politics with my brother and not paying more attention to me like they should. Oh, I support my brother and his efforts, but I think there is more to life than politics."

"Indeed?"

"Certainly. I am more interested in people and their stories. Endlessly fascinating, don't you think? Take you, for example. I see a handsome man with an obviously serious injury in his past on the street in Castries in the company of two coloured people. One of your companions is an extremely good-looking woman, dressed well enough to make me think she is not a slave, while the man is dressed like he came out of the nearest bar frequented by the kind of ruffians crewing our ship. And now here you are in Antigua, looking even more handsome in a naval officer's uniform. This makes you an interesting mystery and I am curious, Commander Ross. What brought you, a Royal Navy officer, to St. Lucia? Out of uniform, no less?"

Evan was alarmed at how perceptive this woman was. Worse, she was still holding his hand and with sudden insight he realized he was a bug in a spider's web already being wrapped in silk threads. He pulled his hand away, reaching for his glass of champagne as the excuse to disentangle his hand from her grasp, and smiled in hope of disarming her.

"Oh, I'm not such a mystery Madam de Bellecourt. I was in Castries as a temporary envoy on behalf of our Governor. Our consul on St. Lucia went missing and I was asked to find out what happened to him. As I was on a diplomatic mission I felt it better to dress accordingly. The people you saw with me are personal servants that attended as my aides."

"Servants, you say?" she replied, as one eyebrow arched up. "Well, I—"

"Marie, my dear, you must join us over here. The Governor wishes to introduce us to some more people," said Anton as he came to her side and took her elbow. Beside him was Emilie, wearing a look of open curiosity. After introductions all around Anton eyed Evan with a wary glance for a moment before speaking.

"So Commander, I saw you on the edge of the crowd listening to our debate. I haven't had a chance yet to sound out any naval people on our mission. What do you think of what you've heard?"

Evan gave him a polite smile. "I'd say the thoughts of our diplomats are more relevant than anything I have to offer, sir. I suspect you'll find most officers will feel the same way. We have more to say when it involves action of some sort."

"Well, there may be action for you if the world doesn't change, sir, and maybe sooner than you think. It's true there has been unrest in France and on our islands here, but I am certain we are not alone in this. I understand the British islands have enjoyed their own share of trouble? I don't think the plantation owners here understand how quickly this may spread, perhaps faster than anyone realizes."

Evan was surprised at the vehemence with which the Frenchman spoke and was about to reply when Marie interrupted, giving Evan a rueful look.

"If you let him, my brother will talk politics with you until your ears fall off. It was nice to meet you, Commander. I hope we'll have a chance to meet again soon. You English love to drink your tea, so why don't you call on us to have some before we leave?"

"Thank you. I shall have to see if I can find some time away from my duties," Evan replied, giving them a slight bow to end the conversation.

She nodded acknowledgement and they left, leaving Evan frowning as he stood watching them walk away. Lieutenant Kent sidled over with a heaping plate of food he had brought with him from the buffet table. Between bites he grinned at Evan.

"Congratulations, sir. You got her attention while everyone else here tonight has not. Any chance of learning your secret?"

A series of invitations to tea and dinner kept the family occupied for the next several days as Anton continued trying to find at least some common ground with local owners. Emilie's obvious, fidgeting boredom with the endless round of invitations was soon apparent to all and when she begged leave to remain in their lodging while the others went out, approval was soon forthcoming.

Elise returned early from the shopping errand Emilie had sent her on to hear muffled moans interspersed with high pitched screams of pleasure coming from the upstairs room Emilie occupied. Knowing what it meant she busied herself in the farthest corner of the house, but the muted sounds continued unabated on and off so she left and returned an hour later.

Her suspicion Auyuba was the other party involved proved correct when she returned to find Emilie and Auyuba devouring a makeshift lunch in the kitchen. Auyuba was standing beside Emilie and stroking her bottom with unfeigned, obvious pleasure as he gnawed at a cold chicken leg in his other hand. He stepped away from her when he realized Elise had joined them.

"Umm, hello, mistress Emilie," said Elise, ignoring Auyuba with a pointed frown. "I have what you wanted."

Emilie took her time finishing her own piece of chicken and with dainty, measured care wiped her lips with a cloth napkin. She paused a brief moment to glance at the satchel Elise held out for inspection, only to ignore it as she stepped closer to Elise, her eyes running all over Elise's body. Elise gave a soft gasp as Emilie reached out and deliberately stroked Elise's bare arm with slow and obvious, sensuous pleasure. Elise looked up from the hand still on her arm as Emilie drew close enough to plant a kiss on her lips, letting her breasts slide with tantalizing slowness across Elise's as she did. After several long moments Emilie finally stepped back.

"Perhaps next time I won't send you away," said Emilie. Pausing to appraise both Elise and Auyuba for one final long moment, she turned and left without another word.

When Elise was certain from the sound of Emilie's receding footsteps they couldn't be overheard she turned to Auyuba, one eyebrow raised at the grin of lust he wore. She gave him a stony look that turned into a frown and his grin disappeared.

"I don't like this white bitch, Auyuba," she said, the heat in her voice clear. "Who is manipulating whom here? I don't know what we are gaining other than you having a good time. And now this slut wants me too."

"Well, I confess she needs taming and this may take a while," shrugged Auyuba, looking uneasy on hearing the unmistakable note of jealousy in Elise's voice. "We need information wherever we can get it as to what they plan, and if it means I get to enjoy myself in the process, well, why not? And if it turns out you are the one to get information from her, what does it matter? You get to enjoy yourself, too."

Elise scowled, but said nothing.

Two weeks after the de Bellecourt family arrived on Antigua, Evan, James, and Alice were standing on the street outside the Governor's office. As they finished making arrangements to meet at the Flying Fish later after completing their separate tasks in town, a gloved hand tapped Evan on the shoulder to catch his attention. Turning, Evan found Marie de Bellecourt and her brother Anton staring at him. Marie wore a mocking frown.

"Commander Ross, how nice to see you again. But I confess I am disappointed in you. You have not called to visit."

"Madam de Bellecourt, I apologize. I have been busy with my duties," replied Evan, before turning to James and Alice with a quick aside. "So let's meet as agreed later, then."

Alice's face was stone as she eyed Marie, but she nodded and turned away with James in tow.

Marie's attention lingered on Alice even after she was walking away before she finally turned back to Evan. "So are you free today, Commander? We are heading back to our lodging now."

"I am so sorry. Once again I must disappoint you, I fear. I am due in a meeting with the Governor and his council shortly and I'm certain it will be longer than usual due to some contentious topics on the agenda. Perhaps tomorrow?"

"Well, I'm afraid this won't work either, Commander. We leave Antigua tomorrow morning for St. Kitts so my brother can carry on with his mission."

"I am so sorry, madam. It is my fault I did not adjust my schedule to make this work."

"Well, you can still work your way back into my good graces if the next time you are in St. Lucia you make your presence known and attend me."

"Madam, I don't know when that shall be, but if I do make it there I promise I shall make amends." Evan bowed in acknowledgment of their nodded agreement and watched them turn and leave, before heading himself for the Governor's office.

Henri and Jacques did their best to look nonchalant as they descended the stairs into the main tavern area of

The Flying Fish and took seats at a table as far from everyone else as possible.

"So, how was she?" said Henri with a leer, knowing Jacques had taken longer to come around to the idea of bedding a black woman.

"Well worth the fee," smiled Jacques. "I am beginning to think coming out here was the best thing that has happened to me. I confess it took me a while to realize it, but these black women are most willing to please."

"Well, I think I shall visit this place for more whenever we are back here again. Mine was like a lioness once she got me alone. I wish we had more time here, but unless something changes we don't. Anton seems set on being away to St. Kitts and Guadeloupe tomorrow, so what remains is we finalize this today. Well, we should know soon."

Even as he spoke Auyuba walked in and spying them at their table came over to join them, nodding a silent greeting as he sat down.

"So is your brother here, Auyuba?"

"I do not see him, master Henri," replied Auyuba as he scanned the room.

"Well, I hope he shows. I don't know why Anton is insistent you confirm it is him, but this is what he wants."

Auyuba shrugged. "He probably wants to be assured I am doing what I say I am doing for him. Ah, here he is."

From the shadows of an entrance at the rear of the room a tall black man wearing nondescript clothing appeared, scanning the room with a cautious eye one final time before coming over to join them. Henri and Jacques realized he had been lying in wait and as he came closer they saw the obvious resemblance in the features of the two black men. Auyuba stood to greet the newcomer and they looked in silence at each other for several long moments as they gripped each other hard by the forearms, the emotion clear in their eyes.

"Asante, my brother. It has been long since I saw you."

"Auyuba. I am overcome," replied the newcomer. "And Elise?"

"We were fortunate to have been purchased for service together by the same family. She is with me."

Asante nodded. "You are fortunate indeed."

Gesturing at Asante to sit, Auyuba introduced the two white men and explained their purpose. Henri acknowledged the obvious similarities of their features and promised to confirm this to Anton to allay his concerns.

Asante gave Henri a stony look before replying. "All I can say is I hope this meeting really is worth it. I have risked much to be here. I too was once a house slave like Auyuba, but unlike him I am now a runaway. If I am caught the best I can hope for is to be beaten until I am a bare second away from death."

"It shall be worth it. I trust our message to you fully explained what we want? Our preference is efforts be focused on damaging property?"

"Your message was clear, but what you want may not be easy to achieve," said Asante in a low voice, as he scanned the room once again to ensure they could not be overheard. "If we are caught in the act we will not let anyone stand in our way. You should also know there are some I lead who desire the exact opposite of what you ask, right? They would prefer we kill every white man in sight."

Henri cleared his throat. "We are not barbarians. We are trying to bring about civilized change to benefit everyone. But having said that, we know there may be people getting in the way and we are not concerned about it on this island. Obviously, they are not French, are they?"

Asante nodded acknowledgment. "Fine, and yes I do understand what you are trying to do. I will do what I can to keep my people under control. But I do have one concern. Your support is good, but I need more weapons and more ammunition in particular. The owners have far more resources than we do. When we rise up to attack, the hunt will be on and they will be relentless. This is why I must have more!"

"Asante," said Henri. "We brought only a limited supply of arms with us and we wish to support others like yourself on a few other islands too. I have already talked to my cousin about this and we agree we should have brought more. We are in some discussion over how best to deal with this, but I cannot promise immediate results. This will take time. And my cousin wants to know it will be worth the effort. He will want to see results."

"Well," said Asante, leaning forward to emphasize his point. "With what you say you will provide, the best I can do is likely limited, random actions. I do not have an endless supply of runaways like myself to lead. We use surprise and attack one plantation on any given night. That is it. We can't attack another the next night because we don't have enough weapons to overwhelm the owner men that will be waiting for us. But I will give you results if you promise to bring me more. I must have more to show the undecided ones before they will commit to action."

"We will do our best. It may be a few months before we can acquire more and get it to you. I understand the messages sent via the fishing boats have been getting to you without difficulty?"

Asante smiled. "I may not have many runaway followers, but I do have many friends here on this island and they do favours for me. As I said, if I can show these friends results I will have many more followers, with your help."

"Excellent. We will be sailing tomorrow and I gather you have the details of the drop location for tomorrow night? And you know the rumour we want your people to spread?"

"Yes, I have all of this information. We will be—" Asante stopped speaking as he turned his head in the direction of the entrance and froze. Alice and James had come in and made their way to a table on the other side of the room, as far from other tables with people as possible. Asante said something in a foreign language with enough vehemence in his voice to make Henri certain the man had uttered an oath of some sort. Asante turned his face away and attempted to keep his head down, but not before James was able to lock eyes with him for an instant from across the room.

Auyuba groaned and said something in return in the same foreign language as James turned his attention to him. The two men nodded acknowledgment of each other's presence before turning away. As soon as Auyuba turned back to Asante the two brothers launched into a low, intense dialogue in the same foreign tongue that went back and forth for almost two minutes.

"Damn you both, speak something we can understand," hissed Henri, losing patience at last. "What the hell is going on?"

Asante rose to leave. "I have stayed too long. My brother will explain." With a final nod to Auyuba he disappeared through the rear entrance to the kitchen.

"Well?" said Henri, frustration bringing an edge to his voice.

"Master Henri, I am sorry for speaking our native tongue. We were surprised because we both recognize this man and woman that came in, but for different reasons. The man was in the company of the British representative that came to St. Lucia to find out what happened to their consul. They asked me questions because I was the one who found his body on the street in Castries. The man had been murdered, but they have not found who did it. This man over there accompanied the representative and all he did was take notes, so I thought he was a servant or an assistant of some sort. The woman with him was also present in Castries."

Henri looked puzzled. "So? What does all that mean? You two were obviously concerned about something."

Auyuba nodded. "My brother knows of him for different reasons. He is not certain, but he thinks this man is a spy and the woman with him may well be involved too. The man questioning me in Castries is actually a British Royal Navy officer based here on Antigua, although he wasn't in uniform when I saw him. He is easily identified as he has only one arm. The man sitting over there is known on this island for constantly asking questions of everyone, but it isn't clear what he does or why he wants information. He has been seen frequently in the vicinity of their naval Dockyard here, so it may well be he has some role there."

"Hmm. I agree this is cause for concern and I will let Anton know, but I don't think there is reason to change our plans. We're just friendly visitors enjoying a drink here, right? This fellow who came and went was some passing acquaintance you haven't seen for a long time. No, I think we are all right. Well, we've done what we set out to, so let's get out of here."

James watched the three men leave, locking eyes once again with Auyuba before they left, nodding acknowledgment one final time.

"So you're certain, James? I admit they do have similar features," said Alice.

"As much as I can be. Those two have to be related somehow, maybe even brothers. It hadn't crossed my mind until seeing them together, but then it's not like I've seen a lot of either of them. I think the other fellow is a runaway, he was too nervous and he cleared out fast. I've not seen him before. Hmm, I wonder if he has some link to this mysterious leader here I keep hearing rumours of. Whoever he is, he's a clever bastard, because no one seems to know much. I don't like this and I'm sure Evan won't either. I haven't seen those two white men he was with before, but judging by their dress they have to be part of this French family of diplomats. And I recall the lawyer told us this Auyuba was a slave owned by the de Bellecourt family. So, if I'm right, we have a bunch of frogs with a ship crewed by a pack of the nastiest buggers I've seen in a long time meeting with someone I'm fairly certain is a runaway slave and, who knows, may even be the leader of the runaway slaves here on Antigua. No, I don't think Evan is going to be happy."

"Do you think they've used someone here at the Flying Fish as a conduit for messages?"

"Could be. I thought our friends were still working here, but except for your half sister Rachel I don't know anyone here anymore."

Alice grinned. "Well, you *knew* her pretty well for a while. I really don't know why you passed her over. She's a fun girl like me."

James smiled in return. "I guess it wouldn't be hard to get to know her again and find out what she's seen in the process, would it?"

Anton finished listening to Henri's report and turned to stare out the window at the view while he gave thought to what he had heard. After a few long moments he turned back to Henri and Jacques.

"Hmm. I agree we must be careful in light of this, but I don't think we have cause for concern. If this man is indeed a spy what could he have learned? You were both there to enjoy the services of the women and you arranged to have Auyuba meet you there. So he chances to meet an old acquaintance. They have proof of nothing. But I am interested in the connection to this British Navy officer. Describe these two people to me and what they were wearing."

After listening to Henri's detailed description Anton's brow furrowed. "Well, this is interesting. It has to be the same couple Marie and I met earlier today on the street. And they were with a Royal Navy officer."

"What?" said Henri, as he exchanged worried looks with Jacques. "What happened?"

Anton shrugged as he told them of the encounter. "This British Navy officer has somehow caught Marie's fancy, God knows why. It's likely because he was wounded somehow and lost an arm."

"Anton," said Henri. "This has to be the same man Auyuba talked about. He told us the officer who questioned him had only one arm. If he is linked with known spies perhaps we should cancel the drop. We can't let ourselves be linked to this."

Anton frowned. "No, I think we should stick to the plan. I will talk to Marie, but I am fairly certain she was the one initiating contact with this officer. Were it the other way around I might agree with you."

Henri and Jacques both looked at each other, before turning back to Anton.

"So this is it, then?" said Henri. "This is where there is no turning back, Anton."

Anton smiled. "I know. I've had enough conversations with these people now to know they are set in their ways and will not change unless there is a catalyst of some sort. And if this means we must be the catalyst, then so be it."

Chapter Eight
April 1788
Antigua and St. Lucia

Asante had to make what he had count, so he doled out some of his weapons and what little powder and shot he thought he could spare to his men, making them practice over and over until they were able to do what he wanted with as much discipline as could be expected of an untrained rabble. The many random nights of practice frustrated his men, because they couldn't use the weapons for long. But this too served Asante's purpose as the sound of the weapons discharging unnerved many planters on the island, keeping them on edge waiting for attackers to appear at any time.

Asante laughed to himself, as they had reason to be living in fear. He had lied to the white men providing him with the weapons and wanted every white man in sight dead.

Asante was also waiting for the moon. After three weeks of practice and patience, he knew the wait was over as the moon was now full and the sky was cloudless. Asante had already scouted the plantation he wanted to target first and he laid his trap with care. The owner and overseers on this particular plantation were known for using an even greater level of brutality in their methods than most. He smiled to himself, knowing the vengeance they would wreak on this plantation would send a message to everyone on the island.

He struck in the middle of the night by murdering the two guards on watch without a sound and setting fire to one of the buildings used to store already processed sugar, a move calculated to serve a dual purpose. Sending the owner's valuable crop up in flames was rewarding, but it also got the instant attention of every overseer on the planation when the alarm was sounded. Knowing they would be coming from the direction of the living quarters Asante arranged his men in a line hidden by scrub brush off to one side, urging them to have their targets already picked with care for when he gave the order. When Asante judged he had the maximum possible number of victims in their sights he exulted, knowing his plan to use the white man's tactics was working. He screamed his order with glee.

"Fire!"

The sudden volley of shot from the six excited slaves hiding in the brush mowed down only two of the leading overseers in their tracks, but it brought chaos to the scene. Those remaining had seen the flashes to their side and thinking the danger was over after the first volley they drew their weapons in a headlong rush toward the runaways. But they were wrong about the danger. Even as they massed together for a charge the slaves were passing the now spent weapons to other slaves waiting behind them and receiving new, already loaded muskets in return. Other slaves began reloading the spent weapons with frantic haste. Seeing they were ready Asante grinned as he roared out his command to fire once again.

Two more overseers dropped dead, blossoms of blood staining their shirts, while three others cried in pain as they were struck in less vital places. But more of the overseers and the owner's sons had arrived on the scene, dashing Asante's hopes of getting off a third volley to inflict mass damage. Screaming his final command to general attack Asante stepped into the fray from the shadow of the tree he had been standing beside, bringing his loaded pistol up to the face of an overseer surprised at his sudden appearance. The man's face was demolished from the point blank shot.

Asante's command was also a signal to launch his final surprise. As the scene dissolved into a chaotic jumble of struggling bodies punctuated with inarticulate screams of both pain and anger another six runaway slaves joined the fray. They had hidden on the other side of the path the overseers had followed, out of the line of fire from the muskets. Launching themselves into the fight in silence and from the rear of the struggling overseers as Asante had commanded achieved the desired effect. The attacking white men were overwhelmed and realizing the fight was lost those still unharmed broke and ran. With years of pent up fury the runaways chased them hard, cutting many down from behind with devastating slashes from long machetes they wielded.

Asante was desperate to bring his men back under control, knowing reinforcements from other plantations would already be on the way. Punching and shoving them into a semblance of order he issued a series of rapid-fire orders. More buildings were set on fire as three still alive overseers, too wounded to escape, were seized, fitted with nooses, and without delay left to choke out their lives from the limbs of the nearest tree. The plantation owner was killed on the doorstep to his manor and the runaways rampaged through the building. His wife was hacked to pieces as others dragged away their two young daughters to be raped and killed later.

"Excellent," said Asante, watching it all and smiling as he stood to one side surveying his handiwork. Knowing they could linger no further, he gave one final signal to his men to leave.

Giscard Dusourd stiffened and rose from his seat as Adam Jones walked into the room, but Anton and Henri smiled and waved the American into a seat across the table from them. Anton had opted for the anteroom of Jean Moreau's office for this conversation, as far from prying ears as possible.

"Captain Jones," said Anton, reaching out to shake the American's hand. "Thank you for coming. We may as well get straight to business. Captain Dusourd has convinced me you may be better able to meet my needs than anyone else. I trust he gave you a full understanding of what we desire?"

"He has, sir, but what you are looking for will not be easy to attain. I am prepared to attempt this transaction with all discretion, but it will still raise questions with my contacts back home. It would be helpful if I had a better sense of what this will be for."

"You will be paid well for the discretion, but what this shipment will be used for is no one's business but ours. We are approaching you because America is much closer to hand than sailing all the way to France and back. I give you my assurance these weapons will not be used against America or American interests."

"You are a man of honour, Count de Bellecourt, so your word on this is helpful. Can you at least tell me where they will be used?"

Anton drummed his fingers on the table in thought before responding. "Surely it must be obvious we are here in the Caribbean and we aren't going anywhere else anytime soon. Is this enough of an answer for you?"

"You know, I've been hearing some interesting things around town," said Jones, the barest hint of a smile creasing his lips. "There are some pretty wild stories out there about runaways going on the rampage on a few other islands. Antigua, St. Kitts, and Guadeloupe to be specific. Why, there has even been some property damage here on St. Lucia."

"So? What about it? There are runaways on every island. Sometimes they get out of hand," said Dusourd.

Jones laughed. "Well, out of hand is an understatement. What's been happening here isn't too bad, but it certainly is on the other islands. I hear there was an entire plantation together with everyone on it laid waste on Antigua, and the British are all frothing at the mouth to find whoever did it. A few got murdered in their beds on Guadeloupe, too. You know, it occurs to me you fellows visited these islands recently. You wouldn't happen to know more about all of this, would you?"

"No," said Anton with a scowl. "I suggest you stop this ridiculous speculation and make a decision. Are you in or not?"

"Oh, I'm in, for certain. Like I told Giscard here, I need the work. I can't guarantee getting as many supplies as you want, but I will do my best. I will sail tomorrow and all being well I should be back by the end of May or the first week of June."

"Excellent. Henri, it's time to bring Moreau into this. Captain Jones, we have a cover story for you. You will have paperwork, in case you need it saying we have contracted for some trade goods from America through you, which will explain all the gold you will have on hand. Also, we will provide you with contact details on each of the islands along with a list of how much we want you to deliver to each. You will then report to us here as your final stop for payment of our holdback."

Jones smiled.

Anton moaned with pleasure as Elise rode him, sweat beads rolling in streaks down her body as she leaned forward with hands on either side of him to brace herself. She moaned as he teased her nipples to attention and stroked her breasts with insistent, feverish strength. Unable to contain himself any longer Anton exploded into her with a moan of ecstasy as Elise shuddered with her own pleasure. Collapsing, she lay beside him in a pool of shared sweat, both of their chests heaving.

After a few minutes to catch her breath Elise turned to smile at Anton. "I'm sorry, master Anton, but I don't think we were as quiet as you wanted us to be. I fear others in the house may have heard us."

"That's all right, at this point I don't think I care anyway. My God, that was good."

As his heartbeat and breathing began returning to normal Anton's thoughts turned again to the puzzle of the woman beside him. Prior to their trip to Antigua she had been distant to a point Anton was certain she was making every effort to avoid him. During their stops on St. Kitts and Guadeloupe he had been far too busy with his mission to focus on her, but in the back of his mind he detected a subtle attitude shift on her part. Brushing against him with slow and deliberate intent, despite obvious opportunity to avoid contact, was the first sign. Flirting with an increasing degree of innuendo by the time they returned to St. Lucia made it clear what she wanted, culminating in their tryst today. Deciding he had to know, he asked her about it.

"That's easy, master Anton. I wasn't sure you were serious about helping us, but after Antigua it was clear you really are. So I guess I wanted to reward you and besides, you are an attractive man."

"I see," said Anton with a leer. "Well, I am appreciative, believe me. But what about Auyuba, Elise? He likes you, I think."

"Auyuba is just another man," she replied with a shrug. "So master Anton, what is next? Auyuba tells me there were really few weapons to offer."

"This is true, but we are trying to get more. It is a pity the plantation owners on St. Kitts and Guadeloupe are all so set in their ways. Well, we distributed what we could to get the maximum possible from what we had and we have seen some results we can maybe exploit, but we do need more. The Americans will hopefully supply what we need. I am already sensing a growing frustration among the other owners here. Perhaps the day will not be far off when all slaves will be free."

Elise smiled. "I hope so, master Anton, and I'd like to reward you for it, in whatever way you like."

Feeling a stir of anticipation, Anton grinned in return, unaware that downstairs Auyuba was scowling at the ceiling as the sounds of intercourse echoed from above once again.

Evan felt like groaning and holding his head, but all he could do was give a polite nod and look concerned as Captain Rand vented his frustration by covering the same ground for the third time. Evan couldn't blame him, though. The Captain was the man everyone wanted a piece of for the Navy's failure to prevent arms from being smuggled onto the island. Several of the plantation owners serving as counselors to Governor Shirley had pointed literal fingers of blame at the Captain and they weren't buying his protestations, making Evan fear the man was going to have an apoplectic fit. The Governor was doing his best to maintain control of the meeting without success to that point, but displaying the persistent patience of an experienced diplomat he tried once again.

"Gentlemen, this is getting us nowhere and we are at a point where the good Captain here is repeating himself. As it happens, I am sympathetic to his case, although I wish it were otherwise."

He held his hand up palm outward to forestall any outburst from his counselors. "No, hear me, please. Look, there was no hint of anything like this on our horizon until we started hearing the weapons fire in the nights leading up to the massacre at the Stanton plantation. By then it was already too late. And let's face reality, please. This island has so many deserted beaches smugglers could use a different one every day of the year. Even if the Navy had been patrolling constantly and with advance knowledge of our foes movements, the task is challenging."

"Thank you, Governor," said Rand, obvious gratitude and relief etched on his face. "I'm glad someone here understands the magnitude of the problem."

"And our friends in the Army have their own challenges once the weapons are on the island, I fear," said Governor Shirley. "Is this not true, Colonel Holmes?"

A stiff looking, mustachioed officer who had been silent until now leaned forward to speak. "You are correct, Governor. Similar to what the Navy faces, there are simply too many places for runaways to hide. The hilly terrain, scrub brush and trees covering much of this island serves them well and hinders coordinated troop actions to flush them out. Of course, they are constantly shifting their base of operations, too. But we are keeping the pressure on them with random searches of likely hiding places."

"Bloody excuses is all we hear," growled one of the plantation owners. "Governor, they must do better. Our operations are suffering because we have to deploy more of our men to providing security, which means they aren't doing the work we need them to. This is eating into our profits and it simply cannot continue. It's intolerable, sir."

"I know, gentlemen, and I do agree something must change," said the Governor, his tone firm as he addressed the plantation owners. "Now, I must ask you gentlemen to leave so I can discuss this further with our military people."

Once they had filed out, unsmiling and still grumbling to a man, the Governor sighed and rubbed his chin. "Captain Rand, Colonel Holmes, I need to know more about your strategy for dealing with this. To start, have either of you had any success in learning what is behind this?"

The two officers looked at each other before they in turn confessed they had no idea why the violence was happening. The Governor raised an eyebrow as he leaned forward, arms folded on the table, with the beginnings of a frown appearing.

"Come, come, gentlemen. Have you made no efforts to find out? These things don't happen randomly."

Captain Rand started to groan before mastering himself. "How would we do that? And why? Governor, this is simple. Find a way to get me but a few more ships and the freedom to stop and search everything, and I mean everything, coming to this island, and we will put a stop to this nonsense. The problem is we are stretched with trying to patrol around St. Kitts given the unrest they experienced there too. I'm certain my colleague in the Army could use a few more resources, too. Between us we can do it with your support."

The Governor snorted in disbelief as he looked back and forth at the two men. "If you two think I have the power to will more resources into being for you both you are dreaming. What about your intelligence sources? What are they saying?"

"Intelligence sources?" said Captain Rand.

The Governor scowled. "Good God, man. What do you think Commander Ross is supposed to be doing for you? Never mind, I'll ask him myself. Commander Ross, what do you know?"

Stirring himself for the first time Evan looked the Governor in the eye. "Sir, unfortunately I have little to offer here. My colleague and I have made some informal enquiries and are striving to learn more, but all I can provide right now is confirmation there is a rumour out there of a link to the island of Grenada as a source. Frankly, this makes no sense whatsoever to me, but it is out there. Grenada is under British control and it's three hundred nautical miles away."

The Governor's eyes narrowed and he raised an eyebrow in question at Evan. "Commander, I don't understand. You did a fine job of providing intelligence to bring the smuggling under control some time back. Why are your sources not helping with this?"

"Well, we have not maintained our network active to the extent it was, sir. Captain Rand made it clear he had no need for our reports and as most of our funding to, um, motivate our sources comes from the Navy there seemed no purpose to it. We do still have sources, but they are limited and it will take time to rebuild what we had."

The Governor rolled his eyes and shook his head. "Captain Rand. Colonel Holmes. I shall be sitting down after this meeting to write some letters. You saw in the meeting I am doing my best to support you, but I must have results. I will be making this clear to your superiors. So, I have a word of advice. I don't know why you aren't exploring all options, but you should start."

"Governor," said Captain Rand, growing red in the face. "I agree with Commander Ross this rumour of Grenada as a source is ridiculous. I think those frog warships on St. Lucia are far more likely to have a hand in this."

"Captain Rand," growled the Governor, as he gathered up his notes and rose from his seat to signal the meeting's end. "I'm not normally given to being blunt, considering my job is to be diplomatic. But this once, I think I shall make an exception. If you think the French Navy is behind all this, then prove it and do something. If you think Grenada is ridiculous, then do what you have to do to prove this too. I don't give a shit how you get me results, just get them. Good day, gentlemen."

Both senior officers were still steaming with anger at the implicit dressing down, but worse was the Governor's threat to write reports criticizing them to their superiors. Evan wasn't surprised when the two men stopped to confer with each other once they were free of the Governor's office and he braced himself for what was coming. Evan watched as Captain Rank looked around to ensure no one was in earshot before venting his frustration.

"Bloody politicians! Can you believe he claims to have some understanding of our situation?"

Colonel Holmes gave an incoherent snarl and a shrug of frustration before responding. "Well, I agree, but what are we going to do?"

"It's not what we are going to do, sir. It's what Commander Ross is going to do. Isn't that right, Commander?" said Captain Rand, turning to glower at Evan. "By God, you young fool, if you ever do this again I swear I'll have you court martialed."

"Sir?"

"You know goddamn well what I'm talking about. Blaming me in front of the Governor for your own failure to be ready when necessary."

"Sir, the Governor asked me a direct question and I responded with the facts. I've sent you regular reports on our activity."

"Don't back talk to me, damn you. How you got to the level you're at without understanding how this works is beyond me. Look, you simpleton, I'm going to be as clear as I can. The Governor seems to think you're some golden boy, so as of now your job is to prove it. I think the goddamn frogs are behind this, so you are going to St. Lucia to find out what the Christ they are up to. I want to know where those frog warships are and what they are doing. And if you don't find anything there then go to Grenada and do the same thing. Meanwhile, the Colonel and I will be here doing real work protecting people and assuring the Governor every chance we get you have been given orders to do what he suggested and you are on the job. If you succeed you report to us and we will report to him the good Colonel and I have got the job done. If you fail I will be throwing you to the sharks."

"Sir? Our network in St. Lucia has not reported any movement on the part of those French warships. If they haven't left port, how likely is it they would have a part in this?"

"God Almighty, it's *likely* because the frogs are all a pack of devious liars, including your bloody sources! So sail there and make sure."

"Sir, I shall depart as soon as possible," nodded Evan, knowing he had pushed the issue as far as he could. "When I arrive in St. Lucia again I will need some sort of cover story. Do you have any preferences?"

Captain Rand rolled his eyes and shook his head in dismay. "Good Christ, you really are a simpleton, aren't you? You're the bloody spy, so you figure it out and deal with it! You have your orders. Lieutenant Kent will be given his orders to place his ship at your disposal once again."

Captain Rand shook his head as he turned his back on Evan to face the Colonel. "Come on, let's go get a drink somewhere. Tell me, is it this bad in the Army too?"

Evan sighed as the two men stalked out of sight.

Both Alice and James weren't happy, but Evan was confident they understood. In a hurried conference as Evan packed to leave for St. Lucia and Grenada, he could see the disappointment on their faces.

"I know you both want to join me, but we've got to get more information fast. In particular, we need to figure out who is behind all this here on Antigua. Captain Rand made a point of telling me I'd be fed to the sharks if we don't get this under control and I think he would be sore tempted to actually do it if we fail."

"We do want to join you, Evan," said James, putting on a brave face. "I'm envious we can't go to sea with you, but I know what has to be done. I'm positive that bastard I saw in the Flying Fish that day with Alice has something to do with this and he could be the one with the leadership skill behind what's happened. The attack on the Stanton plantation was too well planned. Look, Alice and I know what to do here. We will step up the pressure. I just wish we could be there to watch your back."

Pulling out his favourite pistol to pack, Evan held it up and smiled. "I dare say this will help watch my back."

"Evan?" said Alice. "I think the French bitch and her family we keep running into on the street has something to do with this. As much as I hate to suggest this, perhaps you should try and meet her? You said she suggested you contact her if you were back on St. Lucia."

Evan eyed Alice for a long moment with open curiosity, keeping the smile he wanted to give her off his face. "Did I hear this right? You want me to connect with her?"

Alice raised one eyebrow and put a hand on her hip in a pose Evan had come to know she used whenever he was being particularly dense. "You know what I mean. The French bitch is the one who will have to watch her back if she lays a hand on you."

James snorted with muffled laughter as Evan smiled and pulled her close. "Yes, I do know what you mean. Look, you two, I'll be careful and I'll be back as soon as I can. But, I'm curious. What makes you certain this bunch of French aristocrats has something to do with all this? I know you saw them consorting with a suspicious character, but that proves little."

Alice shrugged. "Just my intuition. When you make your living on your back you have to get good at figuring out whom to trust real quick. This bunch had me suspicious from the first second I saw them."

Evan smiled to himself as he watched the faces of the officers on *HMS Alice* deflate when he broke the news Alice wouldn't be joining him on this voyage. When asked, most common sailors and officers would profess to believe women had no place on a ship of war at any time and for any reason, but a woman appearing on board brought welcome change from the dreary routine and the constant presence of nothing but males. Still, being at sea again was welcome news to everyone, as too much time in port at English Harbour always meant more access to rum and more reasons to apply the lash.

As they fired their salute and sailed into Castries harbour once again Evan searched for the French warships to confirm their presence. As he absorbed the scene before him he swore to himself at the same time as Lieutenant Kent spoke.

"Sir? I can see all of the same warships that were here last time except for the big frigate. The *Marie-Anne*, I think it was? I don't see it anywhere."

"Damn, sir. Well, we are going to have to find it. But first things first."

After working through the same Customs formalities as last time Evan made his way straight to the Governor's office in civilian clothing once again. A new British consul had not yet been appointed and Governor Shirley on Antigua had been willing to provide a letter nominating Evan as temporary consul. Governor Marchand promised to put the word out Evan would be in residence for the next few days for anyone desiring contact with the British consul. On his way to the former consul's office Evan stopped at Jean Moreau's law office to request a message be sent to Marie de Bellecourt regarding his presence. Evan wanted to make his next stop The Thirsty Sailor to find out what Paddy and his daughter knew about the missing French warship, but he was concerned someone could already be tailing him, so he went straight to John Andrew's office instead. As word got out of his presence a trickle of people stopped in to talk to him about a range of matters left hanging too long due to the absence of a consul.

At the end of the day Evan locked up and left, walking in the direction of the harbour where the *Alice* was tied up. Pretending to stop and go back to check out something interesting in a market stall he had passed Evan scanned the crowds from the corner of his eye, picking out a young man who looked away, trying to be innocuous. Realizing he was the same young man that had followed him on his last visit to St. Lucia, Evan's thoughts raced as he resumed walking toward the harbour. Evan had no proof, but it seemed reasonable the young man had been left behind with orders to follow Evan should he arrive again on St. Lucia because he knew what Evan looked like.

Ducking into the open door of a grog shop Evan smiled as he saw what he was looking for. At the rear of the room the staff entrance to the kitchen was open and past it he could see daylight through a door left partway open to let in fresh air from outside the rear of the building. Walking fast Evan ignored the startled looks he got as he strode past the bar straight into the kitchen and out the back door into a back alley reeking of garbage. Picking his way around piles of debris he made his way with care down the alley and back out onto the street he had left. No one followed him.

Peering around the corner of a building Evan smiled again as he saw the young man doing his best to be inconspicuous as he watched the entrance to the grog shop Evan had disappeared into. Turning away Evan headed straight for The Thirsty Sailor, where he found Paddy sitting with a mug in front of him in his usual spot. When Evan explained why he was in St. Lucia Paddy called Manon out from the rear of the shop. On seeing Evan she looked around the shop before turning back to him with a question in her eyes.

"No, he didn't come with the Commander this time, my love," said Paddy with a gentle laugh. "Never mind Lieutenant Wilton. The Commander wants an update on the situation here and in particular he wants to know about the big frigate that left yesterday. I've told him we don't know where they went, but why don't you carry on from here. I don't think he knows about Guadeloupe."

"Guadeloupe?" said Evan.

"Sir," said Manon, as she sat and looked around the room to ensure they weren't overheard. "You must have missed receiving our message. The frigate actually left unexpectedly, what, almost four weeks ago now, but it returned a couple of weeks ago. We've learned from one of their sailors it was at Guadeloupe most of the time, but it was also at sea off another island. He wouldn't talk more about it. As father told you, it left again yesterday and we don't know its destination, but this time they went south after they left the harbour."

"South? Hmm," said Evan. "Do you know why it was on Guadeloupe?"

"Probably because of the unrest. We can't be certain of this, of course."

"Unrest?"

"There were several plantations on the island attacked by runaway slaves. A few people were killed, but they seemed to be focusing on damaging the owner's property. There has been some unrest here, too. Well, it's been more than usual, but not as bad as Guadeloupe. At least, no one here has been murdered yet."

Evan sat back to digest it all, tapping his fingers on the table as he considered the implications, before sighing in frustration. "Has there been any word on what is behind all of this?"

Manon looked at Paddy, who turned to Evan to speak. "There's a rumour out there Grenada is the source of all this, but it's all extremely vague. No indication of why it's happening. But you told me you've heard the same rumours about what happened on Antigua? Sir, this makes no sense."

"I agree," said Evan, dropping some coins on the table to pay for his drinks and rising to leave.

"Well, I shall be here a couple more days. If you hear anything further send word to me at the ship. Otherwise, please keep at it. I don't know what's going on here, but we need to put a stop to it."

"Actually, there is one other bit of information for you, but I don't know what to make of it. Most of what Manon and I do is go on the hunt for information for you, right? Well, we were hunted down and offered information."

Evan sat down again. "Hunted down? Good God, what happened?"

Paddy shrugged. "A stranger came in here one night and told me he knew we were looking for information about what happened to the consul. He started telling me this stuff, but I stopped him and asked how much this was going to cost. He didn't want anything, which I thought was strange. Anyway, he didn't offer any hard facts, but if we were looking for likely suspects he said a black slave named Auyuba and a Frenchman named Gilles Dusourd were in a dispute with the consul over money. They both have links to a local lawyer named Moreau."

"Good God, I've met both the slave and the lawyer. Who is this Dusourd?"

"He's Captain of a merchant ship named *L'Estalon*. The de Bellecourt family owns it and I see from the look on your face you've heard of them, too. But there's more, sir, and you may not like this. The man that came to see us claimed to know of you, too, and he said you may find it amusing to reacquaint yourself with the Captain of the *Marie-Anne*."

"Reacquaint myself? What in God's name does that mean? Who is the *Marie-Anne's* Captain?"

"Sir, I don't know and he wouldn't give me a name. This is another odd piece of the puzzle. All of the other French Navy officers are quite open about who they are, but this fellow has made a point of keeping a low profile. I am trying to use some of your gold to loosen tongues, but have not had success as yet."

Evan racked his memory in furious thought, but nothing came to mind. "Damn. Well, you are right, I don't like this."

"Sir? As I said, I don't know the name of this French Captain, but I do know the man who came to see me is an American. His accent is unmistakable. And there was an American flagged merchant ship in port named the *Beacon* for some time, although it left a while back. I noticed it because it looked like a warship to me. Maybe a little old, but it was still serviceable. The thing is this man came to see me right before that ship left port and I haven't seen him around Castries since."

Evan sat silent for several moments before pulling out a couple of gold coins and sliding them across to Paddy. "Well done, sir. You have given me much to think about. Well, I must go."

"Sir?" said Manon, forestalling Evan as he rose and turned to leave once again. "Next time you come back bring Lieutenant Wilton with you. Please?"

Evan and Paddy both laughed as she blushed.

Two days later, Elise greeted Evan at the entrance to the De Bellecourt manor. Evan was certain he saw the same look of interest in her eyes that he couldn't help showing in his own, given this woman was a serious rival to Alice's beauty. Evan also couldn't help watching her sway as she showed him into the drawing room where two glasses of wine were already in place before she withdrew. Marie de Bellecourt entered soon after from another doorway. As they made small talk and sipped at the excellent wine she confirmed Evan's growing sense of genuine pleasure on her part he had made the time to see her.

"Well, you can consider yourself forgiven you failed me on Antigua, sir," she said with a smile. "I really do enjoy meeting different people, especially interesting ones. I wish I had known the timing of your arrival as I could have arranged to meet you at our manor house in Castries instead of making you ride all the way here. So what brings you to St. Lucia this time, Commander?"

Evan smiled. "I'm still not sure why I'm so interesting, but if a beautiful woman wants to pay attention to me I won't complain. And you don't even have a chaperone? Won't there be talk, madam?"

Marie shrugged as she sniffed in disdain, before a coy look appeared. "Let them. I am a grown woman and I know what I am about. Besides, you are an officer and a gentleman. You would never take advantage of a lady, would you?"

Evan laughed. "Yes, I am an officer and a gentleman, and you are right. Of course, if she *wanted* me to take advantage of her I would have to give this serious consideration. But in my experience a true lady needs to be courted properly."

Marie's open laugh showed she enjoyed the banter and a mischievous look appeared in her eyes. "But Commander, I am dying to know. This stunning black woman I saw you with both here in St. Lucia and on Antigua? Is she yours?"

Evan took a moment to clear his throat to buy himself time to think through his answer. "Ah, that would be Alice. She is an assistant to me in my diplomatic and other duties as Commander of the Naval Dockyard."

Marie pursed her lips and raised an eyebrow. "Commander. You haven't really answered my question, have you?"

Evan was saved from having to answer as a frown appeared on her face when the door opened and Anton walked in.

"Commander Ross, I heard you had come to visit and thought I would drop in. You don't mind, do you, Marie?"

"I had thought to enjoy the Commander's presence alone, dear brother."

Ignoring her Anton looked at Evan. "So Commander, what brings you back to St. Lucia?"

Evan gave his cover story as Anton raised his eyebrows in response.

"Well, Commander, you seem to be an important man. You have both command level duties as an officer and diplomatic tasks coming your way too. I see why my sister finds you interesting."

"I serve in whatever ways I am asked to, sir."

"So tell me, Commander, as an individual what do you think of the situation now? You sidestepped it all nicely in Antigua, but even diplomats have their own opinions. This random violence the islands have been experiencing shows it is time for a change, don't you think?"

Evan put his glass of wine down to buy himself time to think through his response once again. "Well, sir, speaking as a diplomat, I think change is inevitable. It would be preferable people not resort to violence to achieve it. This is what diplomacy is for. As for me personally, I do have sympathy for your mission. In my time here in the islands I have come to know many black people quite well. This notion they are simple beasts is nonsense. Why, we have several black sailors serving in the Royal Navy and I can attest they are as capable as anyone else. Slavery has built the sugar industry to what it is for everyone involved, but I do not like or support it. But this is my personal opinion, you understand."

Anton nodded. "I can see you understand, sir. Well, I ask you all of this in hopes you will help promote our mission, sir."

"We all do what we can, sir. Well, I thank you both for your hospitality, but I must be away."

"So soon," said Marie with a frown, turning to glare at her brother. "I had hoped to spend more time with you without having to talk politics."

"I am sorry, Madam de Bellecourt. The—"

"Commander, please call me Marie."

"Marie it shall be," said Evan as he took her hand in departure. "And please do call me Evan. Unfortunately, the tide does not wait for anything and we are sailing with it this evening as my business here is concluded."

"Commander—sorry, Evan. I shall be expecting you to dance with me the next time we are in Antigua."

Evan smiled and took his leave. As he rode back to Castries he mulled over everything he had learned, but the truth was he wasn't much further ahead. One last visit to Paddy and Manon had revealed no new information for him. Knowing his mission wasn't complete without finding the missing frigate, he was frustrated and worried. He felt certain Grenada would yield nothing new, but he had no choice. *HMS Alice* would chart a course to Grenada as soon as he was back on board.

Chapter Nine
May to June 1788
Grenada, Antigua and St. Lucia

Evan had his telescope at the ready as *HMS Alice* sailed past the town of St. George's on the southwest coast of Grenada. Fort George dominated the scene, perched on a point of land with a hill high enough to command both the town and sea around it with ease. Moments after Lieutenant Kent gave the order the first of the cannon fired its blank charge to offer compliments to the fort and when they finished the fort boomed out its reply. As they rounded the point they found another promontory of land in the distance, which together with the one Fort George sat on formed the entrance to a large inner harbour, offering safety from the worst of storms. Evan bided his time waiting for a glimpse at who was in the harbour by staring at the Fort, admiring its excellent placement.

As the Lieutenant tacked into the picturesque harbour filled with the usual wide assortment of ships he issued a rapid series of orders to reduce sail. The Lieutenant was engrossed with maneuvering his ship and appeared startled when Evan broke his concentration.

"God Almighty, I think it's her," said Evan, his voice betraying his rising excitement. "Yes, it's the *Marie-Anne*."

The Lieutenant whipped his own telescope to his eye before turning to Evan with a mischievous grin. "Fortune has smiled on us, sir. Even better, it looks to me like we have room to dock right beside her. Shall we?"

Evan laughed and nodded. "Oh, please do. I need to introduce myself to whoever this Captain is."

As soon as he set foot on land Evan made his way back along Wharf Road to where the French warship was moored. Evan saw a French Lieutenant supervising a working party loading supplies from the dock, so he signaled for his attention as he approached. Evan could see the French officer eyeing his civilian clothes with suspicion and realized he must be wondering why he was being approached. Evan was pleased to discover the officer could speak English, allowing Evan to keep the fact he spoke French a secret. When Evan explained he was a diplomat the man's attitude became deferential in an instant, but the suspicion returned to his eyes when Evan began asking about the Captain of the *Marie-Anne*.

"Sir, I am not at liberty to discuss anything about my Captain."

"Not even his name so I can send him an invitation to dine with me?"

"Ah, no, sir. I can certainly take your contact information and—sir," replied the Lieutenant as he stiffened, his eyes now fixed on a point past Evan's shoulder.

Evan turned and was forced to master his surprise, as standing before him was a smirking Marcel Deschamps. Over two years before Evan had worked to stamp out a plot masterminded by this man in concert with his American counterpart to destabilize the British sugar islands. Evan was on edge, as this man had also attempted to have him murdered.

"It's all right, Lieutenant. This gentleman and I already know each other. Don't we, Lieutenant Ross?"

The French Lieutenant turned to Evan in surprise, confused by the alleged diplomat in front of him being referred to as an officer.

"Well, actually, Captain Deschamps, these days I am a Commander."

"Really? Well, the fruits of success are yours! I heard the fort rendering honours to your arrival and simply had to come investigate. And would this ship you came in on be your command now?"

"No, sadly not, much as I would prefer it. I am here on a diplomatic mission, sir."

"Well, I must say this is interesting, given what I know about the kind of diplomacy you indulge in."

Irked at the man's smug look Evan shrugged before going to the attack. "Ah, but we are in the same business, aren't we? And how about you, sir? I am thinking you are the mysterious Captain of this fine frigate I see before me, despite the fact I see you are dressed as a civilian too. Am I correct?"

The knowing smirk remained planted on the French Captain's face as he nodded and gave a slight bow with a hand out to concede the point, so Evan continued.

"For my part I find *that* interesting, far more so than the promotion of my own humble self. You have gone from being a mere merchant ship Captain to command of a formidable warship. It's quite the achievement, sir."

"Well, I've always kept my hand in with our Navy in a reserve role," said Deschamps, with an open laugh. "I guess I neglected to mention this when last we met. Look here, how long are you in Grenada, sir?"

"Perhaps a few days at most."

"Well, we were going to depart tomorrow morning after I conclude some business tonight, but I could be induced to stay an extra night. Why don't we dine tomorrow night? Catch up on old times?"

"Yes, I was going to suggest this myself."

"Excellent! I know of a perfect place for dinner too. It has a wonderful view of the harbour and among other things they serve a fresh crab dish so good you won't believe it."

After getting directions and arranging a time Evan took his leave, thankful to get away from the encounter and needing time to think through the implications. Having learned the Captain was Marcel Deschamps was a huge step toward the success of his mission, but he was wary of the danger the man presented.

With plenty of time before the next evening's dinner Evan went in search of information, starting with the Governor of Grenada, whose office was in Fort George itself. The Governor acknowledged he too had heard of rumours the unrest on other islands had its roots in Grenada. He was adamant the rumours were false, however.

"Sir, I assure you I have every confidence in the officers of the Fort George garrison. They are diligent and I ensure they keep their ears to the ground. If there were something brewing here we would know and be dealing with it. Commander Ross, you must ask yourself how it could be we are the source of this violence and unrest while not experiencing any ourselves. Personally, I would be more inclined to think this French frigate paying us a courtesy visit would have something to do with this nonsense, but we have been watching them like hawks and so far, at least, they haven't done anything to confirm the suspicion."

Evan agreed, but indicated he wanted to talk to some of the officers to get more details. The Governor smiled and gave directions to the office of the senior officer on station. After talking to several officers Evan was satisfied the Governor was correct regarding the competence of these men.

That night and all through the next day Evan prowled the bars and inns of the town, buying drinks for anyone looking promising enough to have information. He also went into two different brothels pretending to need service, instead paying the women well just for information. What he got for his efforts was consistent validation of what the Governor had told him. Knowing a plot to carry violence to other islands was too big to hide without some hint slipping out Evan felt confident enough to be able to report the rumours were indeed false.

The one interesting tidbit he did learn was not a surprise. Evan, it seemed, was not the only person spending money in search of answers about the rumours. No one could say much for certain, as the man asking questions had been vague about who he was or why he wanted information. No one wanted to ask such questions anyway as the man doing the talking had been accompanied by a huge, vicious looking thug serving as protection. But when Evan learned the timing of the appearance of the man asking questions coincided with the appearance of the French warship, the answer was obvious.

At the appointed time for their dinner Evan made his way to what turned out to be a high-class inn with a tavern so well hidden he walked past the understated entrance twice before realizing his error. Once through the entrance and the small lobby of the inn Evan stepped onto a wide, shaded, open verandah with a sweeping view of the inner harbour. A light breeze wafting through the room welcomed him as he saw Captain Deschamps already seated and waving at him from the far side of the room. Evan surveyed the room as he joined him and sat down.

"Captain Deschamps, I think you have managed to secure the best seats in the house."

The Captain smiled. "You are right, sir. It's not hard to do when you have been a client with them before and even better, the wife of the owner is your cousin."

As Evan raised a questioning eyebrow Deschamps shrugged. "The fortunes of war, sir. Don't forget Grenada was a French colony for a long time before we had to cede it to you in 1783. My cousin and her husband have been here many years and were far too settled to pull up their roots and leave, despite their dismay at the change. But their resolve to stay here is good news for us. I guarantee you are about to be treated to the finest French cuisine on the island! Oh, and please don't fear the impact to your money purse. Tonight is my treat."

"It's not really necessary, sir, I—"

Deschamps forestalled Evan with a wave of his hand. "Nonsense, I insist. Commander, I am well aware of the difference between the pay of a Captain and that of the lower ranks. I have other resources of my own to draw on, too. Besides, our last encounter was quite civilized. It was something I recall you made a point of, when under the circumstances it could easily have been otherwise. So I think this is the least I can do, and besides, I 'd like to keep our present and future interactions civilized too."

"I confess I was a little unhappy about the attempt to murder me, but I did try my best to put it behind us," replied Evan, allowing a wry look to crease his face. "Well, this is most generous of you, sir. I accept your hospitality."

Deschamps laughed. "Trying to have you murdered seemed like a good idea at the time. You were proving to be a thorn in our sides, but it's part of the business, isn't it? Now please try some of this lovely Bordeaux I brought for the occasion from my personal stock."

Evan acquiesced and he sipped the wine with appreciation when he realized the vintage was of excellent quality. Captain Deschamps called over the host and, after confirming Evan was willing to leave the menu up to him, he ordered a series of dishes for both of them.

"You shall enjoy this, sir. My cousin's husband is a most accomplished chef. This is French cuisine, influenced naturally by the spices and foods of the Caribbean. And yes, Commander, I know you want to find out what I am doing here, much as I have interest in learning the same of you. But let's save it all till after dinner, shall we?"

As they talked Evan began forming a clearer picture of the man before him. Marcel Deschamps was erudite and well informed on a broad range of topics. As the two men relaxed, enjoying their wine and the conversation, the Captain revealed he was also part of the French aristocracy.

"Yes, I am indeed from a noble background, sir. However, I am also the youngest of a large family! My four other brothers and two sisters all take precedence over me. As it happened, my father dabbled a little in diplomatic intrigues in his time and somehow saw in me similar potential. He also knew I had a love of the sea, so here I am. Ah, and here it begins! These are the hors d'oeuvres. Let us enjoy, sir."

As he spoke a dish of food for each of them, steam rising from both, was placed in front of them. Filling the empty shell of a soft shell crab was a baked dish filled with crabmeat, scallions, garlic, and herbs all held together with breadcrumbs. Using small slices of fresh, crusty bread the two men scooped the mixture out even as a second dish appeared. This proved to be a cold mixture of mashed avocado combined with already cooked, cold fish. More scallions, garlic, herbs, and lemon juice had been added.

"My God, Captain. You were right, this crab dish is absolutely amazing," said Evan, relishing the dishes. Captain Deschamps smiled as he continued devouring his own share of the food.

The main course proved as delectable. A delicious, spicy sauce on the side accompanied grilled fish cakes, a mixture of local fish, herbs, and spice held together by more breadcrumbs. To Evan's amazement the spicy sauce complimented the delicate flavours of the fish instead of overwhelming it. Fried plantains, a wonderful salad with a homemade dressing, and more fresh, crusty bread rounded out the main meal. Two desserts appeared, one a crème brulee and the other a fresh, sweet cake infused with bits of pineapple. Both left Evan wishing he had worn looser fitting clothes.

With the last of his wine Evan offered Deschamps a toast. "To your health, sir. This was a truly fine meal."

The Captain merely smiled as a cognac decanter and two snifters were placed on the table. Full night had fallen by the end of the meal, but the moonlight and the lanthorn lights of the ships in the harbour ensured the view remained pleasing. Pouring them both full measures of the amber nectar the Captain pushed a glass toward Evan.

"Well, I also have a toast, sir. To the health of our respective monarchs."

"To their health, sir." Evan sipped his drink with care, knowing he was already feeling the effects of a half bottle of wine and that he needed his wits about him.

Deschamps toyed with his glass for a moment before speaking. "You know, I toast the health of our monarchs for a reason, sir. I confess I am concerned with what has been going on in France. Oh, I'm not giving away any secrets here, as this is nothing new. Everyone knows the fact is we have problems. I fear many competing interests beset my good King on many fronts. I can only hope our problems with the harvests are behind us."

"Not that I am an expert, but I fear we have our own problems, sir. Let's hope it keeps us from going to war once again."

"I would like to be optimistic about this. I really would, but I am not sure. Perhaps I am too old and more jaded now than you. Well, to business, sir. You are wondering why I am here, of course. As it happens, I am wondering why *you* are here, sir?"

Evan shrugged. "I expect you know something is going on out there. Some bastard is smuggling weapons to the slaves. We had people murdered on both Antigua and St. Kitts. An entire plantation was basically wiped out on Antigua. The rumour is whoever is behind this is operating out of Grenada. I suppose I shouldn't be telling you this, but frankly, I am convinced this is horseshit. But I had to come here to be certain."

Captain Deschamps nodded acknowledgment while obviously weighing what Evan had said. "Yes, something is going on. Some bastard, perhaps the same bastard you refer to, has smuggled weapons to Guadeloupe and St. Lucia. So far, at least, the only people killed have been on Guadeloupe. And I too heard the same rumour floating out there about this island being the source. After doing some digging here I was in agreement the rumour is nonsense until you showed up and my suspicions returned. After all, this is a British island. Add to that I know you were in St. Lucia in February and now you are here. So are you behind all of this, Commander?"

Looking him straight in the eye Evan replied. "No sir. I think you know there is no logic to support this as a course of action. It is not in our interests. Besides, the timing does not make sense. I was in St. Lucia in February and the trouble didn't begin until several weeks later. Can you see a bunch of runaway slaves sitting around with a pile of unused weapons for that long? I think not. But sir, you are correct I am wondering if *you* are somehow the one behind this."

The Captain grunted before responding. "Well, I cannot argue with your logic. It does not make sense you would be involved. But then, the possibility I could be behind this is also ridiculous. Do I really have to convince you of it?"

This time Evan was the one to toy with his glass as he thought about his response. "Actually, no, but I do have one question. May be a little tough for you to answer, but I'm going to ask anyway. What *are* your orders, sir? Specifically, why are you in the Caribbean with a naval force of this size?"

The Captain laughed loud enough to draw looks from other patrons in the restaurant. Evan gave him a questioning look, but the Captain forestalled him with a wave of his hand. "I'm sorry, Commander. It is the irony I am laughing at, not you. I see now you are thinking I am here to use the tiny force at my disposal to create havoc by giving arms to runaway slaves and for God knows what other nefarious purposes. Look, my masters do expect me to keep my ear to the ground, as always, but I have no orders to start a war. The truth is we were ordered here at the request of the Governor of St. Lucia to help maintain order. I know you know there has been unrest. The reason I have others under my command is because there was some indication our support is needed on other French islands too."

"If you know help is needed on other islands, why isn't some of your squadron already stationed elsewhere, sir?"

The Captain shrugged. "Times are hard. The funds to pay for us to be here are coming from the island of St. Lucia itself. The others are in a hard place, as unrest is growing, but they don't want to have to pay."

Evan stared in silence for a long few moments at Captain Deschamps, before giving him a slow nod of agreement. "Well, I think I believe you. So, if neither of us are behind this, who is?"

The French Captain rubbed his chin in frustration and sighed. "I wish I knew. The question is who profits if there is unrest on the islands and our sugar production is disrupted. The Americans? They would be happy to see you in disarray, but on balance I don't think they want their own slaves to start getting ideas. They don't want disruptions to trade with them, either."

"What about the Spanish? We've had no word of unrest in any of their possessions on the same scale and a disruption in the market for sugar could only benefit them."

Deschamps shook his head. "What you say is true, but I cannot see the Dons having the initiative to carry out covert missions on our turf. They are happy with what they already have."

"The Dutch? Their trading ships are everywhere. They could be doing double duty."

"The only thing keeping the Dutch going is trade. Disrupt this and they suffer."

The two men stared at each other in silence for several long moments, before Evan sighed in frustration. "Well, weapons don't appear out of thin air. Sooner or later, whoever is behind this will make a mistake."

By the beginning of June Evan was back sitting in Captain Rand's cabin watching him read the report Evan had prepared, but a midshipman ushering in a messenger interrupted them. The Captain took his time finishing Evan's report and then scowled as he read the note from the messenger while muttering to himself.

"Damn the man."

Rising and putting his hat on, he dismissed the messenger. Evan rose at the same time, but remained silent waiting for orders as Captain Rand turned to Evan. "Governor Shirley must have bloody spies working for him, too. He has somehow already learned you have returned and is demanding we both meet him at once. Meet me outside the Dockyard in ten minutes and bring your damn report."

After a long ride strained by silence as the two men rode the Captain's carriage into town they presented themselves at the Governor's office. They found him alone, despite a buzz of activity and several senior military officers meeting in an anteroom. The Governor scanned the report fast, went back to a few passages to reread them again, and then looked up at the two men. He tapped his fingers on the table in thought a few moments before speaking.

"Thank you for the report and for joining me so promptly, gentlemen. Well, what do you make of this French Captain?"

"He's a devious goddamn frog and I don't believe a word of it, Governor. The man has a hand in this somewhere. Even Commander Ross will surely agree this frog Captain's past history smuggling arms to our island points to him," said Captain Rand, with a sour glance in Evan's direction.

The Governor gave him a stony look for a long few moments before turning to Evan. "And you, sir?"

Wary of what happened the last time, Evan tried to be noncommittal. "Sir, the facts are as detailed in my report."

"This doesn't answer my question, sir."

Evan sighed to himself, knowing he would have to respond with caution. "Sir, I agree with

Captain Rand we must be careful with this man. In my prior experiences with him I found him to be quite dangerous. He is obviously still involved with intelligence work. Having said this, I do think we must consider the possibility he really is telling the truth. Unfortunately, while we now know more than we did before, we do not have conclusive evidence of his innocence or his guilt."

The Governor signaled his agreement and fingered Evan's report once again. "What's this about the Captain of the ship these French diplomats are sailing around in and his possible involvement with the murder of our Consul? Why did you not follow up on this?"

"Sir, it was not my mission to follow this lead, although obviously it is of interest. I felt it was more important to find answers to the question of who is behind these attacks, so I chose to save this for investigation at a later date. But I am wondering about the possibility the mystery informant is an American. I am also wondering why he knows so much and whether he has some links to this French merchant Captain these diplomats from France have employed. Sir, my report doesn't cover this, but we have encountered members of this ship's crew in the course of looking for answers. They appear to be a bad lot and bear watching. The thought has crossed our minds they may have something to do with this, but motive escapes us."

Captain Rand rolled his eyes. "Governor, this is ridiculous. Accredited French diplomats being involved in this?"

The Governor's face was a mask as he thought through the implications before responding. "Yes, well, none of this is proven and Commander Ross, you are quite right we do need answers, the sooner the better. Thank you, gentlemen. As you say, at the least we now know more than we did and we must carry on. I apologize for having kept you in the dark, but information is vital right now. Sirs, we have experienced what I fear are more bad attacks involving significant amounts of weapons. Two plantations were attacked simultaneously last night. You wouldn't know of this yet, as they are beside each other on the opposite side of the island from where you are."

Captain Rand and Evan looked at each other, before turning back to the Governor.

"Casualties, sir?" said Evan.

"No details yet, but I fear the worst. Gentlemen, we must find a way to put a stop to this."

Adam Jones returned to St. Lucia at the end of the first week in June, when he said he would. Sitting in Jean Moreau's office once again he watched Anton look up from the page he was reading in open-mouthed surprise at him.

"What is the meaning of this?" said Anton. "Why was the shipment so limited?"

Henri, sitting beside Anton at the table, gave a start. "Anton? What do you mean it was limited?"

"Just this, dear cousin. The Captain has given us a report here saying all he could obtain is slightly less than half of what we wanted. Captain? Explain, please."

"Sir," replied Jones, his hands held wide to try and convince them of his sincerity. "My sources did not have warning I would be arriving with such a large request for weapons. It takes time to acquire these without too many questions being asked.

Knowing you had goals and not wanting to disappoint you I felt it best to acquire what I could and make my way back here when I said I would. I did drops along the way starting with Antigua on all of the islands you specified, but the amounts on each were reduced proportionately to reflect what I was able to obtain. I left a portion of your gold with my contacts as surety on the assumption you would want the rest acquired. They are doing this as we speak. I hope you are satisfied I have done the best I could under the circumstances."

Anton gave an incoherent growl before replying. "*No*, I am not satisfied. I expected better, sir."

Adam had thought this would be his reaction. He shrugged and pulled out a heavy bag tied close and it tinkled with the sound of many coins as he dropped it on the table in front of Anton and Henri. "Well, I am sorry this did not work out. Here is the remainder of your gold, sir. It will take some time, but you have my word I shall reimburse you the remainder when I return from my next trip home. I trust you may find success elsewhere."

As he reached for his hat and rose to leave Anton grumbled inarticulately in frustration and slammed his fist on the table. "Damn it, sit down, please."

Adam raised an eyebrow, but complied. After a few long moments Anton took the bag of gold and shoved it back toward Adam.

"I said I was unhappy, but I didn't say I was done with you. I still want weapons, as much as you can get. When will they be ready?"

Adam pretended to think for a long few moments, although he already knew the answer. "Sir, we are now well into the month of June. I can go back to America now, but I cannot return before hurricane season. The earliest I could risk sailing back would be early October. Actually, a later return would benefit us all, as it would guarantee my safe return with the remainder of your order. You could even top up your request to ensure I return with a full load. Assuming you want to spend more gold, of course?"

Jones watched as the two men before him eyed each other, questions on their faces, before Anton finally spoke.

"This is taking longer than I wanted, Henri."

"Do it, Anton," shrugged Henri in reply. "If it could mean success and we can return home I am for it."

After staring away in obvious thought Anton turned to Jones. "You'll have your gold. This time I shall want to meet you in Antigua. Your drop there will be the same location and we shall meet you there to arrange for final payment."

"Anton," said Henri. "Is this wise? The drop location is not far from the English naval base. If we are caught with him it will go badly."

"An acceptable risk," said Anton, waving away the concern. "We will just be out sailing to explore the beauty of Antigua's many beaches before continuing our mission, which will conveniently come on the heels of yet more attacks on these stubborn plantation owners."

"I am happy to be of service, gentlemen." Adam Jones smiled, as the conversation with the two Frenchmen had gone as he and his cousin Nathan, now a senior officer within the American intelligence services, had anticipated. The strategy to short the order of weapons in order to keep the violence and disruptions to the right level was working. Having the British and French islands in disarray without having the unrest spread elsewhere was the fine balance they sought to achieve.

Evan and James both chafed at being told to stand to the side by the senior Army officer, but they had little they could do about it.

Ever since the destruction of two plantations and the murder of their owners all in one night earlier in the month, the hunt had been on. Another plantation had been attacked but defended with success, albeit with many casualties on both sides. Diversionary fires had been set in cane fields. With all the attention on fighting the blazes, other saboteurs had damaged the sugar cane processing equipment on several plantations. With mounting concern everyone had also noticed the numbers of runaway slaves seemed to be growing.

Both men had spent long days scouring every possible source on Antigua for any hint of what was happening and where to find the runaways. Tonight, Evan hoped, with the help of the moonlight they would find what they were looking for.

The runaways had been clever, shifting their hideaways with regularity and, Evan was certain, never letting all of them be caught in the same place at the same time. But an informant had come through, pointing to this strategic, well placed cleft between two low, gentle sloping hills covered with innocuous scrub and tall thorn bushes as one of their hideouts. Parties had been sent around either side to cover all possible exits for when the main attack began. Evan had hopes of springing the trap with complete surprise, but they were dashed just as the Army officer was about to give orders for his party to advance as quietly as possible, muskets fitted with bayonets at the ready.

In the distance, much farther up the hill a man screamed as several weapons went off, well before the attack was to begin. The officer cursed and, with the need for secrecy gone, he bellowed his order to advance through the brush. Within moments, the scene dissolved into chaos. A defensive line of pits had been dug at intervals along the entrance to the cleft and a number of the advancing soldiers stumbled into them, only to find a series of short, sharpened stakes had been sunk point upwards into the bottom of each pit.

The pits served to funnel the remaining uninjured soldiers into two channels as they pressed forward, sending them straight toward the defenders waiting for them. A sudden volley of shot from several muskets cut down even more of the soldiers at the head of the files leading the attack. But even with the losses the stream of attackers continued to push forward.

The fighting raged, frustrating both Evan and James, with it impossible to tell who had the upper hand. Someone screamed a command in a foreign language and seconds later they understood what the order was. Three heavily armed, separate groups bunched together in tight masses burst from the brush in different places seeking to get away. As the nearest group to Evan and James ran past one of them turned and hurled a short spear at a red-coated soldier stumbling out of the brush in hot pursuit. The spear appeared in the centre of the soldier's chest and he crashed with a strangled cry to the ground. A second later Evan shot the runaway that had hurled the spear.

"Evan!" said James with a shout to draw Evan's attention away from the man he had killed. "It's the bastard from the Flying Fish! He's in the bunch that ran past us. I'm going after him!"

But Evan had his hand on James's shoulder, holding him back. "Don't do it! I know you want a shot at him, but it's not worth the risk. One of these redcoats could mistake you for a runaway."

Even as he spoke a party of soldiers ran past them in hot pursuit of the fleeing slaves. James looked frustrated for a moment before his face fell and he turned to speak.

"You are right, of course. Don't need some fool of a soldier sticking twelve inches of bayonet in my back, do I? Maybe next time we wear something to distinguish us as friends so we can join the fun, eh?"

By the time the sun was peeking above the horizon the Army officer had sorted out the scene and came to speak to Evan and James.

"Well, gentlemen, a busy night. Your information appears to have been correct as it looks to me like this was a major base for them. A bunch of them got away and we've lost several men, but so did they. I have to give a little credit to whoever the bastard is leading this lot. He had a defensive strategy in place for exactly this kind of situation and they executed a coordinated escape."

"We think we know who it is and we will do our best to get more information as to his whereabouts, sir," said Evan. "Have we been successful in capturing their weapons store, as we hoped?"

"A good portion of it, I think, sir. Come see for yourself. It's odd, but this lot appears to be

American made, unlike the French weapons we were finding earlier."

Following him into the brush past the burial details now working to remove the victims they found numerous pistols and muskets with ammunition piled together, with more being added by soldiers scouring the site for others. Sitting off to the side were four slaves under guard, most of whom bore bruises or wounds too severe to let them get away. Evan got permission to question them. The four men eyed him with wary, fearful looks as he came over to speak to them.

"If you cooperate and answer my questions truthfully I will speak to the Governor and recommend he spare your lives. I suspect you will still be lashed for your misdeeds, but at least you will live. Do not cooperate and you will most likely find yourselves dangling with a rope around your neck. It is your decision."

Three of the four men winced and hung their heads while the fourth man spat on the ground at Evan's feet. Evan ordered this man be removed to different spot on his own before turning back to the remaining runaways. The youngest of the three men looked up, his eyes pleading, as he told Evan to ask his questions. Evan soon learned his foe was named Asante, while garnering more details of other locations around the island where small caches of arms had been stashed. But the three men knew nothing of who was providing the weapons beyond the obvious fact an unknown ship had brought them.

What startled Evan was information the young slave added that the others knew nothing of. In fear for his life, the floodgates had been released. The young man revealed he was one of a number of informants passing information to fishermen from other islands about what was happening on Antigua. He didn't know for certain, but he had heard rumours the people paying for the information were French. The young man provided more names of others he knew were sources for the same network.

Once he had what he wanted Evan briefed the Army officer, requesting the three men and in particular the young man be treated well until Evan could speak to the Governor. Leaving the officer to finish his work he marched with James back to where they had left their mounts. "Well, it's a start and I think we have them on the run. Let's go brief the Governor and then we'd better figure out who the Christ is spying on us."

Evan was dismayed to find Captain Rand was already present as he came into the Governor's office to make his report. Both men were pleased to hear the raid had been successful, but Captain Rand hammered the table with his fist when he heard mention of possible French espionage on the island.

"I knew it! And you have let this go undetected until now, sir?"

"Sir, I confess this is the first we have heard of this. We will of course be following up and putting a stop to it. The questions we have been asking have focused on finding out where the runaway slaves are hiding, not on whether there are informants working for foreign interests on our shores."

Captain Rand shook his head. "Still offering excuses, I see. Is this not further evidence this bloody frog Captain who also happens to be a spy is behind all this? Governor, I think I should sail into Castries and demand they cease and desist."

"You'll do no such thing, Captain. Diplomacy is my domain, sir, and I fail to see how this is the proof you think it is. What you don't know is I have received reports once again from St. Kitts of more weapons appearing there and more violence occurring as a result. There are also rumours the French islands have experienced the same. So I agree it is disconcerting there is evidence of espionage here, but it makes no sense to me the French would somehow be inflicting this on themselves too. And for the record, Commander, I am pleased you have at least been successful in tracking down the runaway's hideout."

"But perhaps the reports from the French islands are stories being fed to us, Governor," protested Captain Rand.

"Perhaps, but I don't think so. I have met my counterpart on Guadeloupe and find he is actually a reasonably civilized man. His correspondence with me on this topic has been frank and it bears the ring of truth. Besides, if you want to have at the French you'll have another opportunity next week."

As a puzzled look appeared on the Captain's face the Governor smiled. "Those French diplomats that came through here a while back trying to convince everyone in sight we should end slavery? They have returned, apparently seeking to have another go at us. Another ball is being organized and you both should expect an invitation to attend."

Evan watched from the fringe of the crowd once again as Anton made an impassioned plea for understanding.

"Do you not all understand?" cried Anton, spreading his arms wide to the watching crowd. "The kind of violence you are experiencing is exactly what we have feared. It is symptomatic of a system with no foundation in high principle. Can you not realize slavery is a form of tyranny?"

"I think we see someone imposing their own form on tyranny on us in finding ways to provide weapons to these animals, sir," replied one of the plantation owners, as he scowled in the direction of Captain Rand who was standing to one side. "And if our illustrious Navy ever gets around to doing its job the problem will be solved."

Captain Rand started and made to protest, but Anton cut him off. "Sir, this violence is becoming endemic. Why, our own plantations in St. Lucia have been damaged. We have had several of our crops burned to the ground and equipment damaged. We've had no one killed, thank God, but I am told several died on Guadeloupe as a result of this latest round of violence. Gentlemen, I suggest this is growing beyond the capacity of your Navy, and ours, to manage. Why, there are simply too many places for runaways to hide and too many places for whoever these smugglers are to drop weapons to them."

The scent enveloping him once again told Evan whose hand was touching his shoulder to draw his attention away from the conversation. Without turning he spoke.

"Madam de Bellecourt."

"Madam, is it now?"

"Ah, Marie," smiled Evan as he looked at her. "Yes, we had agreed on first names, hadn't we?"

"We did," said Marie, offering Evan a blazing smile in return. "We also agreed you would dance with me. Take me away from all this boring politics, please."

As they danced several numbers Evan realized that despite himself he was enjoying holding this woman's body close. To take his mind off the thought he asked how long the family would be on the island.

"Why, Commander, if I didn't know better I'd say you were interested in seeing more of me," said Marie, a hint of jest twinkling in her eye.

"Well, who wouldn't want to see *more* of you?" replied Evan, taking his cue.

She laughed. "Commander, you make me feel like I'm my naughty sister."

"Ah—your sister is naughty?"

"Oh yes. She does not have my discriminating tastes. My dear brothers do their best to ignore it and have spoken to her many times, but she will not change."

"I see. And what *is* to your taste?"

"Handsome men like you. But I fear you and I will not have opportunity to be naughty anytime soon. We leave tomorrow morning."

"So soon?"

"Our Captain warns us we must be back in St. Lucia no later than early July because of hurricane season. My brother wants to stop at other islands along the way to promote his message further. But he tells me we shall be back in early October to try diplomacy one last time before we go home. Perhaps we will find a way to see more of each other then."

Evan smiled in reply as they finished one last dance. "Perhaps."

"But Commander? You still haven't answered my question."

"Question?"

"You know who I mean. Is she yours?"

"Ah. You mean Alice," said Evan, pausing a moment before replying. "Yes. Yes, she is mine in the way you are thinking."

"I thought so. But I still think we should find a way to see *more* of each other, Commander. I look forward to seeing you in October."

Without warning she reached up to kiss him full on the mouth as the dance finished, letting her lips linger and her breasts slide across his chest as she rose up. And with a quick parting smile she was gone.

Chapter Ten
October 1788
Antigua

Every sailor on the island knew something bad was coming, even those with no experience of the onset of a hurricane before.

Reports of unusual, heavy swells on the open sea and steady gusts of wind increasing in strength drew both Evan and James away from their duties in the Dockyard to view the chop on the normally placid surface of English Harbour with wary eyes. Evan took one look at the suspicious, dark bank of cloud on the far distant horizon and turned to James, pointing towards the looming hill overlooking the Harbour.

"I need a better look at this. Let's go up to the Heights."

Evan was worried as they rode at best speed to the fortifications on top of Shirley Heights, the hill dominating the area surrounding English Harbour. With a sidelong glance at the grim look on James's face Evan realized his companion was anxious too, so Evan made an effort to keep his voice calm.

"If this is a hurricane the Captain won't be back from the annual October meeting in Barbados any time soon. This could explain why they haven't returned yet. I was expecting them last week."

"It's unusual to have a big storm this late in October, Evan. God Almighty, another two days and it will be November."

"It is, but it's not impossible apparently. Well, we'll know soon enough."

Reaching the top of the Heights they left their horse and buggy and strode through the Guard House at the summit to survey the vista before them. Even as they walked into the open they could feel the growing strength of the wind trying to push them off their feet.

"Good God," said Evan, his face grim. Below the Heights he saw *HMS Alice* moored to the dock in English Harbour, the lone warship that had not gone to Barbados for the regular October meeting of Captains on the Leeward Islands station. The *Alice* with her people had remained in Antigua to meet Evan's possible needs should further trouble develop. The ship was already dancing and straining against its tethers. Dotting the Harbour were a number of small civilian ships now at anchor, and more were on the way in, fleeing for safety.

Looking beyond the Harbour to the open sea he saw they were fleeing to save their lives. The reports were of steady swells at least four feet high, but to Evan's eye they were already exceeding this. Frothing whitecaps and choppy waves were everywhere and using the telescope he had brought with him he could see it looked even worse closer to the storm. The telescope also showed the band of cloud on the distant horizon resolving itself into a dark, ugly, growing mass creeping ever closer. Heavy gusts of wind were tearing at the trees and the sky would be fully overcast in less than an hour.

"Well, if this isn't a hurricane coming our way my bet is it's going to be the nastiest storm we've ever seen, James."

"Yes, we're going to have to batten down for this one. Maybe we had better—what?"

The boom of a signal cannon on the distant lookout post dominating the western approaches to English Harbour cut the conversation short. Both men turned to see signal flags rising at the post, but the scene unfolding before them was already clear. James was the first to react.

"Oh, my God, look at those two ships coming in from the west just rounding the headland and making for the entrance. Isn't one of them the ship those French diplomats were using?"

"It is. God Almighty, the worst storm I've ever seen and now I have to figure out how to keep a bunch of diplomats safe."

"Jesus Christ, Evan, there's a big ship further out!" cried James, staring hard through his own telescope off to the distant horizon. "I think he's in trouble too, his sails don't look right."

Evan trained his own glass to the spot James indicated. "You're right, but he is making progress and he's coming this way too."

"Evan, it's a warship. One of ours, do you think?"

Evan studied the ship for several long moments before replying. "No. I caught a glimpse of their flag just now. I think that is the *Marie-Anne* coming our way. Well, this is getting more interesting by the second."

By the time the two men made their way back to the Dockyard the *L'Estalon* was docking beside *HMS Alice* in the one remaining spot available to do so. The Harbour was a hive of chaotic activity, as sailors on every ship were leaving nothing to chance, setting every anchor they could and ensuring sails were furled as tight as possible to the yards. James nudged Evan and pointed to the American flagged ship that had followed *L'Estalon* into the Harbour.

"Evan, this Yankee ship is the *Beacon*. It's the one Paddy told you about. And isn't it interesting these two ships came in together?"

"Yes, isn't it just?" said Evan, keeping his face blank as Anton de Bellecourt stepped ashore with the rest of the family following close behind. Auyuba and Elise also alighted and the little group huddled together staring at the unfamiliar surroundings as they tried to shelter themselves from the buffeting wind. "Right, let's greet our diplomats."

Evan strode forward hand outstretched in greeting, struggling with every step against the growing, insistent strength of the wind. "Count de Bellecourt. Welcome back to Antigua. I wish it were under better circumstances."

"Thank you, Commander and I agree. Captain Dusourd tells us he believes this is a hurricane coming and insisted we seek shelter immediately. He tells me this harbour is the safest place on the entire island for our ship."

"This is true, sir. It is the primary reason this was chosen as our base of operations. However, this is a naval base and it has no suitable accommodations for diplomats such as yourself."

"Is there nothing in the area to serve, sir? My Captain tells me this storm could last several days. We do not wish to be cooped up in the confined quarters of our ship, but we can stay aboard if we must."

"Count, there is a local Inn not far from here in Falmouth Harbour called The Dockyard Dog. I'm fairly certain there is sufficient room there for all of you. It has recently been renovated and although it may not be quite to the high standards you are used to, it should serve. It has the added benefit of having been reinforced specifically to withstand storms like this. If you approve we must get you on your way immediately. I think this is going to hit us soon and we must not be caught in the open when it does."

"Commander," said Marie with a smile. "I for one am happy to leave myself in your capable care."

Anton raised an eyebrow briefly as he looked at his sister, but he turned back to Evan and nodded.

"I must remain here to oversee operations as the senior officer on station, but Lieu—ah, my assistant Mr. Wilton here will help with this." Evan quickly turned to James, hoping no one had noticed he had almost referred to him as an officer. "Mr. Wilton, please find Midshipman Cooke and have him round up a party to gather our visitor's belongings to convey them as soon as possible to the Dockyard Dog. Ask Mr. Cooke to remain here, as I may need his help to render assistance to the frigate if she is in need. I suggest you accompany Count de Bellecourt to arrange for accommodations with Emma and Walton. Please do what you can to ensure all their needs are met. I will join you if I can, but first we have to get this situation here under control."

As James nodded and left Anton gave Evan a questioning look. "A frigate in need, sir? I thought I saw a ship in the far distance behind us as we were coming in."

"Yes. We saw her from the lookout. I believe she is the French Navy frigate the *Marie-Anne*."

Anton frowned. "Yes, I have seen her in Castries harbour. What would she be doing here, sir?"

Evan shrugged. "You will have to ask her Captain that question, sir. And now I see Mr. Wilton signaling he is ready to proceed." Evan pointed to where James was standing beside a large carriage he had brought into the Dockyard itself. Evan directed a file of Dockyard hands looking for the family's belongings to the *L'Estalon*. "Count de Bellecourt, if you and your family would join Mr. Wilton we will have you on your way to safety soon."

As they filed past Marie stopped in front of Evan. To his surprise she used her body to hide from everyone's sight the hand she placed on his chest. "Thank you for your aid and your hospitality, Commander. We must find a way to repay you. I hope you will be joining us at this Inn?"

"Possibly, Madam. Duty calls, but I will do my best."

Marie smiled and turned away, but Evan had no time to wonder at what had happened. Striding over to Midshipman Cooke he rapped out his orders.

"Mr. Cooke, I am going to have myself rowed around to these ships that have come into the Harbour in the last little while. I will instruct them to send to you if they are in need of water or any other supplies before the storm hits. Arrange a party to assist you. I am going to start, however, with the *L'Estalon* here."

On gaining the deck he was met with several wary looks from the sailors as they hurried about, but they all looked away when the Captain strode over to meet Evan. After hurried introductions Evan enquired after their needs, but Captain Dusourd assured him they were fine.

"We suffered a little damage on the way in, Commander, but we have the wherewithal to make the repairs." He paused to look over his shoulder at the sky in the direction the storm was coming from before continuing. "I doubt we will have time to do them before it hits us. At any rate, we will be fine on board our ship, sir. We appreciate being able to shelter here."

Evan nodded and looked around with a critical eye one last time before leaving. Everything about the ship spoke of professional competence, but Evan realized James was right; the crew and the ship's Captain were rogues of the sort no one should turn their back on.

Evan worked his way from ship to ship in the Harbour, scrutinizing every detail of the American ship the closer he got. By the time he reached them the chop had become significant enough he was safer to remain seated in the rowboat. Calling up he asked to speak to the Captain of the *Beacon* and soon a face peered down at him from over the railing. Once again, Evan explained who he was and asked of their needs. He couldn't help giving a small start of surprise when the Captain introduced himself as Adam Jones and told him where they were from.

"Jones?" said Evan, his eyes narrowing. "This is interesting, Captain. I once knew a fellow from the same area as you named Nathan Jones. Any relation to you, sir?"

"Not that I know of, sir," replied Adam Jones, wearing a bland look. "I believe I may have heard the name somewhere, but Jones is a pretty common surname in America."

"I see. Odd, you look somewhat like him. Perhaps a distant relation you don't know about, sir. In any case, you have no damage or need of assistance in any way?"

"No sir. As soon as this storm is over we shall be on our way. I have trade goods for Guadeloupe and St. Lucia to deliver and I have a deadline to meet. I thank you for your hospitality, sir."

"Oh, you aren't travelling in company with the *L'Estalon*, sir? I saw you both come in together."

"Well, I have been working as a trading partner with the de Bellecourt family. We had arranged to meet in Antigua after hurricane season. It was coincidence our courses converged here at the same time as this storm. Everyone knows English Harbour is the best safe haven in this part of the Caribbean. We shall conduct our business once the storm is over and I shall be away."

"Of course. Well, I shall be on my way also." With a nod to the men at the oars Evan pointed to shore. Evan glanced back and saw the man still standing at the railing, only now his face wore a frown.

By the time Evan got back on shore the wind had increased even more and the sky was now fully overcast. Bits of loose debris were beginning to fly about at random, stinging the skin and forcing everyone still outside to shade their eyes. The rain had yet to start, but this could change at any moment. The sudden boom of the signal cannon on the Heights made every eye turn to the entrance of the Harbour, where the heaving masts of a frigate could be seen attempting to work its way into safety.

In a flash Evan saw the warship was indeed the *Marie-Anne* and she was in trouble, struggling to maneuver her way into the unfamiliar Harbour. He also realized his initial impression it had sustained damage was correct, as some of the yards and sails were completely gone, while others still swayed from where they had split, held in place only by the tangle of rigging the crew had not had time to cut free.

Looking around in desperation, Evan waved at Midshipman Cooke, who appeared within moments at his side. "Mr. Cooke, the *Marie-Anne* coming in over there is in danger. They have sustained damage and need help. Round up the men. We have two cutters at our disposal, I'll take one and you take the other. We must row out and take her in tow to help them in."

Within minutes both cutters were scuttling as fast as they could to the struggling ship at the far end of the Harbour. Before they could reach her the first drops of rain began to fall and with a sudden rush the first squall hit. In moments the rain was hammering at the men even as the wind grew in strength enough to force the rain to come in hard at an angle.

Reaching the beleaguered ship Evan saw Captain Deschamps had realized he was in peril, close to running aground, and he had taken in all of the sails he could. Two parties of French sailors were already lowering the ship's boats into the water to attempt towing the frigate to safety. Within minutes they had it in tow by all four of the boats on the scene and the sailors were straining hard at their oars. Evan had a bleak moment of doubt it would be enough, but the squall hitting them chose that moment to ease. The opportunity was all the men needed, knowing the sooner they got the ship to safety the sooner they could get there too.

Once the ship was in a safer spot Captain Deschamps dropped anchor. Evan came to the side and struggled his way up the boarding ladder, almost losing his grasp twice. On deck one of the mates met him and pointed to the quarterdeck where Captain Deschamps was issuing a stream of orders to a group of his officers. As Evan strode up the group dispersed to their various tasks and Deschamps turned to face Evan.

"Commander Ross." Reaching out, Deschamps shook Evan's hand. "I shall ensure my masters are aware of your assistance. I am not at all certain my ships boats would have been enough to get me out of danger. Were it not for your extra help I fear I would be badly aground on the far side of the Harbour, perhaps dismasted completely and maybe damaged beyond repair. I confess we had not anticipated how difficult the entrance to the Harbour would be."

Evan shrugged. "A hurricane is a common foe of us all. You have sustained damage. Do you need further immediate help? Do you need any supplies on an urgent basis?"

"No, but I would appreciate your help to effect repairs once this storm is past. I will need to bury some of my men, too," said Deschamps, pointing to some already shrouded forms lying in the waist of the ship. "We got hit by an extremely powerful squall. I've never seen anything like it. One moment my ship was fine and the next the squall had ripped away half of my sails. Two men were lost overboard and those you see wrapped below were crushed by the yards when they fell."

"Sir, I am sorry for your loss. We will look to your needs once the worst is over here. Captain, before I leave, have you noticed who your company is in Harbour, sir?"

"You mean the *L'Estalon*? Yes, I have. Of course, the real question you want answered is what exactly am I doing here and whether it is a coincidence I happen to be in the area at the same time as them. Commander, neither of us believes in coincidences, do we? I know the Captain of this ship and have had dealings with him in past. I don't trust him and for lack of any better suspects I thought I would tag along and see what they were up to. There are benefits to keeping a low profile, as he doesn't yet know I am Captain of the *Marie-Anne*. We were doing our best to stay over the horizon with no topsails they would see. To be honest I was wondering if he is delivering weapons on the side. Having some diplomats to carry around would be perfect cover."

"I see. Well, perhaps we should speak more about this once this storm is over, Captain. But speaking of coincidences, are you familiar with the American flagged ship over there?" said Evan, pointing at the *Beacon*.

Deschamps looked at it and back at Evan, raising an eyebrow in question. "Yes, I have seen it in Castries harbour, but I don't know anything about it. It looks like an old warship actually, but my men told me it is now a trading vessel."

"Hmm, well, I talked to the Captain. His name is Adam Jones and he is out of Boston."

"*Jones*?" said Deschamps, his eyes narrowing as he gave a start and looked at the Beacon.

"Indeed. I asked him if he knew of our mutual acquaintance Nathan Jones, but he claimed no knowledge of him. Odd, he looks a lot like him."

"Commander, I assure you, this is news to me."

"Even more interesting, Captain Jones claims to be involved with the de Bellecourt family in a trading venture. They came into the Harbour together, sir."

This time the look of shock on the Captain's face as the implications sunk in was so obvious Evan had no doubt what he was seeing was real.

As the rain began to pelt harder once again Evan studied Deschamps's face for a long moment, before he nodded. "Captain, I don't believe in coincidences either. We need to talk after this storm is over. I must now look to the safety of my own men. Stay safe, sir."

James and the de Bellecourt family were forced to use the rear entrance through the kitchen of the Dockyard Dog because Walton had already sealed the entire front of the building with boards to blunt the force of the storm. They arrived with bare moments to spare to escape the same heavy squall lashing the Dockyard.

James sought Alice to help settle the family in their quarters, knowing Emma and Walton would be flustered at having to deal with French nobles while trying to ensure their other guests were cared for. Alice stood silent, obviously thinking through what needed to be done as James explained the situation.

"Alice, is it?" said Marie, before Alice could speak. "We meet again. Commander Ross has his assistants everywhere he needs them, doesn't he? He speaks highly of you." She offered an innocent smile that didn't extend to her eyes as she finished speaking.

Alice locked eyes with her and didn't return the smile. "Yes, we can accommodate all of you. The lodgings may not be quite what you are used to."

By the time everyone had found their separate rooms and returned to the dining room the weather had worsened. Rain could be heard pounding the walls outside and the rising howl of the wind made conversation difficult. Emma and Walton risked keeping the kitchen fires lit long enough to serve a hot soup to bolster everyone, as it would be cold meals from this point on until the storm blew past.

The dining room was crowded with people using it as shelter, but room was made for the de Bellecourt family. Several of the poorer local residents were sheltering at the Inn, as this was the safest place in Falmouth Harbour.

Once the de Bellecourt family left the crowd to retire to their rooms James breathed a sigh of relief and turned to Alice. "There are times I wish I was the Commander and Evan the Lieutenant. I would have far preferred to stay in the Dockyard and deal with the ships. Shepherding a bunch of diplomats around isn't for me."

"Do you think Evan is coming here tonight, James?"

"No. From the sound of things outside he's not going anywhere for the next two or three days and neither are we. They have plenty of food in the Dockyard and it's pretty sheltered in the lee of the headland. So don't worry about his safety in this storm. He'll settle into his office and will be fine."

"I wasn't worried about his safety from the storm, I'm more interested in keeping him safe from the white bitch that wants him. With any luck we can get them out of here fast when this storm passes and I won't be forced to kill her."

"Is that any way for a diplomat's assistant to talk?" said James, grinning as he looked in the direction of the guest rooms. "No, don't answer that. I'm off to bed. Let's see what the morning brings."

Making his way up the stairs to the upper floor he groped his way down the dim hall, lit only by the candle he clutched in his hand and a small window at the end of the hall letting in the little remaining light from outside. He was about to enter his room when a soft hand touched his shoulder.

Turning in surprise, he held up the candle to find Emilie de Bellecourt holding a finger to her lips. As his eyes widened she grinned and pointed at his door. James let her in and followed behind, failing to see a stone faced Elise watching the entire scene from further down the darkened hallway.

Once they were both inside and the door closed behind them she made him put the candle down before reaching up to wrap her arms around his neck and mold her body to his. James decided he wasn't about to complain and went to kiss her when she spoke.

"Hello, Lieutenant Wilton. I thought it was about time we got to know each other better."

James gave a start and pulled back a little, but she forestalled him with a finger to his lips. "Don't deny it, Lieutenant. Your Commander slipped and almost called you Lieutenant today, but I had already suspected something was unusual about you. The rest of my family thinks I am a brainless fool, but I do pay attention to what they talk about. I find it convenient if they think I'm a fool, it makes it easier to get what I want."

"I see. Well, I shall neither confirm nor deny what you say. But what is it you want, Mademoiselle de Bellecourt?"

"Call me Emilie, please. And isn't what I want obvious? We are going to be cooped up here for at least a couple of days and as it happens, I like interesting and mysterious men. I especially like handsome, mysterious men. So I thought we could get to know each other much better. Besides, your Commander ordered you to see to our needs, did he not? Well, I have needs, Lieutenant."

"Hmm, yes, he did say this, didn't he? And here I thought I was going to be bored out of my mind cooped up in here for the next couple of days," said James, reaching to cup a firm breast in his hand.

As Elise groped her way in the dark past Auyuba's door further down the hall she realized he had been watching from the darkened doorway. He wore a look of surprise.

"Elise? What are you doing?"

"What does it look like? I was going to try and get some information from this man Wilton and see if he really is a spy, but the French bitch is already after him."

"I saw this, but aren't you coming to my room?"

"What, the bitch has passed you over and now you want me again? Well, as it happens the master also suggested he would like to see me, so that is where I'm going."

"Elise!" said Auyuba, too stunned at her reaction to say anything else.

She gave him an uncaring shrug. "We're trying to manipulate them, remember?"

Turning, she walked away before the scowl she knew would be on his face could appear. Her tapping on the door to Anton's room was just loud enough over the still growing shriek of the storm outside to catch Anton's attention. Opening the door with a big candle in his hand he looked around before drawing her inside.

"Elise? I thought you were going to see if you could worm some information out of the man Wilton?"

"I was, but someone beat me to it. You won't like it."

Anton groaned. "Goddamn, it's her again, isn't it?"

"I watched Emilie go into his room, master. She didn't come out again."

"Damn the bitch. Henri is worried and I promised him we would have you try to confirm if this man really is a spy and what he knows. This was a perfect opportunity!"

"Not to worry, master. I can try again once they are done. I don't think we will be going anywhere anytime soon. And besides, if I'm not busy doing that and we have to wait out this storm, we'll have to find something to occupy our time, won't we?"

Elise saw a smile cross Anton's face in the flickering light of the candle. He reached up to cup her face with his free hand.

"I'm sure we can think of something. You really do want to come with me when we return home to France, don't you?"

"Master, take me away from this. I'm tired of life on the island. I want to see more of the world. And I want to spend time with you and enjoy fine things. I know I can never be anything but your servant to the rest of the world, but we can still share the future together in private, can we not?"

"I'm glad you want to come with me. Serve me well and you shall, Elise. I can think of many ways for you to serve me." Putting the candle on the bedside table, Anton pulled her closer.

The full force of the storm hit in the late hours of the night, hard enough to wake everyone on the island.

People cowered inside whatever shelter they were in, listening to the insane pounding of rain being driven into the walls around them. The wind was a constant banshee shriek.

In the midst of it all Evan sat sleepless at his desk in the Dockyard, staring at the lone candle he was nurturing to stay alight and still puzzling over what he had learned before he had been forced to take shelter. That this American could have something to do with weapons smuggling to the various islands seemed credible. Despite hearing his denial of a link to Nathan Jones, the American spy allied with Marcel Deschamps two years ago, Evan had no doubt in his mind they were indeed related. Nathan Jones had proved a dangerous foe, and Evan felt certain this man Adam Jones would be the same.

What was making Evan fret, though, was whether or not Adam Jones had a link to Captain Deschamps. Nathan Jones and the Captain had been firm allies in the desperate plot Evan had foiled. The Captain's surprise had seemed genuine, yet a worm of uncertainty still gnawed. Captain Deschamps was a wily foe and had much more experience in the dark arts of spying.

Evan also fretted over the visitor that stopped in to see Paddy in St. Lucia and the information he had passed on. Evan had no evidence the visitor was indeed Adam Jones, but Paddy had been certain the man was American. Implicating the de Bellecourt's ship Captain and their household slave Auyuba was one thing, but having Captain Marcel Deschamps on the scene along with a possible relative of his former ally at the same time was another matter. Why this unknown American might send Evan an indirect message to draw attention to Deschamps remained a mystery. The possibility of some convoluted double game being played by Captain Deschamps or any of the others was most worrisome.

In the middle of it all were the de Bellecourts. Their connection to all of these suspects was the worst of all. The possibility they could be tainted by scandal if the people surrounding them were involved in something nefarious would be the biggest concern of people like Captain Rand and Governor Shirley, who would make his life hell if they were unhappy with his handling of this most delicate factor.

Evan swore under his breath at having more questions than answers and not being able to learn more until the storm ended. Outside the storm lashed the Dockyard with its intensity. Seeing the candle was about to gutter out Evan lay down on the pallet he had spread on the floor and pulled a blanket over himself to try and sleep.

Drowsy, trying to ease the tension from his mind and body, his thoughts drifted to the future. He was grateful Captain Nelson had supported his promotion to Commander and for the opportunity to remain employed in an active role. But the truth was, except for the last few months, most of his duties had been little more than bureaucratic and administrative. Much of it boiled down to reading endless letters and distilling information into yet more letters to send onward. Attending the balls he had been invited to courtesy of his new status had been interesting at first, but soon lost their novelty. Worse, the trips to St. Lucia and Grenada had rekindled his love for being at sea. When he had accepted the assignment he had done so with blithe optimism that a posting to a ship would be forthcoming long before the three years was up.

"Please God," he whispered. "It's been three long years. Give me a ship, any ship, and I'll be away from this."

But even as he said it a vision of Alice's face swam into his mind and he moaned at the realization the problem would have to be faced sooner or later. Having a ship meant leaving everything behind and sailing wherever he was ordered.

As the wind screeched and the walls around him shook from its force, he fought to drift into sleep that wouldn't come. He smiled at the irony of it, as the storm wasn't the reason he was struggling to sleep. The battle in his heart and the knowledge he didn't want to leave her behind when the time came was what kept him awake.

Chapter Eleven
November 1788
Antigua

"Good Christ, what a mess," said Evan as he made his way to The Dockyard Dog two days later. Evan had first made certain the Dockyard was out of danger, but his next immediate priority had to be the safety of the French diplomats.

The ships enjoying the protection of English Harbour had come through the storm in relative good shape. None had dragged their anchors and the only damage any had suffered was from flying debris. No one had died or been injured in what seemed a miracle, but no one had escaped at least some damage to their ships. Uprooted trees and large branches ripped from others had smashed into several ships and buildings in the Dockyard area with incredible force during the height of the storm. Coconuts had been torn from the trees or from where they were lying on the ground, turning into flying projectiles with the same impact as if they had been cannonballs. The Dockyard shipwrights, though at an initial loss as to where to start, were already hard at work on effecting repairs.

The scene he found in Falmouth Harbour was different than the naval base. Of the seven small craft forced to remain in Falmouth Harbour only one had found enough holding ground for its anchors on the distant eastern lee side of the hill that gave English Harbour its protection. The rest were all lying on their sides smashed on the beach or in the still heavy surf pounding at the shores. The seas would take another day at least to settle back to more normal conditions. He was thankful the driving rain and demonic winds had disappeared, and that the still overcast skies were no longer threatening. Occasional gusts still buffeted, but the wind's force was dropping steadily.

Most of the homes in the area of Falmouth Harbour were damaged, some devastated beyond all hope of repair. All manner of debris lay scattered about and in the midst of some of it were bodies. A few of the older, more stubborn residents of the village had paid the price for preferring to remain on their own in the now flattened shacks. Debris from flash floods flowing down from the surrounding hillsides was everywhere. Evan was shocked to find two nine-pound cannons, usually in place guarding the harbour, dismounted from their carriages and laying almost a hundred feet from their emplacement.

The Inn had fared much better. Already hard at work with his helpers removing the boards he had put up, Walton waved when he saw Evan ride up and dismount. Nelson the dog ran out to greet Evan and lick his hand, with James appearing right behind him.

"James, thank God. Is everyone all right here?"

James pulled Evan to the side to ensure they couldn't be overheard. "Yes, but I think our guests aren't going to want to stay cooped up here much longer. Also, you need to know my cover is blown, at least to one of them. When you almost referred to me as an officer it firmed up a suspicion on the part of one of the women about me. I denied it, but she doesn't believe me."

Evan put his hand to his head in dismay. "One of the French women? Which one?"

"The younger one, Emilie."

"Damn, I wonder if she has told anyone else."

"I don't think so, at least not yet perhaps. She's had no time because she spent all of the last two days with me."

Evan burst out laughing, knowing what that meant and thinking back to his conversation with Marie de Bellecourt in June. "Why am I not surprised?" Evan had to curb his laughter in an instant, though, as Anton came outside and walked over to where the two men were standing.

"Commander Ross, thank you for your assistance in finding us this shelter. We are grateful to have survived. Has our ship fared as well? We are hoping to be away as soon as possible."

"Count de Bellecourt, I am glad you are well. Your ship has sustained some minor damage, much like all the others, but I think the repairs will not take more than a couple of days. Are you thinking of leaving so soon? I was going to send word to Governor Shirley of your presence. He will undoubtedly want to organize better quarters for you and a society function for you to attend."

"Thank you, Commander, but I think you need not bother," said Anton, with a wave of his hand at the devastation around them. "I think the Governor will be far too busy dealing with all of this for some time to come. I wouldn't be doing him any favours by adding my needs to his woes, let alone expecting people here to drop what they are doing and attend a ball. I will compose a letter to him to this effect and we will be away again as soon as our ship is ready for sea."

"As you wish, sir. I shall leave my assistant Mr. Wilton here to see to whatever needs you may have in the interim."

"Excellent. I shall commend you to the Governor for your help. He should be grateful he has an officer at hand with such varied talents. I should like to visit my ship tomorrow to speak to my Captain and see how he is progressing."

"Certainly. I think you will find the *Beacon* came through the storm well, too," said Evan, watching the Count close to gauge his reaction.

Anton didn't disappoint, as he let his eyes narrow at the mention of the American ship before mastering himself. "Indeed, Commander. Thank you for this information."

"Commander," said Marie as she walked over to join them, wearing a pouting look. "We were disappointed you did not join us here."

"I'm afraid duties kept me in the Dockyard and that is where I must now return," said Evan, seeing Alice emerge from the entrance to the Inn. "Good day, everyone."

Walking over to Alice he assured himself she was all right and explained his need to return to duty. He gave her a long, lingering hug and kiss before turning to leave, hoping Marie de Bellecourt would get the message once and for all.

Late the same evening Auyuba reached out and pulled Elise into his room as she made to walk past yet again, unable to keep his patience any longer.

"Auyuba, what are you doing?" said Elise in protest as he closed the door and put his arms on either side of her against the wall, preventing her from slipping away.

"Elise, this is *my* question to you," said Auyuba, his voice low to ensure they were not overheard. "You have completely ignored me the whole time we have been here and you are spending all your time in our master's bed. So what are you doing? What is going on here? You were about to go into the spy's room, weren't you?"

Auyuba watched her face set, hardening into a stony look he didn't like.

"What is going on, Auyuba, is you don't own me. I've been just a tool for you to use so you get what you want. I've had enough of this life we have been living and I want something better."

"Something better? Are we not fighting for that?"

"Auyuba, you are a fool. You have been working with these white pigs for years, trying to use them to our advantage at every opportunity, and what have you accomplished? We are still slaves and your followers are still living in the jungle like little more than beasts."

"Elise," said Auyuba, stepping away from her. "What has the white bastard offered you?"

"He is going to take me with him when he goes. I am under no illusions. He will use me as you have done. But he is rich, Auyuba. He can offer me a far better life than you will ever be able to. And if he wants me to go to bed with this English spy to get information, how is it any different than what you would have me do?"

"He will use you and throw you away when you no longer interest him, Elise."

"I'm willing to take the chance. And if I can find a way to relieve him of some of his riches before he loses interest I will."

"So this is it?"

"This is it." Without another word Elise opened the door and left, not looking back.

Auyuba scowled as the door closed and he clenched his fists in silent rage. Someone was going to pay for this.

James had time to remove his clothes and lay down on his bed before the door to his room opened. In the faint moonlight streaming through his now open window he saw the dark shape of a female form cross the room to him. He smiled in the dark as the woman stopped by the bedside, lifted the mosquito netting, and without a word ran her hand down his bare chest to his groin.

"Come back for more, have you?" said James. "I think you should take your dress off and join me."

Within moments she had discarded her shift and slid onto the bed to straddle him before she spoke. "Well, I haven't had more yet, but I expect I shall want it soon enough."

James froze in the midst of reaching up to fondle her breasts. Looking closer he came to the belated realization his visitor had brown skin and was not the woman he thought she was. "Good God, I'm sorry, I thought you were someone else. Who—oh, you are Elise, aren't you?"

"Yes, I know you thought I was the white slut Emilie. I wanted to come to you the other night, but she got here first. I can't blame you because she does have a certain beauty, but she really is a slut."

"You sound like you are speaking with experience."

"I am. The bitch wants to take me to bed, too," said Elise, running her hands over the firm muscles of his chest. "But I'm not interested in women. I like men, especially handsome and mysterious men. I think you're a spy, you know. Are you?"

James froze once again. "Wherever would you get this idea? I'm just an assistant to Commander Ross."

"No, I think you are more than this. Even if I ignored everything else, like the fact your Commander almost referred to you as a Lieutenant when we arrived, I cannot ignore your aura of command. You are a man used to giving orders and expecting they will be followed. I can't imagine why you would be nosing around on St. Lucia asking questions about everyone and everything if you weren't a spy, but you can tell me more about it later. Right now, I'd like you to give me my orders."

"Meaning what, exactly?"

"Tell me what you want so I can do it, Mr. Wilton. How about this to start?" Leaning forward on one hand she guided his lips to one of her nipples and she gave a soft moan, as he lingered with it for a few moments.

Reaching up to firmly grasp both of her breasts James smiled. "Well, that was a good start. I'm certain I can think of more things for you to do."

James and Elise both moaned with pleasure as they found their release. As James rolled off to collapse beside her, struggling to slow his breathing, he became aware of yet another presence in the room. In the now brighter moonlight streaming in he saw Emilie was standing beside the bed.

"Well, I enjoyed watching this almost as much as I'm sure you two enjoyed doing it," she said, as she slid her hand underneath the mosquito net to run it over James's chest. Removing it, she pulled her dress over her head and slid onto the bed, wriggling her way between the two of them before either realized this was what she was doing. Shifting a little to her side, Emilie tried to slide her hand down between Elise's legs. "I enjoyed it so much I'd like to participate, too."

Recovering from her shock, Elise grabbed Emilie's hand and shoved it away from her. "*No*, I don't think so. At least, you won't be participating with me. I'm not interested in women. James, if you want to spend your time with this—this *woman*, you are welcome to, but I'll be leaving."

"You bitch. Wormed your way into Anton's bed and now you're in here, and you think you have cause to look down at me. Who do you think you are? You're a slave, bitch, and we own you. I could have you whipped."

"Look here, ladies, I—damn," said James, disconcerted by the sudden change of tone.

"Get out of my way, you slut," said Elise, shoving Emilie back and clambering over her to struggle into her discarded dress. She scowled at Emilie as she straightened it, unable to keep the rising heat from her voice. "Anton would never have me whipped. He's not that kind of owner. But he might have you whipped. He knows what a slut you are and he isn't happy about your behaviour."

As Elise turned and left, slamming the door as she went, Emilie hissed back in return. "I'm going to enjoy watching you get a beating, bitch."

James rolled his eyes and struggled out of bed, pulling on his clothes as he did. Emilie turned her attention to him, a look of surprise on her face.

"What are you doing? You don't need your clothes for what I need you to do."

"Ah, Mademoiselle de Bellecourt. I rather think I am no longer in the mood and I am a bit spent tonight. Perhaps another time."

"What, you're a fool too? Fine." Rolling out of bed she shoved him out of the way and pulled on her own dress. She paused at the door and looked back, a scowl marring her face. "I think I shall tell everyone who you really are, Lieutenant. They all suspect you anyway, but I will confirm it and you'll have to live with the consequences. There are people out there that don't like spies, you know."

As the door closed behind her James slumped down onto the only chair in the room, hands holding his head.

"I never used to have shit like this happening to me when I had a ship," he said with a groan, lifting his head in a supplicant plea to the heavens. "I'm sorry for all those complaints about the food and the lack of women and life in the Navy. Please God, give Evan and me a ship and I promise I'll never complain about it again!"

Anton and Henri met in Henri's room on the ground floor of the Inn to talk the next day. Auyuba was certain both men thought they were in a secluded enough spot they couldn't be overheard, but Auyuba had long since learned the fine art of eavesdropping. He made his way quickly to where he could overhear them without being observed when he saw them leave together to talk. The conversation had already begun by the time he got in place and he realized right away Anton was angry.

"God damn it, Henri, I'm sorry to have to tell you this, but my sister really is a bitch. I know you have feelings for her, but this latest incident is the last straw. I know Elise is a slave, but it seems wrong to me to expect her to meekly submit to Emilie. Christ, I had both of them in to see me separately, both of them angry enough to claw each other to death the next time they see each other, and they both want *me* to mete out punishment!"

Henri sighed. "Anton, Emilie is young. I do still like her, but she is becoming headstrong. Perhaps it was a mistake to bring her out here. I know you have spoken to her about her behaviour, but maybe as head of the family you need to push her harder. Threaten to send her to a convent for a spell?"

"That might work. I will think about it. But I think you may be right, it was possibly a bad idea to bring her and the right answer is to take her home. Yes, I mean all of us. We've been out here a year now and are not much further ahead than when we started. Also, both of the women confided to me they are certain this man Wilton is in fact a spy. They have no proof, but to add to the problem I think this Commander Ross subtly tried to quiz me about our link to the American ship and this means maybe the women are right. The other concern we have is the *Marie-Anne*, which happened to be in the same neighborhood as ourselves. Captain Dusourd is suspicious a French Navy frigate would be so close."

"So what does this mean, Anton? Are we going to go through with the last drop?"

Anton sighed. "It means I think we should do it regardless and see what happens," replied Anton. "They may be suspicious, but they have no proof. If this final drop gets us what we want we can deal with repercussions as they come. That assumes this rogue Adam Jones has actually brought the full order this time. We'll find out soon enough. But I confess I am not optimistic we'll get results more to our liking. I am beginning to think we should go home and talk more with the Marquis about it all regardless, maybe see if he has a better approach. You expressed concern before about our being linked to these weapons and if this Commander Ross and his minion really are spies getting suspicious of us, then the time to leave has come. So we go back to St. Lucia and prepare to leave for home."

"Maybe we can make arrangements for the weapons to keep coming even after we are gone?"

"We could, but our strategy always was to use diplomacy at the same time to push the locals into moving toward our thinking. God knows what would happen if we weren't here to keep making the case. There's also the fact we haven't come up with any new ideas to improve the sugar process and I confess it frustrates me. It was my fallback strategy in case prodding these owners with weapons didn't work."

Anton paused, allowing a wistful note to come through his voice. "Remember I told you a while back about my inspiration for a sugar revolution? Well, so far, we haven't succeeded, but I am coming to think we will have to put the best scientific minds to work on it. And the place to find them is back home, not here. Maybe if we fund it someone will come up with new and cheaper ways to do this, enough to put all these owners using slaves right out of business."

Henri gave a slow nod. "All right, I'm with you on this. So what will you do about Elise, Anton? It's a long voyage back to France. Those two could make our lives miserable the whole way and maybe even when we get home."

"They could, if we let them. Well, I like the idea of having Elise around. She won't risk my leaving her behind, so she will do as I tell her. We can find something for her to do in the household at home and whenever I want a taste of something different I can send for her. You and Jacques can use her too if either of you want to. As for Emilie, I like your idea about a convent, come to think of it. Emilie may want to get into bed with a woman, but I don't think a steady diet of nuns is what she had in mind. She'll do what I tell her to."

Auyuba gritted his teeth in frustration as the two men laughed and left Henri's room. He remained where he was for a long time to master his face, as he couldn't betray the depth of his anger to anyone. After thinking hard for several minutes he reached a decision. He remembered Asante maintained contact with some of the fishermen who sailed out of Falmouth Harbour, as they were part of the communication network passing messages throughout the islands. As Auyuba went in search of a contact, he composed the message he wanted to send to his brother.

On learning late the next day what had happened with the two women Evan ordered James to abandon his role shepherding the de Bellecourts and to instead keep a low profile in the Dockyard. The family helped matters by remaining at the Inn the rest of that day and then appearing the next desiring to return to their ship, as Captain Dusourd had sent a message he expected to be ready for sea the following day.

Evan was amazed at the difference a couple of days could make. The storm had passed and the new day was promising fair, pleasant weather with plenty of sunshine and enough wind to allow easy passage out of English Harbour for anyone ready to leave. The

Harbour was a noisy, bustling hive of activity, with the shipwrights pushing their men hard. Sailors from the ships helped. The sound of incessant hammering and sawing filled the air.

Evan had little time to enjoy the improved weather, though. The sudden spike of activity and demands on the supplies of the Dockyard resulted in a growing mountain of paperwork on Evan's desk, enough it reached a point he couldn't see the surface of his desk. He was still working his way through it all when James came into his office.

"Evan! I've been keeping a watch as you told me to. The American Captain came ashore and went aboard *L'Estalon* five minutes ago. Also, the shipwrights tell me his ship the *Beacon* sustained minimal damage which has already been repaired."

"Really? Well, this sounds like a good reason to escape this goddamn paperwork for a while, although I'm going to pay for it later. I think I'll find something to keep myself busy and catch him when he leaves."

A half hour later Evan was nearby when Adam Jones left *L'Estalon* and made for his crew waiting to row him back to the *Beacon*. Evan was nearby, pretending to inspect work being done, but in reality waiting exactly for that moment. Making a show of coincidence at being there Evan stepped into his path and extended his hand in greeting.

"Captain Jones, have your needs been met, sir?"

"Yes, Commander, your men have been most helpful. I sustained relatively little damage so I am departing immediately."

"I see. Concluded your business with Count de Bellecourt, have you?" said Evan, nodding his head in the direction of the *L'Estalon*.

"Yes, sir," replied Jones, his eyes narrowing at the question. "The Count wanted to ensure I have everything he wanted this time. I had difficulties sourcing everything on my last trip, but fortunately I had no similar problems on this one. Plenty of timber and fish for him."

"Well, I'm glad to hear we got the job done for you, sir," replied Evan, as he openly studied the man's face. "You know, seeing you up close I have to say I really do see a resemblance to that fellow Nathan Jones I told you about."

"Indeed, Commander? I shall have to ask among my relatives when I get home. So, I must be on my way, unless there is anything else, sir? I am past due to be in Guadeloupe."

"Safe travels, sir."

True to his word Evan saw Jones issuing orders the moment he stepped back aboard and within minutes they had weighed anchor to depart. As Evan turned away he saw Anton de Bellecourt striding toward him.

"Commander Ross, I wanted to stop and thank you once again for your assistance these last few days. My family and I appreciate everything you have done, but we won't be a burden to you much longer. Captain Dusourd assures me we shall be ready to leave at first light tomorrow so we shall be on our way."

"I see. I'm sure Governor Shirley will be pleased to host a ball for you all on your next visit to Antigua, Count."

"Ah, well, perhaps not. We may be returning home soon to continue our work there."

"Well, I'm glad you had opportunity to conclude your business with Captain Jones, sir. Please offer my regards to your sister, Count. You never know, I may be in St. Lucia again at some point and if you are still in the area I shall make a point to call upon you."

The Count allowed a smile to play on his face, but it didn't extend to his eyes. "Of course, if we are still in the area. Good day, sir."

Evan was standing on the dock in the bright morning sunshine watching as *L'Estalon* cast off from the dock and prepared to get underway. The de Bellecourt family appeared on deck as the ship began pulling away. Evan doffed his hat to Anton, who offered a tiny bow in their direction in return. Marie glanced once in Evan's direction, and then in a clear snub looked away to the direction they were going. Once Evan was sure they would weather the entrance without difficulty he turned to go back to his office only to find he was not alone. Marcel Deschamps had joined him and Evan immediately surmised he had waited until he was certain they were far enough away they would not be able to make out his features.

Evan raised an inquisitive eyebrow. "You will be ready for sea soon, Captain Deschamps?"

The Captain sighed. "I fear it will be a while yet, Commander. The squall hit us pretty bad. Your shipwrights, however, are first class. They think they will have me underway two days from now."

"We haven't had a chance to talk yet, Captain."

"No, but now is as good a time as any. I made a point of laying low the last while, but I did catch a look at the American Captain. I agree with you, he has to be a relative of Nathan Jones. I think he is lying when he claims not to know him, for the simple reason he knows your role and he does not want you suspicious of him."

"But what is the game being played here, Captain? Look, I didn't tell you this earlier, but I was passed a message from an unknown party via, hmm—someone I know in Castries that I should *reacquaint* myself with the Captain of the *Marie-Anne*. This same person hinted Captain Dusourd and the de Bellecourt's slave Auyuba, along with the lawyer in Castries named Moreau, all had some involvement with the murder of our consul John Andrews some time back. It was allegedly a dispute over money. But here's the thing, Captain. The conduit for this information strongly suspected the unknown party was an American."

Captain Deschamps couldn't hold back any longer, cutting loose with a stream of expletives in French for a few long moments before mastering himself and ceasing. "My God, I'm sorry, Commander. This is clearer, now. I see the hand of my former colleague in this. I think this is an attempt to sow discord and violence in the islands and to destabilize both of our respective domains. Ask yourself, who benefits if both the British and the French islands are in disarray and are weak? The Americans do, of course. They haven't stated it, but they want the Caribbean to be their back yard and for American businesses to have sway over everything here. The hope, of course, is you and I will point fingers at each other and battle it out."

"Hmm. You know, it's interesting that in the last round of slave violence we captured American made weapons. But what about the murder of our consul?"

"Yes, I had heard about this, but I hadn't made the connection until now. Remember I told you I had dealings with Captain Dusourd during the war? It was only peripheral as I had other tasks while another of my colleagues dealt directly with him. Suffice to say I am aware he was involved with others in running weapons to the Americans. I am also aware we compromised someone on the British side to ensure our deliveries made it to our friends safely, but not all were successful. I recall rumours of concern someone was playing both sides, but nothing was ever proven. I wonder, perhaps your Mr. Andrews was that man."

Evan grunted after pausing a few long moments to think about what Deschamps had said. "All right, this is starting to make a lot more sense than any other theories I've come up with. So the Americans are using the de Bellecourt family as cover to distribute weapons on the side, right? But if this is the case, why were the first weapons we captured French made and where was our American friend when this all started? Are the de Bellecourts somehow involved in this?"

Deschamps rubbed his forehead in frustration. "God, I don't know. I can't imagine why a family of nobles would sail around preaching diplomacy while covertly supporting violence. But on the other hand, Commander, we live in strange times. I don't like what I have been hearing about what is going on back home."

"Well, we don't have proof of any of this and I don't know how we're going to get it. What I'd like to do is find some reason to search both *L'Estalon* and the *Beacon*."

"Hmm. I will think about this. There must be some excuse I can dream up once I return to Castries."

"I'd like to join you there, but I don't know what excuse I would use. Well, I have duties here the next couple of days so I have time to think of something."

"Yes, I think the sooner I am in Castries again the better. Commander Ross, thank you for your help. I am going to push my men hard. I think something is going on and there are too many coincidences here. I think perhaps I shall make Captain Dusourd's life miserable when I am in Castries once again and will get information that way."

After shaking hands, the two men went their separate ways.

The drums pounding in the night that had woken Evan were trouble. Even worse, he soon realized the drums were coming from several different places on the island.

The morning brought word Evan was expecting in the form of a messenger from Governor Shirley requesting an urgent meeting with Evan and Captain Rand on the events of the night. Before leaving Evan ordered James to scout for information from his immediate sources on what had changed.

An hour later Evan was ushered into the Governor's office to join the small group of men already at the table, a mix of Army officers and men Evan was already aware were local plantation owners. They all had worried, drawn looks, appearing tense from lack of sleep.

"Ah, Commander, please join us. I'm sure you can guess why you are here. Yes, the drums in the night spelled trouble for all of us. Several attacks have taken place all over the island and some are still ongoing. The runaways have been using ambush tactics and several people have been killed and wounded. They must have received yet another shipment of weapons from somewhere, because they are even more heavily armed than before. The Army is making some progress in quelling this, but it's going to take a while given how well armed they are."

"Governor," said Evan. "Does anyone know by chance if the type of weapons in use are American made?"

"Why, yes," replied one of the Army officers. "Everything we have captured in this latest uprising has been American. How did you know, sir?"

"I was hoping you might have something to help us, Commander. Please tell us what you have," said the Governor.

"Governor, I do not have proof, but I am deeply suspicious of an American ship Captain who was here during the hurricane. The Captain of the French ship the de Bellecourt family is using may also be involved. I think there may be collusion between them to bring American weapons to the islands in order to destabilize our situation once again."

"Goddamn Yankee bastards at it again—" grumbled one of the senior Army officers, before the Governor scowled to silence him.

Turning back to Evan, the Governor frowned. "Commander, are the de Bellecourts involved in this?"

"Sir, I do not know. It is possible, but I cannot confirm this."

"The letter I got from Count de Bellecourt states he was returning to St. Lucia immediately. Has he left already?"

"Sir, he left yesterday. Of interest, the American ship left the day before."

The Governor paused and sat back in his chair, scratching his forehead, obviously deep in thought. But moments later his face set as he reached his decision, and he leaned forward once again.

"Commander, I expect since only you showed up that Captain Rand has not returned yet?"

"I am expecting his return at any time, sir."

"Commander, what are your next steps? Is there any way to get the proof we need?"

Evan sighed. "Perhaps, sir. As my suspects have left, it would involve going to St. Lucia to pursue matters. Also, you should be aware I have unofficially been in discussions with my counterpart, the Captain of the French frigate *Marie-Anne* who I told you about. I have become more and more convinced he is not the source of our problems here. I wouldn't be surprised if we see more violence on the neighbouring French islands too. If anything, Captain Deschamps wants this stopped as much as we do."

"Commander, I'm not your superior officer, but as far as I'm concerned there is no higher priority for your time right now," said the Governor, reaching for his quill pen and some paper. "I will give you a letter right now stating you have my full support to depart for St. Lucia and investigate this further. If you find proof bring it back with you. I cannot give you explicit instructions, as I don't know what you will encounter, but if you find it necessary to apply a judicious level of force to put an end to this I will support you. I doubt anyone will question my judgment in this and I think the French Governors in our neighbourhood will be supportive too."

"Governor," said Evan, rising to leave. "I shall depart immediately."

"I don't believe this, goddamn it," said Evan, as he threw the scrawled note he had received down on his office desk. "This doesn't make sense."

Captain Deschamps, the other occupant of the room, wore a frown. The Captain picked up the note to read it one more time, looking close at the handwriting before turning back to Evan.

"Tell me more about how you got this, please?"

"Sir, I ordered one of my associates to do his best to find out more about who or what was behind the attacks. He was in a tavern in a nearby village and got up to use the necessary house. When he returned to his drink this note was waiting for him beside it. No one would admit to having planted it there. When he read the note he knew he had to get it to me immediately."

The Captain seemed lost in contemplation of the possibilities, so Evan continued. "Captain Deschamps, this note claims to be from Captain Dusourd, but I don't believe it. From everything you've told me about him and what little I have seen, this is not a man to suddenly find patriotism, as the note claims, wishing to expose a plot by the de Bellecourt family to incite a violent revolution among the slaves. I am interested in the fact it directly implicates Adam Jones as the source of the weapons and that it claims there will be drops on both

Guadeloupe and St. Lucia. But really, this explanation that he couldn't find a way to slip away and meet us in private before he left, so he uses this method to do it? This is beyond belief."

"Commander, I completely agree. I don't know if this is Captain Dusourd's handwriting or not. It could be, I haven't seen it for a long time. But this is completely out of character for the man I know. I think someone is trying to frame them. But who could be behind this? Why?"

Evan shook his head. "Tell me, Captain, is this some scheme on your part? I have had reports of French spies trying to buy information here on Antigua."

Deschamps shook his head, a weary look on his face. "No, it is not and, Commander, *of course* I am trying to get information on what is happening here. You are doing the same on St. Lucia."

Evan shrugged in response. "Of course. I had to ask. Well, once again I believe you. But this means there is only one other possible source and that would be the runaway slave network on this island. They, or their sympathizers, are the only ones who would have an inkling of the role my associate plays. And I really don't know who in all of this business would have a contact with them, unless it is these two Captains we suspect. Well, if nothing else, this does give you reason to pay a visit to Captain Dusourd's ship and have a look around, don't you think?"

Deschamps smiled for the first time since being called to Evan's office. "You are right, it does. And actually, now I think on it, this does make sense someone out there would have contacts with the slaves. They have to coordinate and make sure the weapons get to the right hands, correct?"

The two men stared at each other for several long moments, before Evan nodded. "Hmm, the de Bellecourts have a slave named Auyuba. My associate and I have been highly suspicious of him. I wonder if he has friends here? Well, perhaps I shall track him down and ask him some questions."

Captain Deschamps raised an eyebrow. "Track him down? They all went back to St. Lucia."

"Which is where I am off to as soon as I finish here with you, Captain. Our Governor requested I go to St. Lucia with all dispatch to investigate this further and act as necessary."

A frown crossed the Captain's face as he responded. "Commander, would it not be better to wait until tomorrow morning, when I can join you?"

Evan held out both hands wide. "Sir, I have my orders."

A knocking on the door prevented Deschamps from responding. "Enter," said Evan, as James immediately walked in and saluted.

"Sir, the squadron is back from Barbados. Captain Rand is leading them into harbour right now."

"Very good. We will greet the Captain and explain what has been happening and then depart. Let's go, gentlemen."

With Deschamps leading they left the room and James leaned close to Evan to whisper in his ear. "Evan, the *Alice* is ready and our belongings are on board. So is Alice, by the way."

Evan gave James a sharp look. "What is she doing there? I had planned to take only you."

"She saw me getting ready to leave and figured out at once what was going on. She told me she wants to help again."

Evan sighed, but he had no opportunity for further discussion as Captain Rand's frigate docked beside the *Marie-Anne*. Captain Rand was the first ashore and seeing the three men waiting for him he made straight for them. Evan sighed to himself again, seeing the Captain's wrath clear on his face, but then he smiled to see Sir James Standish disembark too.

But Captain Rand got to Evan first. Glaring with unconcealed suspicion at Captain Deschamps for a brief moment, Rand settled his gaze on Evan.

"Commander Ross. Please explain what in God's name a French warship is doing here? Make it a good explanation, sir," he added, as the sarcasm dripped from his voice.

"Captain Rand, this gentleman is Captain Marcel Deschamps of the French Royal Navy frigate *Marie-Anne*. He was badly damaged and nearby when the storm hit. We were the closest refuge and he had few options open to him."

As Sir James joined the group Captain Rand burst out with his reply, before Captain Deschamps could speak up. "Commander, has it escaped you this is an *English* naval base? Everything about this is supposed to be secret, damn you. The whole time he has been here he has undoubtedly been observing the details of our harbour and our capabilities here."

"And a fine harbour it is, Captain Rand," said Deschamps with a disarming smile and a quick bow. "Really, Captain, your Commander Ross had little choice. I sailed in here uninvited because I had to. I must commend him for the services he has rendered us. Were it not for his help my ship may have ended a wreck. Your capable shipwrights have also helped admirably and I shall be away tomorrow at first light. I shall of course provide a full report to my government and yours commending you and your operation here. Your hospitality when I was in need deserves high praise and you shall have it."

Captain Rand opened his mouth to speak before closing it again, lips pressed together in frustration. "You are leaving tomorrow, you say?"

"He is, Captain," said Evan, nodding to Sir James before turning back to the Captain. "I am also leaving, but much sooner. Sir, there have been developments while you were gone. Another shipment of weapons appears to have been delivered and there has been violence all over the island. The Governor ordered me to ask you to report to him as soon as you returned."

Captain Rand scowled and held a hand to his forehead, looking as if he had a migraine coming on. "You are leaving? Where are you going? And why?"

"Sir, I have reason to believe the American Captain Jones may be the source of the weapons. There may be a conspiracy of some sort involving those French diplomats as well. The Governor agreed and requested I leave immediately for St. Lucia with the *Alice* to get to the bottom of this."

"Well, I came to Antigua to help you with this, Commander Ross," said Sir James. "But it sounds like you have the matter in hand and it's best you should be about it."

"My God, why me?" said Captain Rand, shaking his head. The scowl remained in place as he took his hand off his forehead. "Yes, this is a good idea, come to think of it. The sooner you are out of my sight the happier I shall be."

Chapter Twelve
November 1788
St. Lucia

Evan was on edge as the *HMS Alice* sailed into Castries harbour and finished the salute. Both he and James were anxious to see who would be in port. Standing by the railing nearby where she would be out of the way was Alice, wearing a broad smile as she basked in the late afternoon sunshine. She appeared to be enjoying the experience of sailing into Castries once again to the full, her simple joy a sharp contrast to the tense features of the two men.

"The *L'Estalon* is docked in the same place as before," said Evan, as he trained his telescope on the ship.

James was sweeping the rest of the harbour with his own telescope. "No sign of the *Beacon*, sir."

Evan grunted. "Seems to be a lot of activity on *L'Estalon*. I wonder if they are getting ready for sea? Yes, they appear to be loading cargo and those look like trunks women would use."

"Things getting too hot for their liking, Evan?" said James.

"Maybe. Well, we'll stick with the plan for now. I would prefer to leave them to Captain Deschamps to stop them from departing, but if they leave port we will have to act."

With the Customs formalities over Evan stopped as they stepped ashore to confer with James and Alice one final time. "All right, I am going to see Captain Dusourd and see how he reacts when I tell him about the note. After this I am off to the Governor's office to pay respects. We will see what happens. I will meet you back at the ship by dinnertime. You will both be careful, please. All we want to know is where the American ship has gone."

Standing unnoticed in the shadows of the busy port, Auyuba watched James and Alice nod in reply to Evan before the two of them left. Auyuba had smiled when he saw *HMS Alice* come into harbour and now on seeing the directions they went he smiled once again. Auyuba had anticipated their arrival in response to the message he had sent in Antigua and he was certain he knew where Alice and James were headed. Even better, he knew what they would learn when they got there. That Paddy Shannon was an information source for the British had long since come to Auyuba's attention, and using him to plant the seeds of yet more discord was perfect for Auyuba's purposes.

Seeing Evan was heading directly for the *L'Estalon* made Auyuba laugh with grim delight. Turning away, Auyuba began following James and Alice to ensure his plan was coming to fruition. When Elise spurned him his anger had found no bounds, especially because of whom she had left him for. Worse, though, in his heart he understood what she had said was true and that cut him even more. For years, Auyuba had tried to work with the white men and turn his knowledge to his advantage, but in truth he was no further ahead. The knowledge was a volcano awaiting eruption inside him, demanding a sacrifice to its fury.

Auyuba's sacrifice would be his revenge upon them all and he exulted in the knowledge he could create enough mayhem the volcano's release would be joyous.

Reaching the *L'Estalon* Evan approached the first mate and asked to see Captain Dusourd. The man eyed him with suspicion, but left to get the Captain from his cabin. The crew continued loading provisions around Evan as he waited.

"Commander Ross? I am surprised to see you again so soon. What brings you to St. Lucia?" said Captain Dusourd as he stepped ashore.

"Captain Dusourd, thank you for seeing me," replied Evan, looking around to ensure they could not be heard. The Captain saw what he was doing and a wary look stole across his face in response. "I came in response to your message to us, sir."

"My message to you? What message?"

Evan searched the man's face and saw no hint of anything other than puzzlement. "Captain, we received a message from you telling of your patriotism and how you wanted to help us with information about the source of the weapons being smuggled onto the islands. Was this not from you?"

A look of complete, stunned surprise crossed the Captain's face before he mastered himself. "Good God, no, it was not from me. I have no idea what this is about. Wherever did you get this message?"

Evan studied his face yet again for a few long moments, trying to decide if there had been a brief look of guilt flash at the mention of weapons before the man's guard came up. "It was given to us by an unknown source. Well, it would seem there has been a mistake. I trust you understand I had to follow up on the message. People smuggling weapons ending up being used to murder other people in their beds are criminals and not patriots."

"Sir, I am not a criminal. As for being a patriot, well, maybe I was once, but now I am a cynic. Someone has deceived you, I fear."

"I see. Well, thank you for your time, as I can see you are busy. It looks like your men are loading stores for a long voyage?"

"Oh, the de Bellecourt family has decided to return home. They are staying at lodgings in town tonight while we load stores. I expect we shall be ready by end of the day tomorrow and to depart with the tide at first light the next day."

"Well, then," said Evan, turning to head for the Governor's office. "If I don't see them before you leave please pass on my wishes for a safe journey. Good day, sir."

Anton was in his sitting room at the manor house in town with Henri, Jacques, and Marie enjoying drinks before dinner when word came of a visitor. He realized something had happened the moment Giscard Dusourd was shown into the room by a servant. The Captain's unconcealed agitation was held in check only long enough to ensure the servant was out of the room before he turned to speak.

"Count de Bellecourt, am I free to speak of matters in the presence of these others?" said Dusourd, indicating the rest of the family with a wave of his hand.

"You may. What is wrong?"

In terse, clipped tones the Captain described his unexpected meeting with Evan. He also told them that although knowing he had to tell Anton what had happened as soon as possible, he also understood he couldn't rush right over to see him. He had therefore waited a reasonable amount of time, going about his business on the ship, before departing at a steady pace to see the Count. As he told his story the family's faces fell almost as one.

"Anton, this is a disaster," said Jacques. "This Englishman is getting too close for comfort."

"How is this possible?" said Henri. "Who would have done such a thing?"

Anton remained stone faced in silence for several long moments, staring into the distance. With a sigh, he turned back to Captain Dusourd.

"I agree with my family, but only to a point. Something odd is obviously going on. But all the man said was you had information to pass on. He never gave any sense you were actually involved, did he?"

"You are correct," said Dusourd, as a questioning look appeared on his face. "I wonder if someone is carefully trying to expose us, while hiding something themselves? Perhaps this someone is involved, but doesn't want to be exposed too? Count, if this is the case you need to consider who could be trying to betray you."

The conversation dissolved into chaos, with everyone else trying to speak at once. Anton could only gnaw his lip in worry, realizing the situation was slipping from his control.

"Captain," said Anton, loud enough the rest of the conversations ceased in mid sentence. "We are scheduled to leave here early the day after tomorrow. Can we leave sooner?"

"Impossible, Count. We have only begun loading your belongings late today. My crew has already been dismissed for the day and is undoubtedly off getting drunk as we speak. We need tomorrow morning at least to finish loading your household goods along with taking on sufficient quantities of food and, in particular, water. You know it is a long voyage back to France. I suppose we could leave late tomorrow night, but the tide is not good and the men will already be tired. It would be best to leave as scheduled."

"Well, I don't know what is going on here, but we shall have to see what happens," said Anton, doing his best to hide a growing sense of unease from the rest of the family.

Auyuba smiled, watching and listening to James and Alice from his hiding place, having followed them as they went straight for The Thirsty Sailor. They had not stayed long and Auyuba elected to continue following them. When he saw them step into the shadows as Giscard Dusourd hurried past, only to begin following the Captain, Auyuba's smile widened even more.

Auyuba felt a fierce glee when he realized his plan was working, as Dusourd headed straight for the de Bellecourt manor house. Auyuba saw Alice and James secret themselves near enough to observe the place from a distance, so he worked his way closer in order to hear what they were saying.

"What do you think, James? I wonder if this is the place the de Bellecourts keep in town Evan told us about? It looks expensive enough and seems well maintained."

"You could be right. Hmm, well, we can stay here for a little to see if anything develops, but we need to get the information Paddy gave us to Evan soon. If it's true the Yankee is doing a drop of weapons north of Soufriere tomorrow morning we have plenty of time to join the party and spoil their fun, but I know Evan will want to know sooner rather than later. Those rumours Paddy heard of more violence on Guadeloupe mean we beat this Yankee bastard getting here. What I'm more concerned about is this is the second time some mysterious informant has come along and handed Paddy information we need."

"Yes, and why this time the mysterious informant is a black man and not white like the last time is also strange. Something odd is going on here. It's almost like someone is deliberately trying to sabotage whatever it is these people are up to."

Auyuba laughed to himself and then froze as an idea struck him. He spent several long moments thinking through the implications and considering the opportunity that had come his way unbidden. Realizing Alice and James could leave at any moment and his opportunity could be lost, Auyuba steeled himself to seize it.

Pulling out his knife, he looked around to ensure no one was watching and he strode in silence over to where the watchers were emerging from their cover to leave. Seizing Alice by the hair he poked the knife into her back enough to draw a gasp from her as she felt its sharp point.

James turned to look at Auyuba and his eyes widened in recognition.

"Don't even think it," said Auyuba. "I'll have this knife in the bitch's heart before you have a chance to try anything, so don't bother, either of you."

"I swear if you harm this woman you will beg me a thousand times to kill you before I finally do," said James. "And I'll start by cutting off your balls."

"Shut your mouth. Head for the back of the manor. We're going inside."

Manon had watched with growing concern as the scene before her unfolded. She was returning from a journey to the north of the island seeking information when she saw Auyuba hiding and watching someone, so she stepped into her own hiding place in the growing shadows to watch him in turn. Auyuba did not see her as he joined James and Alice and the three of them disappeared into the manor house. Manon bit her lip, uncertain over what to do. James and Alice had appeared tense, and there had been a forced look about the whole interaction. No one had been smiling.

It was odd they would be entering this particular manor house, as she had long since learned whom it belonged to. She had seen Auyuba at The Thirsty Sailor, but didn't know who he was. His access to the manor house of the de Bellecourt family demonstrated an obvious link.

Manon's fear grew, but she made herself wait until full dark before giving up her vigil in case they reappeared. Rising from her hiding place, she went to find her father.

The Governor had another visitor so Evan had to wait, but once he was ushered in the meeting was cursory enough, allowing Evan to be back at the *HMS Alice* in plenty of time. As the afternoon wore into early evening Evan grew concerned when neither Alice nor James had returned. Unable to contain his impatience any longer, he set out for The Thirsty Sailor.

Paddy greeted him with warmth, but wore a perplexed look. When Evan explained why he was there, the look changed to one of worry.

"Commander Ross, both of them were here, but they left quite some time back. They were going back to see you immediately because of what I told them."

As Paddy quickly explained what had happened a sense of dread stole over Evan, as James would have understood the importance of getting back to the ship with his news. Evan thanked Paddy and instructed him to tell James and Alice to return to the ship if they reappeared.

"And Paddy? I think this mysterious black man giving you the information may be a slave named Auyuba the de Bellecourt family owns. If you can find out more information about him please do so. I will check with you again as soon as I return."

Evan made his way back to the ship in the fast fading light of dusk, looking about with care the whole time for them. By the time he reached the ship he was frantic with worry, hoping they would have returned in his absence. But on gaining the deck Lieutenant Kent confirmed they had not returned and Evan turned to let his gaze sweep the port.

"Damn, damn, damn," said Evan, clenching and unclenching his fist in frustration and worry as he reached his decision. "Lieutenant Kent? We shall leave port immediately. But before we go I want a small party of Marines left on shore to await the return of my colleagues. Their orders are to maintain a watch for them here on the dock. We are going after the Yankee ship to catch them in the act at first light tomorrow. I expect to be back in port by tomorrow afternoon."

As *HMS Alice* came alive with activity Evan remained standing and staring at the shore. Both James and Alice would understand his duty was to put a stop to the weapons drop if at all possible. They would also understand someone was going to pay if any harm came to them.

Auyuba forced Alice and James into a storeroom accessed through the kitchen that held a table and two chairs, in addition to a range of various supplies for the household. Auyuba made Alice tie James to one of the chairs using lengths of cord stored on the shelves and then he did the same to her. After ensuring their bonds were tight and secure he used kitchen rags to tie gags over their mouths.

Stepping back to view his handiwork, Auyuba paused for a few long moments to let his gaze linger on Alice. She glared at him, ice in her eyes, as he stepped closer to her.

"You waste yourself on this white officer, don't you? A pity. A woman like you deserves a real man," said Auyuba, as he slid his hand down the inside of Alice's shift to grasp her breast. Alice tried to wrestle away from his grasp to no avail and the gag muffled her protest.

Auyuba stepped back and laughed. "Yes, you deserve some attention. Perhaps I will find a way to give it to you. But that shall be later."

Auyuba left and made his way to the sitting room where Anton, Henri, and Marie were all still sitting discussing the situation with worried looks on their faces. Auyuba saw a look of suspicion on Anton's face as the Count told him of their meeting with Captain Dusourd.

"Yes, I saw Captain Dusourd was here," said Auyuba. "He has gone back to his ship?"

"Yes. How did you know he was here?" said Anton.

"He was followed here by those English spies, the woman and the black man we think is an officer," replied Auyuba, enjoying the mixed looks of shock and fear appearing on their faces as he spoke.

"My God, are you certain? Why were they following him?" said Henri.

"Well, I saw them deliberately change their path to follow him when they saw him pass by. They didn't know I was in turn watching them. And as for why they were following him, why don't you come and find out?"

"What? What do you mean?" said Anton.

"Follow me, master."

As the family crowded into the little storeroom they stopped in their tracks when they saw James and Alice.

Anton turned in fury to face Auyuba. "God Almighty, are you insane? What did you do this for?"

"Master, what would you have me do? They must have been following him for a reason. If they went back to their ship and reported what they had seen to their commanding officer he would have come here to ask questions. This is all moving too quick. I thought it better to simply make them disappear."

Anton swore inarticulately and Henri shook his head in dismay. Marie locked eyes with Alice, who glowered in mute anger back at her. Auyuba watched, as Marie turned away and scowled at Anton, who was frozen with indecision.

"Anton," said Marie. "What's done is done. If you want to know what is going on why don't you do as Auyuba says and question them?" She turned back to Alice, a cold look on her face. "They can be made to answer questions."

Anton groaned and shook his head. "God, let's not make this worse than it already is. Auyuba, you will have to keep them here until we leave. It's the only choice."

Auyuba cleared his throat. "Well, I could find a way tonight to make them disappear permanently."

"No, for God's sake. The English will be searching for them and if you are caught taking them somewhere God knows what will happen. Look, just keep them here until we leave. After that you can do whatever."

"As you wish, master," said Auyuba, watching them leave the storeroom. Auyuba turned back to James and Alice and smiled.

"Well, there you have it. I am to do whatever I want with you once they leave," he said, looking straight at James. "I think I shall make you watch as I take her, then I shall kill you. Who knows, maybe I shall keep using her for a while."

Auyuba laughed and left the room, locking the door as he went.

Manon groaned when Paddy explained she had missed Evan. Racing through the dark streets she headed for the docks as fast as she could. As she turned the final corner into the port area itself she wailed in despair as in the moonlight she watched *HMS Alice* disappearing into the distance.

Dismayed, she turned about and headed back to The Thirsty Sailor, not seeing the Marine Sergeant and the two Marines with him stationed off to the side.

With a moon close to being full and a cloud free night he could see much further than otherwise would have been possible. Marcel Deschamps was standing on the quarterdeck watching the progress of the *Marie-Anne* as she bore down from the north on Castries harbour. He was startled to see in the moonlight the unmistakable shape of a ship sail out of the still distant harbour, tacking to the south. The Captain frowned and turned to his first officer.

"My night glass, please."

Within moments both he and his First Officer were staring with concentration at the ship. They had been fortunate to catch sight of the unknown ship's starboard side profile before it completed its tack about and showed only its stern.

The two officers lowered their night glasses and turned to each other as one.

"Captain, I am fairly certain it is the British ship that has been to Castries before. We've seen it often enough I am positive I recognize the shape and the cut of the sails."

"I agree, I was thinking this too. Pass the word we will not be sailing into Castries yet. I think we had better follow and see what Commander Ross is up to."

Evan fretted as the night wore on, unable to sleep from worry over James and Alice. Worse, with the winds being as light as they were he was not at all certain of catching the American ship in the act. But the same light winds would slow the American ship as well and it was a mercy when the first bare hint of dawn stole over the horizon.

"Beat to quarters, Lieutenant Kent. But do it quietly, without the drums. We don't want to give away our presence to our Yankee friend if he happens to be in the area."

But as the full light grew it became apparent they were alone. Lieutenant Kent conferred with the sailing master and came to report to Evan.

"Sir, given current conditions, I believe we are still about thirty minutes away from the bay you believe the drop is being made. I—"

"Deck there!" came the cry of the masthead lookout. "Ship on the horizon dead astern!"

Both men whipped around to look behind them, but all they could see was the barest hint of what might be sails in the far distance. A midshipman was sent to join the lookout and soon returned with news they were too far away to discern who they were, but it appeared clear the ship was coming their way. Evan grunted, wondering if they had arrived too soon. After contemplating it for a few long moments he looked at Lieutenant Kent, standing in silence awaiting orders.

"We continue as planned, Lieutenant. Ensure the men are given a cold breakfast at their stations. We don't know what we are in for here and we will know soon enough whether our prey is there."

As the morning wore on all Evan could do was pace back and forth. But they crept ever closer, aided by a slow, increasing wind. As they rounded the point barring their view into the bay that was their goal every available telescope was in use on the quarterdeck.

"Sir, it's the *Beacon*!" said Lieutenant Kent. "And they appear to be offloading cargo."

Evan watched the scene unfold for a while before giving the Lieutenant a grim smile in return. "I agree. I think they have noticed us, too. They've offloaded some of their cargo, but the ship's boat heading to the beach with more has turned about and headed back to the ship. I think the crew on board is making preparations to get underway, too. A shot to make them think otherwise is in order, Lieutenant."

Within minutes the forward chase gun roared and a round dropped into the bay, well away from the American ship, but unmistakable in its meaning. As Evan watched the American ship a second boat filled with American sailors returned from the beach, but many of them disappeared below deck. Evan frowned, but he had no time to think about it further as *HMS Alice* rounded up and heaved to within shouting distance of the Beacon.

Captain Jones was standing on his quarterdeck, his anger apparent as he spied Evan. Stalking to his quarterdeck railing he shouted across loud enough for all to hear.

"What was the meaning of your shot? I am a trader going about my business."

"Actually, Captain, I'm not so sure about that," shouted Evan in return. "We are going to board you and inspect your cargo. We are also going to have a look at what you have already dropped on the beach."

"What are you talking about?" shouted Jones, even angrier than before. "You have no right. This is French territory and I am an American trading ship."

"I think my French counterparts will support my action, sir, and I frankly don't care who you think you are. Prepare to accept boarders, sir."

"Bastard!" screamed Jones, as he whirled about and gave an obviously prearranged hand signal.

Evan was shocked as most of the gun ports on the side of the American ship opened almost as one and he realized why most of the American crew had disappeared below decks. The Beacon may indeed have been decommissioned as a warship, but she still retained what looked to be two thirds of the six-pound cannon complement she had once carried, proving she still had teeth to fight with. Two large swivel guns mounted at either end of the Beacon were also now manned and in the process of being loaded.

"Jesus Christ, Commander, I think those bastards are going to shoot—"

The sudden bark of the aft swivel gun on the Beacon shooting a load of grapeshot felled Lieutenant Kent in mid sentence, dead before he even hit the ground. The side of the American ship erupted moments later in a roar of noise blotting out every other sound. With the shots coming at such close range they couldn't help but have a devastating effect. Evan felt the *Alice* groan from the multiple strikes as splinters flew below decks, followed by screams from badly wounded men.

The British crew was shocked by the sudden turn of events, but only for a moment, before cold fury at being attacked without warning took hold. Evan howled orders to fire and the *Alice*'s response came within moments. The *Beacon* rocked as if she had been punched, with numerous holes appearing in her sides. Screams of pain drifted across the water. The worst punishment, however, came from the deck carronades of the Alice as they thundered too in response. They had been loaded with grapeshot, enough to do far worse damage than the much smaller swivel guns on the *Beacon*. Evan saw the swivels on the *Beacon* were no longer manned as the carronades had scythed a bloody path across his foes deck.

The two ships traded another round of shots, with the British response coming bare moments after the American ship's broadside. Marines were firing from the fighting tops, but a small group of American sailors had boiled up from below and, taking cover wherever they could, began returning fire with their own weapons.

Evan had seen enough of the Alice's crew to be confident in their competence, but sitting back trading shots would end with far more dead or wounded than he wanted. The distance between the two ships was a long throw for the grapnels, so he turned to the master's mate standing beside the quartermaster at the wheel.

"Bring us about, closer to them. We are going to board them and take that ship."

"Aye, aye, Captain," came the reply.

Evan started in surprise for a moment, realizing this was the first time anyone had ever addressed him as Captain. The crew of the *Alice* had long since realized Evan was an officer and the death of Lieutenant Kent made it automatic to them that as most senior officer present Evan was now in charge. Although it felt strange to be stepping into a dead man's shoes, this was how it worked in the Navy.

Evan had no time to savour the moment as he stalked about to avoid being shot while issuing orders for grapnels to be readied and boarding parties to be formed. Within moments they were close enough for grapnels to make it and as they sailed across the Americans seemed to accept their fate, ensuring their own parties were ready to meet the challenge. The carronades plowed paths through the waiting Americans before the British sailors, still furious at being blindsided, poured over the sides with their cutlasses flashing in the morning sunlight.

Evan joined the attack and formed a party to make for the American's quarterdeck. The fight grew to its hottest as the report of a large cannon opening fire echoed from further out on the bay made everyone stop to find the source. The *Marie-Anne* had made best speed with the rising morning wind and was now well within range of the two ships locked in battle.

"Surrender, you fools!" screamed Evan. To his relief, one by one, the Americans dropped their weapons to stand in sullen silence. The next several minutes were a blur as Evan issued a stream of orders to secure the situation. Wounded and dying men were everywhere. A party Evan detailed to search the hold reported back the only cargo it held were crates of weapons.

Evan worked his way to the quarterdeck, scowling as he looked about in anger for Adam Jones. He found him still alive, seated on the deck and leaning against a bulwark. Looking at the wounds inflicted by one of the carronades, Evan could see he wouldn't live much longer. Sensing a sudden presence beside him Evan turned to find Marcel Deschamps had been the first from the *Marie-Anne* to board the *Beacon*. He shook his head as he looked down at the dying American Captain.

"Fool," said Deschamps.

The American coughed several times, somehow finally finding the strength to raise his arm and wipe away the trickle of blood seeping from his mouth before he spoke. "Maybe. Maybe not. I did my duty and so did my crew. They fought well, didn't they?"

"They did, but I would rather they had not," said Evan. "There would be a lot of good men still alive if they hadn't."

The French Captain merely shook his head. "Captain Jones. What in God's name was your cousin thinking?

Adam Jones struggled to speak once again as he offered a weary smile in response. "Ah, this was my idea, not his. I—I saw an opportunity and took it. He supported me, though, and he saw it as a way to set you two at each other's throats."

"What do you mean, an opportunity?"

"I mean your crazy French Count and his family," said the dying American, his voice almost a whisper. "Captain Deschamps, I don't need to explain to you what my mission here was, do I? If some way could be found to lessen the grip both of your countries have on these islands then I was to pursue it. And along comes these fools dreaming of freeing the slaves by spreading around a few weapons to create havoc. Who am I to argue when opportunity knocks?"

As he finished he coughed several more times, an even greater quantity of blood trickling from his mouth. This time, he didn't have the strength left to wipe it away and he nodded at his two foes before death took him.

Evan sighed as Captain Deschamps put a hand to his forehead as if to stem a sudden pain. Evan turned to the Captain, shaking his head.

"Well, Captain, I think there are plenty of fools to go around in this story. Sir, can I leave this for you to sort out? This ship was smuggling and has been captured in your waters. I must get back to Castries."

Deschamps raised an eyebrow to signal his mute question and Evan told him what had happened. As he finished he gave the French Captain an imploring look. "So you see, I am concerned for my colleagues. I can only think the de Bellecourts or perhaps this Captain Dusourd they employ has had a hand in their disappearance."

Captain Deschamps was silent for a long moment before reaching a decision. "Yes, Commander, I shall clean up this mess and be right behind you. And yes, I'd like to have a conversation with the de Bellecourts and my old friend Giscard Dusourd. Do you need assistance with repairs?"

"I don't think so, but I will let you know."

Despite driving every man at his disposal hard to effect repairs it still took an hour to get underway back to Castries. Evan could see Captain Deschamps was driving his men hard too, and knew he wouldn't be far behind him. A prize crew from the *Marie-Anne* was already in place on the *Beacon* dealing with the damage and preparing to make sail.

By the time *HMS Alice* got to Castries it was once again late evening, but they had made better speed on the return trip with more favourable winds. Evan gave a grim smile as he saw the *L'Estalon* was still docked in the same place he had last seen her. The ship was close enough he could see several of the sailors lining the rails, drawn there to speculate on what had happened by the obvious damage *HMS Alice* had suffered. Evan saw Captain Dusourd watching from the shadows on deck, wearing a worried look. As *HMS Alice* docked once again the French Customs officer tried to board, protesting against Evan's posting of Marines in the harbour. Evan brushed him aside as he strode ashore to speak to his Marine Sergeant.

"Report. Any word of my colleagues?"

The Customs officer tugged at Evan's empty sleeve to draw his attention and Evan rounded on him, his anger boiling. "If you do that again I will have these men throw you in the harbour. If you have a problem with anything I have done take it up with Captain Marcel Deschamps of the *Marie-Anne*. Now get out of my sight."

As the man scurried away Evan turned back to the Sergeant, a questioning look on his face.

"Sir. We have not seen them at all. However, a young woman claims to have information for you."

"A young woman?" replied Evan. As he spoke, a familiar voice shouting his name drew his attention.

"Commander Ross!" said Manon as she ran up to him. "Thank God you are back. I think I know where Mr. Wilton and Alice are. I missed you last night so I asked my father what to do. He told me to keep watching the manor house and to keep checking for you to return."

"Manor house?"

Manon quickly explained what she had seen and where the manor was. As she described the black man that had forced them into the manor Evan grew cold, certain it was the black slave Auyuba.

"Bastard!" swore Evan. "I will carve him into a thousand pieces if he's harmed them."

Manon stepped back a pace, frightened by the blazing anger on Evan's face. "I can lead you there, sir."

Evan was at a loss. Cold fear of what the fate of Alice and James could be gnawed at him, but what he could do was another matter. Chasing after an American weapons smuggler in French waters and having it out with him was a risk no one would blame him for taking as long as he succeeded. Barging into the home of French nobles at the head of a file of Royal Marines was risk on a whole other level. If Alice and James weren't there Evan still had Captain Deschamps as a witness to the dying American's testimony, but the question was whether he could rely on it. Deschamps had proved a wily foe before and would certainly see how a forced entrance could be turned into an international diplomatic incident. The question was whether he would.

Evan looked behind him and as expected saw the *Marie-Anne* approaching the entrance to the harbour in the distance. Evan clenched his fist in frustration, knowing it would be almost another thirty minutes before the *Marie-Anne* docked. Evan begrudged every second, but the safer course would be to wait for Captain Deschamps.

But his fear for the safety of Alice and James was overwhelming and even as he clenched his fist once again in frustration an image came to his mind unbidden, a memory of being in the cabin of the *HMS Boreas* with Nelson. In it the Captain assured him yet again an officer could do little wrong by laying himself alongside his foe.

Evan turned back to Manon and once again she shrank back on seeing the hard steel of his face. "Yes, please, Manon. We are going to get them out of there and no one is going to bloody stop us."

Evan turned back to the Sergeant. "I need you and a file of Marines to accompany me, at the double. When we go in there I will lead. I don't know if we shall find resistance, but if we do we will stamp it out with whatever force it takes. Also, I want one man left behind to await the return of Captain Deschamps. Determine who and I will give him his orders."

Within moments a man came forward and once the Marine felt confident he knew where the manor house was based on Manon's instructions, Evan gave him orders to seek out Captain Deschamps and explain what had happened so the Captain could follow. After he finished he turned back to Manon and the waiting party of Marines with a grim look.

"Everyone ready? No more time to waste. Let's go."

Chapter Thirteen
November 1788
St. Lucia

They were a strange sight.

With Manon at his side and the Sergeant with his file of Marines close behind, Evan marched them through the streets of Castries at a fast pace. Several people stopped open mouthed in surprise, as the bright red serge of the Marines jackets stood out despite the growing dusk. A number of the French soldiers standing guard throughout the town turned to look at each other in puzzlement as the British marched past. But the British weren't threatening anyone and the French soldiers had no orders to deal with the situation, so they remained standing watch.

"This is it?" said Evan as they marched past the gatehouse and made for the manor entrance doors.

"It is, Commander," said Manon.

"Stay back, please. There could be trouble."

"Commander, I want to help."

Evan didn't break stride as he looked over his shoulder and made it clear he would brook no arguments. "Stay back."

The entire de Bellecourt family was once again in the sitting room of their manor enjoying wine before dinner when Elise burst into the room.

"Elise? What is the meaning of this?" said Anton.

"Master!" she cried, falling to her knees in front of him. "You have been betrayed!"

Anton felt a cold rush of fear. "What do you mean?"

"It was Auyuba! He is jealous of you for taking me to France, so he went to the contact of the British spies here and told them what has been happening and why. He told them of the last drop of weapons at Soufriere and that you have been behind it all!"

"My God, how do you know this?"

"Master, he is not who he has pretended to be. He is the real leader of the runaways on this island and I have been his helper until you came. But I have many contacts and friends. I have learned he was seen talking to the spies at The Thirsty Sailor and my friends overheard them talking after Auyuba left. But master, this is not all. We have to leave as soon as possible! I think the British are coming for you."

Anton looked at Jacques. "Go and bring Auyuba here. Use force if necessary."

Jacques nodded and stood, hand on his sword hilt, and left through the door to the rear of the manor. Even as it shut, a sudden pounding that could only be someone hammering on the door could be heard coming from the direction of the front entrance.

Evan drew his sword as he reached the entrance, using it to beat on the door with the pommel. With the Sergeant right behind him Evan remained staring in fixed anger at the door as he spoke.

"Sergeant, you and your men will follow me into the manor and be ready for what comes. And if these bastards don't open this door we are going to break it down."

Evan was in the midst of hammering on it a second time when a fearful looking black slave girl opened it and her eyes grew wide when she saw the uniformed men in the doorway. Evan brushed her aside and the Marines crowded in after him.

"Sir!" cried the girl, a hand to her heart as she stepped further out of their way. "What do you want?"

"Where is Count de Bellecourt?"

With another frightened look she pointed at a doorway at the far end of the hall. Evan stalked over and yanked it open to find it led to the main sitting room. He found most of the de Bellecourt family was already standing, looking shocked by the intrusion. Half empty glasses of wine were strewn around the room. The only other person in the room was the black slave woman Elise, who was clutching at Anton with a scared look.

Anton was the first to find his voice and he made his outrage clear. "God Almighty, what is the meaning of this?"

"Count de Bellecourt," said Evan as he looked around the room. "Whether you know it or not, I have reason to believe my colleagues are being held against their will in this house. My men are going to conduct a search to find them."

Anton's jaw dropped in complete, stunned shock. The rest of the family grouped in fear around Anton. Henri had his hand on the hilt of the sword at his side.

"You can't do this!" shouted the Count.

"Count. We have evidence you, and your family, are complicit in smuggling weapons to runaway slaves. Your game is over, sir. I am not here to arrest you for your crimes, I am quite certain the French authorities will be along soon to take care of this. I am interested solely in finding my people and no one is going to stop me."

Evan turned to the Sergeant standing beside him. "Detail search parties. I want every possible place they could be held checked."

"No, by God!" roared Henri, drawing his sword. "We are French diplomats and you have no authority whatsoever here. You are trespassing on our property, threatening us with arms, and are thus a criminal. Leave now or we will be forced to see to our defence!"

"Proceed Sergeant, I will deal with these fools."

The Sergeant nodded and turned to comply, but everyone stopped as the clear sounds of struggle and a pistol shot followed by a scream was heard from behind the door Jacques had used to go and find Auyuba. Something hit the floor with a thud and moments later, before anyone could react, the door burst open and Auyuba came into the room with a pistol in his hand. Seeing Anton he raised the weapon to shoot.

"It is fitting you should die with your own weapons, French bastard!"

Evan rushed to cross the room and cut at his arm with his sword, but the two de Bellecourt women stumbled into him as they tried to back away from the fight. As Auyuba took his shot Henri rushed forward to do the same as Evan and paid the price by running straight into the line of fire. Henri crashed to the floor, a swift bloom of crimson growing on his chest even before he landed.

The two de Bellecourt women screamed. Auyuba threw the pistol as hard as he could at Anton's face and laughed to hear a sickening crunch of bone. A blossom of blood fountained from the Count's face.

Shoving the two wailing French women out of his way Evan rushed forward, but Auyuba had already run back through the door and slammed it shut. Trying in desperation to open it, Evan realized Auyuba had wedged something heavy in the way. As the Marine Sergeant joined Evan in shoving at the door the sound of a woman's scream came from the rear of the manor.

But the voice, Evan realized, didn't belong to Alice.

Manon watched Evan and the Marines disappear into the manor, worried they had come too late. With a start, Manon realized she had forgotten to tell Evan about the rear entrance Auyuba had used. Fearing the rear entrance could be used as an escape route, Manon circled around to look. She soon found it and, seizing her courage, she tried the door and discovered it was unlocked.

She found herself in the kitchen. One of the kitchen slaves looked at her with curiosity, but they all seemed preoccupied with the sudden sounds of loud arguments coming from the front of the building. Summoning her courage, she began looking around the warren of rooms, poking her head into every room she came to.

At last she came to a locked door off the kitchen area. Looking around to ensure no one was nearby she knocked as soft as she could and put her face as close to the door as possible to call out.

"Mr. Wilton? Mr. Wilton, are you there?"

The immediate reward was the faint sound of loud, but muffled grunts with a desperate pitch to them. She was also certain there were two voices, one male and one female. A pounding on the floor from within confirmed someone was there. She tried rattling the door as hard as could, but it remained locked. The door latch appeared old and a little rusty. There was enough space between the doorjamb and the door itself to insert a wedge.

She rushed into a nearby storeroom and soon found a thin, but strong looking bar on a shelf of various household tools. Returning quickly to the door she inserted it in the space as close to the locking mechanism as possible and threw the full weight of her desperation into trying to pry the door open. The door withstood her initial onslaught, but rewarded her with a loud metallic squawk of protest. Encouraged, she continued throwing her weight against it until the lock gave and the door popped open. Manon fell into the wall as it gave and hit her head hard, but she picked herself up and pulled the door open wide.

She was shocked at the sight awaiting her. Even as she stood rooted to the spot the sound of two gunshots in close succession came from the front of the house. She started in fear, but realized she had to continue.

Both James and Alice had been beaten and were in bad shape. James was by far the worst of the two. Congealed blood had flowed from his nose, smearing his puffy lips and the lower half of his face. One eye was almost swollen shut. Manon winced when she looked at Alice, as the entire front of her dress had been ripped open to expose her breasts. Alice's face wasn't as bruised as James, but the bruises on her breasts would be painful for a long time to come.

Casting about for something to cut their bonds she saw a small, but sharp looking knife on a shelf.

As she cut the gag binding James's mouth he began coughing to clear his throat. He found his voice as Manon began sawing in haste at the bonds holding his hands together behind the chair.

"My God, thank you for coming for us. We thought we were—Christ! Behind you!"

Even as she turned to face whatever threat James was warning her of Manon screamed, feeling her hair grabbed from behind. She was unable to resist as she was pulled off her feet and thrown hard against the far wall of the storeroom, crumpling against the wall in pain as she turned to confront her tormentor.

In horror she saw Auyuba scowling down at her and setting himself to aim a hard kick to her ribs. She cried in fear and tried to shuffle aside, but with sick apprehension she could see she would be too late.

Even as she cried out, though, James hammered Auyuba hard from behind into the wall. While Auyuba was occupied with Manon, James had summoned reserves of strength to free his hands from the remaining few bonds holding them. His still bound feet tied to the chair hindered him, though. The two men crashed to the floor and Auyuba was soon on his feet. James aimed a desperate punch at Auyuba's groin area and Manon's hopes soared as Auyuba gasped in pain, doubling over as he did.

"Bastard!" said James, as he struggled to regain his balance.

But Auyuba summoned his own reserves of strength. Wincing in pain, he mastered himself and glared with hate at James. Pulling a knife from a scabbard on his belt, Auyuba raised it to strike as he moved forward. Manon screamed, knowing James was certain to be killed. She flung herself desperately at Auyuba to try knocking him off his feet. He wobbled and fell hard into the wall, but was up on his feet again within moments. He gave Manon a vicious kick in the stomach and she doubled over in pain, crumpling back to the floor. Auyuba turned once again to James, who was on his knees and trying to struggle to his feet. Raising the knife, Auyuba stalked toward him.

Pushed to frantic strength by the woman's scream Evan shoved enough of the door open for him to squeeze through. He almost stumbled as he rushed through it, his mind registering the obstacle was a body wedged against the door. In a desperate rush, sword drawn, he ran down the hallway in the direction of the scream. From a room near the back of the manor he heard a voice he was certain belonged to Auyuba.

"You threatened to cut my balls off, remember? Well, you're about to find out what it's like!"

Evan drove hard and as he entered the room he saw James struggling to his knees in a desperate attempt to fend off the knife Auyuba was about to stab him with.

But the thrust never came as Auyuba stiffened and arched his back in a futile attempt to get away from Evan's blade, driven into him hard from behind, enough that a full six inches stood out from his chest before Evan ripped it out of his body.

Manon screamed again as Auyuba fell back and crashed to the floor on top of her, already dead before he hit her. With loathing she shoved him off as Evan prodded him with his sword to ensure he was gone. Sheathing his sword Evan pulled out his dirk and cut the remaining bonds holding James. Two Marines appeared in the doorway, but Evan ordered them to stand down and report to the Sergeant the situation was under control.

"Good Christ, Evan, thank God you're here. You saved us," gasped out James, before he turned to Manon and reached out a hand to pull her to her feet. "And you, too. If you hadn't come in and freed me this bastard would have been cutting my heart out."

As Manon got to her feet, rubbing her bruises and holding her side in obvious pain where Auyuba had kicked her, she stood in front of James. "I saw him capture you and I was worried."

As James reached out a hand to stroke her cheek before enfolding her in his arms in a crushing hug, Evan turned to Alice and rushed over to cut her bonds too. She coughed and gasped in relief as she regained her circulation. Evan was dismayed at how she had been abused, but she brushed away his concerns as she did her best to pull her ruined dress together enough to cover herself.

The two freed captives were unsteady on their feet, suffering from a day without food or water. Both had to be helped to use the necessary house and to clean themselves as best they could. After wolfing down some biscuits and cheese Manon found in the kitchen they were refreshed, but still weak. With Evan and Manon helping them they made their way back to the main sitting room where the Marine Sergeant was guarding the remaining de Bellecourt family members.

Anton's face was one massive bruise. His nose looked broken and he was holding a bloodstained rag to the side of his face. Elise still clutched at him on one side, while Marie was standing on the other. Evan scowled at him as he came into the room, supporting Alice with his arm.

"Count de Bellecourt, you are fortunate my colleagues are alive. I swear to God you would be receiving far worse than what you have today if they were not."

Even as he spoke Alice stirred and he felt her come alive beside him. He turned in surprise, but was too late to stop her leaving his grasp. Marie realized too late Alice was coming straight for her and had no chance to defend herself.

"Bitch!" screamed Alice as she slapped Marie with all her might. The French woman fell backwards, stumbling over a side table to crash hard into the wall. Satisfied with the result Alice turned back to Evan and James. "She knew we were being held here. She stood by and did nothing. By God, I've been wanting to do *that* for months!"

As Emilie struggled to help her older sister get up, the sound of booted feet came from the entrance to the manor. Captain Deschamps entered the room and took everything in as two of the Marines from the *Marie-Anne* followed him. Evan could see others waited outside.

"You are the Captain of the frigate? I am Count Anton de Bellecourt," said Anton, seizing the initiative. "Thank God you are here. This officer and his men have violated our diplomatic immunity. They have invaded our home, killed my brother and my cousin, and both my sister and I have been assaulted as you can see. I trust you will do your duty."

Captain Deschamps stared at the Count for several long moments before responding. "Yes, Count, I am Captain Marcel Deschamps."

Evan explained what had happened in response to the Captain's questioning look. Appearing as if suffering from a bad case of indigestion the Captain stepped closer to face Evan, his displeasure clear over the situation.

"You could not have waited? I was right behind you."

Evan shrugged. "My people were in immediate danger and I had to act. You would have done the same were you in my place."

The Captain stood stiff and silent, staring at Evan for several long moments before letting out a long sigh. "Of course. You are right."

Captain Deschamps turned to the Marine officer at his side and issued orders to have the bodies removed and taken to the morgue so arrangements could be made for them.

"Captain?" said Marie, her voice rising with indignation. "This man is lying. Aren't you going to arrest them?"

Captain Deschamps dismissed her with a curt response. "No, I am not."

"Captain, I cannot believe this," said Anton. "This is outrageous. You are going to take the word of the lying British over ours? You are failing to fulfill your duty, sir."

The Captain's face was blank, but his eyes burned into Anton. "You idiot. You stand there speaking to me of duty, when you have no concept of what it means."

The Captain paused a moment to let it sink in before he continued. "Count de Bellecourt, I am sorry for the tragic loss of your relatives in this unfortunate accident. It is terrible your relatives had weapons out for whatever reason and somehow mishandled them, but whatever the case it seems clear their own actions have led to this awful accident. Yes, people handling *weapons* when they don't really know what they are doing sometimes have to face the consequences of their folly. I shall be speaking to the Governor and will explain *everything,* you understand. You will of course wish to delay your departure for home only long enough to ensure you can make arrangements for their burial and an appropriate public service. But depart for home you will, at the earliest possible opportunity."

The Captain stared at Anton long enough to emphasize his point and ensure Anton would not challenge him. When he was certain none was forthcoming he turned to Evan.

"Commander Ross. I suggest you and your contingent return to your ship. I shall handle matters here. Please do not depart yet. I may need a little time to attend to matters, but I shall want to confer with you tomorrow or the day after. I shall send word."

Evan took a long moment to consider this, weighing the need to leave immediately, before he nodded agreement. "As you wish, Captain."

With a look at the Marine Sergeant Evan pointed to the door. Encircling Alice's waist once again with his arm to help steady her he left.

Chapter Fourteen
November 1788
St. Lucia and Antigua

"Captain, this was a truly fine meal," said Evan, swirling the remnants of the wine in his glass before downing it. "You have a knack for finding excellent places to eat. But, really, sir, I would like to help pay for this."

Captain Deschamps waved a hand in dismissal as he toyed with his own glass for a moment and stared out at the lights of Castries harbour. They were high on the side of one of the hills surrounding the harbour on an outside patio lit by lanterns hanging at strategic locations. Whoever owned the property had constructed the patio so it afforded both an excellent view of the harbour and of the approaches to it on the seaward side of the point. Evan felt he could sit enjoying the view and the light of the moon beginning to shimmer on the water for hours. The Captain was enjoying the scene too, and he reached for the bottle to refill their glasses before replying. The bottle was empty when he finished.

"Commander, do not concern yourself. I have more money than you know and it is not an issue for me. Oh, I am not filthy rich like the Count, but I have enough to be quite comfortable. And as I have gotten older I have become less circumspect about spending it. Many people see acquiring money as the end goal of life, but I see it as a tool to be used. People are more important than money and I enjoy spending my money on people. Well, to business."

Turning to face Evan he held out his glass in a toast. "But first, a toast to successfully putting a stop to this nonsense."

Evan nodded and touched his glass to the Captain's before taking a sip.

"So, I trust your colleagues have recovered?"

"They are much better, sir. They are both young and healthy. It seems the Count basically washed his hands of them and gave Auyuba free rein to do whatever he wanted once the de Bellecourt family left, so it was fortunate Auyuba decided only to toy with them until that happened."

"Good. So, I know I have kept you waiting longer than you would want, but I have used my time fruitfully the last three days and learned a great deal. Much of this came from having a couple of friendly conversations with Captain Dusourd."

Evan raised an inquisitive eyebrow. "Friendly?"

Captain Deschamps smiled. "Well, they only became friendly after I threatened to have him tied to a stake, disemboweled, and made to watch while I fed his guts to the land crabs on the beach. It turns out our meddling Count and his family found inspiration to change the world from the Marquis de Lafayette. I am fairly certain it was just inspiration, whereas the idea to cross the line and incite violence rested strictly with the Count. He needed help from someone with no scruples and he had to confide in someone, so Captain Dusourd became this someone. They brought the first load of weapons from France with them. It was Dusourd who put the Count into contact with Jones, and Jones decided to use these imbeciles for his own purposes. And by the way, it seems likely this nest of snakes was indeed responsible for the death of your consul John Andrews."

Evan sat forward with interest. "Who did it, Captain?"

"Well, I don't have direct proof, but if the lawyer Moreau is to be believed, at least on this point, Jones put the knife in him while Auyuba distracted the man. I know, believing a lawyer on a matter like this is perhaps being too hopeful, but it's all I have. Moreau is the snake behind all the money involved, you see? I had to hold his feet to the fire too in order to get his side of the story. Dusourd, Moreau, Jones, Auyuba and your consul were all conniving during the war and it seems your consul may have double-crossed them in some murky deal involving a lot of money, although it was only recently that his role came to light. I got the distinct impression your consul wasn't exactly a saint and that he in fact betrayed your side on several occasions."

"I see. Captain, I couldn't help noticing the *L'Estalon* sailed earlier today with the remaining de Bellecourt family on board. Captain Dusourd was also on board and appeared to be still in possession of his innards while in full command. He couldn't have been turned over to me?"

The Captain winced and shrugged. "This thought crossed my mind, Commander. Truthfully, the thought of him swinging in the wind while hanging from a British gallows or yardarm was appealing, but I'm afraid the Governor convinced me it would not be good policy."

"The Governor? And how does the Governor desire this matter to be handled?"

"Quietly, and when you think about it, he is right. Do we really want it widely known a French noble and his family conspired to incite violence among the slaves on both French and British islands? The stain on the aristocracy might not be confined to France, if you take my meaning. Plus, do you really want it widely known your consul was betraying you?"

Evan sat considering the Captain's argument in silence for several long moments, before finally responding. "I take your points, sir. Personally, I don't see how it would be in our interests to make any of this known, but you must understand I cannot speak on behalf of either my superiors or of Governor Shirley on Antigua. I will certainly carry this thinking to them, however."

"This is all we can ask, Commander."

"We still have to provide some public explanation for what was happening and to reassure people we have put a stop to it all, though. Let me guess. We are going to lay all this at the feet of the Americans, correct?"

Captain Deschamps chuckled. "You know, this is why I confess I like you, Commander. You are a bright fellow. Indeed, our friend Nathan in America has conveniently provided us with an American ship armed far beyond what a civilian ship should be, filled with American weapons, and caught in the act of smuggling them all into St. Lucia. And in a spirit of cooperation and goodwill between our two nations we shall tell the world the navies of England and France combined to put a stop to this nefarious American attempt to destabilize our domains here. Why, this is a good news story, don't you think?"

Evan couldn't resist laughing in turn, before turning serious. "Well, once again, I agree, but cannot speak for my superiors. I have dealt with Governor Shirley often enough I think he may enjoy this approach too. But I think this willingness to make the Americans the scapegoat a bit unusual, given the alleged friendship between America and France."

Captain Deschamps shrugged. "It hasn't been as friendly as you might think, especially the last while. The Americans have been proving quite independent in their thinking. Besides, someone has to take the blame for this mess."

Evan smiled in reply. "Indeed. A pity I couldn't have taken Captain Dusourd back with me to keep Captain Rand happy, though."

The French Captain looked at Evan and shrugged. "The Governor wanted the de Bellecourt family out of his sight as soon as possible. We especially do not want stain on the French nobility at the moment. We do understand your need, of course. Despite the fact your consul may have been a traitor, he was still the British consul and your government will not want his murder to go without being avenged. The problem was how we would have gotten him to you without creating a scene or creating more problems. Well, the thing is you do know where he is going, and I made it clear I do not want to see him back out here anytime soon. I expect the Count will not want anything to do with him either, so I rather think the Captain will be kicking around the Marseille waterfront looking for employment for some time to come. I'm sure he won't be hard to find."

"Hmm, this is true. You know, I hear the port of Marseille can be a violent place for the unwary. People get robbed and end up with a knife in the back all the time."

"Sad, but true Commander. We live in dangerous times."

"And what about this bloody snake Moreau? If he was involved in this he should be made to pay too."

"I agree, Commander, and so does the Governor. Unfortunately, we will have to be more circumspect with this bastard. He is extremely well connected on this island and back home in France. He also knows where a lot of the bodies are buried, so to speak, involving influential people on this island. The man has gotten too powerful, though. The Governor had been searching for a way to rein him in and his involvement with this nonsense provides opportunity. The Governor is mulling some scheme to have him locked away for a very long time, but I personally like the more permanent solution a knife in the back offers. On the other hand, he is a lawyer after all, so it might be more apropos were he to serve as dinner for the rest of his shark family. In any case, please rest assured the man will not escape paying for this."

"Hmm," said Evan. "So my job is to explain all this to Governor Shirley too, is it?"

"Yes, but I need you to pass this on to him also." Reaching into the inner pocket of his dinner jacket the Captain pulled out a thin sealed envelope and slid it across the table to Evan. "Governor Marchand has detailed in brief his thinking on the public handling of this matter to your Governor. The background details behind this thinking are left to you to convey. Governor Marchand would appreciate a prompt response from Governor Shirley."

Evan regarded the envelope for a moment before picking it up and stashing it away in his own pocket. "I can do this, Captain. But tell me, if you can, why is there such concern over the nobility? I mean, really, it isn't the first time someone from a high station in life has proved to be a criminal. What is going on to make this so sensitive?"

The Captain sighed and looked at his now empty wine glass. "Would you share a little glass of cognac with me before we call it a night?"

Evan nodded. The Captain remained silent until the glasses were before them and they were alone once again.

"We have had word of developments in France, Commander. Matters went from merely bad to being much worse, and have now evolved to what can only be described as dire. Perhaps a little background would be in order. We've had problems with the grain harvests for several years, but thought the bad times were behind us and price controls were removed last year. Well, the harvest has been extremely bad this year. In particular, apparently there was a major hailstorm in the prime fields around Paris in July and everything was wiped out. Prices rose steeply when this happened. Thus, the people cannot afford to eat and there is no work for them. There have been severe riots all summer."

"Good Lord, Captain. I knew there may be problems, but didn't know it was quite this bad."

"Ah, but this is not all. The French government is essentially bankrupt. With little money coming in and no one willing to lend them more, the government is paying lenders what they already owe with yet more promissory notes. The lenders don't like it, but they have no choice. Worst of all, the government has been forced to disband many army units, adding to the unemployment."

"My God," said Evan, a growing, worried look on his face. "Is no one trying to bring the situation under control?"

The Captain laughed, but Evan could sense the sour tone to the laugh.

"Indeed, Commander, you may find it amusing to know the Marquis de Lafayette is still at it. Apparently there is talk he is forming something called The Society of Thirty. I am told most of the members are nobles, but they are promoting major reforms. They are opposing privilege and entitlements at all levels and are trying to promote giving more power to the Estates General. In particular, they want the Third Estate to have much more power."

"The Third Estate? This is the one that represents the common people, is it not?"

"You are correct. The problem is this Estate is far from united in what it wants. A bourgeoisie owner of a bakery does not necessarily have the same interests as, say, a farmer in the countryside or even any of his workers."

"But what about the French government, sir?"

The Captain shrugged. "They appear to be paralyzed. Everyone has their own agenda and none can agree. Thus, you see why Governor Marchand has no desire to add fuel to the fire by exposing what these imbeciles were doing out here. In particular, it is their links to the Marquis that are a problem. The Governor may have misgivings about what the Marquis is doing, but he is giving him credit for at least *trying* to find a reasonable way out of this mess. Sadly, no one else seems to be doing this."

"I see. And where do you stand in all of this, Captain?"

The Captain shrugged as he swirled the remaining mouthful of cognac in his glass. "There are many now who are inspired by the Americans and talk of having a different system, but I remain a royalist, Commander. The system we have lived under for a long time has served us well, particularly in terms of stability in an unstable world. Yes, things have not been perfect and there are people trying to take advantage of our King, but it was ever thus. So despite my annoyance at the trouble the Marquis inadvertently inspired out here, I do support his attempts to reform the system and I hope he succeeds. Thus, I shall continue to be a faithful servant of my Crown, which means of course I shall be having a talk with your friend Paddy Shannon about his activities with a view to ensuring he ceases meeting your needs."

"Of course. I shall be actively rolling up your network on Antigua when I return, too. Well, Captain, I believe I once said there was no reason we couldn't be civilized and maybe even friendly about this, despite what we do. This has been a most civilized evening, but I must be on my way at first light tomorrow."

Both men downed the remainder of their glasses and stood to shake hands.

"Yes, Commander, it has been civilized and friendly. It is good to have friends, sir. Who knows, perhaps I shall have need of them some day in future. I will be honest with you. I am afraid for the future of my country, very afraid. Well, enough. I wish you a safe journey."

The next morning dawned bright and clear. Standing on the quarterdeck Evan savoured the air, knowing it would be a fine day for sailing. But the true joy of the day would come from being in sole command of a fine warship filled with over a hundred souls all depending on his decisions. For a long moment he gave a mental salute to his predecessor, the dues owed when stepping into a dead man's shoes. How long he would get to stay in command was another matter.

Evan was about to order the First Officer to cast off and get underway when James and Alice appeared on the quarterdeck. What gave him pause was the presence of Manon with them. Evan raised an eyebrow at her and turned to James.

"Lieutenant Wilton, isn't it past time for our friend Manon to be ashore? It's time to leave."

James coughed and looked at Manon, reaching an arm around her waist to pull her closer. "Commander Ross, Manon would like to join us and come with me to Antigua. That is, assuming you have no concerns, sir."

Evan smiled, before turning to Manon. "Well, this is interesting. I am really hoping your father is aware of this development? I happen to like my Lieutenant and would really prefer he wasn't tracked down and murdered by an angry father."

Manon gave Evan a broad smile. "You may rest assured my father is aware and has offered his blessing to this. Well, he did warn me about smooth-tongued rogues and I suspect he made a few dire threats to James about what would happen if I wasn't treated right."

"Well then, who am I to stand in the way of true romance?" said Evan. Turning to the First Officer he gave the signal to cast off and get underway.

Governor Shirley finished reading the letter from his counterpart in St. Lucia and then read through it a second time before looking up at Evan.

"All right, Commander. What is the real story here, please?"

Evan cleared his throat and began. The Governor and the other two men in the room, Captain Rand and Sir James Standish, all sat in silence as Evan gave them the entire picture. All three men remained silent for several long moments after Evan finally finished.

Governor Shirley was the first to stir and he turned to look at Sir James. "This tallies with my understanding of the wider situation. Agreed?"

Sir James nodded. "Agreed, Governor. The more we learn of this fellow Deschamps the more I am coming to appreciate him. He does appear to know his business. You will agree to what Governor Marchand is proposing?"

Captain Rand interrupted before the Governor could respond. "You aren't seriously going to cooperate with the bloody frogs, are you? Governor, they cannot be trusted."

Governor Shirley scowled and he rounded on the Captain, his response brusque. "Captain, do me a favour, please? Stick to nautical matters and leave the politics to me."

The Governor left the scowl in place, daring him to argue the matter, but when the Captain chose to remain mute the Governor turned to Sir James. "Yes, I believe so. I need to give it a little thought, but I think overall this serves our purposes. Sir James, I don't like what is going on. We are going to have to watch this carefully."

As Sir James nodded in silent agreement the Governor turned back to Evan. "Well, Commander, once again you have served us well. I shall commend your efforts to the people back home. You will be providing a full written report on all of this, of course? I would like a copy."

"Of course, sir. I shall have it ready by tomorrow at the latest." Sensing his part in the meeting was at an end Evan rose to leave. "I shall return to my duties if there are no further questions, sirs?"

No one spoke and Evan took his leave. As he did, Evan could not fail to see the sour look on the face of Captain Rand. Once out of sight Evan shook his head at the prospect of yet more storm clouds on his horizon.

Sir James put his travel valises down beside him as he settled into the chair across from Evan's desk in the Dockyard.

"Well, Commander, the mail packet back to Barbados is waiting for me and I mustn't keep them long. I apologize I haven't had time to debrief you until now. The Governor has agreed to everything his counterpart in St. Lucia has suggested. The less palatable details of this whole affair shall remain buried. Unfortunately, this means you and Lieutenant Wilton shall not be given public recognition for your efforts. The gallant Lieutenant Kent shall be accorded full honours as the leader responsible for tracking down the smugglers and putting the Americans in their place. The public will enjoy having another brave hero who gave his life to defend them."

"We were expecting that, sir."

Sir James nodded. "I thought you would be. What you were probably *hoping* was that *HMS Alice* would be given to you as reward. Correct?"

"Sir, I would be a liar if I claimed I wasn't. But I knew it was not to be when I saw Lieutenant Walsh read himself in."

"Well, you *should* have been given command of her. Unfortunately, Captain Rand has his own perspective on that and he has his own favourites. You are not one of them, but then you know that. The news does not get better, though. You recall I committed to submitting a case to the Admiralty to have something given to you? The response came with this packet ship from Barbados and they have declined to approve it. I don't understand why the Admiralty is being as parsimonious as it is, but it may be symptomatic of the larger money problem the government continues to face. I admit it was a bit of stretch to have a warship assigned full time to ferry a spymaster around the Caribbean, but I tried to package the idea with the thought you could do double duty and perform standard tasks any Royal Navy ship would do. Kill two birds at once, as it were. Well, they didn't buy it and I am sorry."

"I appreciate you made the effort, Sir James, and I will not forget. Sir, if I may, what is the role for Lieutenant Wilton and myself to be from here on? Captain Nelson told us this assignment would be for three years and we have now reached it."

"There is no change to orders for either of you, Commander, except that the three year limit has been removed. The First Lord of the Admiralty may change his mind some day, but I doubt it. If anything, I suspect your success with this mission will reinforce the desire to keep you doing exactly what you are doing for some time to come."

Sir James paused a moment and sighed before continuing. "I can see how disappointed you are from the look in your eyes, Commander. But you need to lift yourself up, look beyond this, and understand the situation around you. I have every reason to believe you and Lieutenant Wilton are competent naval officers. The thing is, competent naval officers can be found everywhere. However, competent naval officers who are also capable in the dark arts of spying and ferreting out our enemies before they do us harm are decidedly not found everywhere. Do you not see this combination makes you far more valuable? You and Lieutenant Wilton continue to form an effective team. We would be fools to cast this away."

Evan gave him a slow nod. "I think I see, sir."

"I knew you would. Captain Nelson made it clear to me he felt you two understood your duty, no matter how hard it may be, and everything I have seen these past three years has confirmed to me he was right. And it may get even harder."

"Sir?"

"Commander, I believe you said this man Deschamps told you he thought the situation in France was becoming dire? He is a master of understatement if this is all he said. Our information is the entire country is seething with unrest. It is a tinderbox of powder waiting for a spark. If it was any other country we would not be as concerned, but France? Look, the point is we do not know how this will resolve itself, but we fear the impact on us when it does and this means we need people doing what you and I do now more than ever."

"Even out here, sir?"

"Absolutely. The sugar economy of the Caribbean is of vital importance to us and will continue to be for a long time to come. And if France explodes, as we fear it may, the ripples from the explosion aren't going to leave anyone or anything untouched. Commander Ross, we *need* you and

Lieutenant Wilton. None of this may happen right away, but we must be ready should it happen."

"Sir, Lieutenant Wilton and I understand our duty, as you say. I shall brief him fully on this conversation. I think it safe to speak on his behalf and say you can count on us, sir."

Sir James smiled as he rose from his chair and picked up his valises. "I had no doubt on the point, sir. I shall write soon."

Evan rose too and saluted as Sir James left. Once he was alone he sat back in his chair and he stared with unfocused eyes at the door for several minutes as he processed what the Captain had said.

With a sigh he stirred and reached for a pile of correspondence sitting on the corner of his desk. He pulled one particular letter that had come in via the Barbados packet from the pile and sat contemplating it for a moment. Evan had been about to open it when Sir James had interrupted him.

Unable to contain his interest any longer Evan slit the envelope open and pulled out a three-page letter. Captain Nelson had promised to write when he left over a year ago, but this was the first Evan had heard from him despite having sent two letters of his own to the Captain. Evan gave it a quick scan and then read it again from the beginning at a slower pace. When he finished he put the letter down and sat back in his chair, staring off into space for several long minutes before shaking his head. He rose and put on his uniform jacket, slipping the letter into his pocket. James would be on edge awaiting word of their future and it was unfair to delay any longer. Leaving his office, Evan headed for the Dockyard Dog where James would be waiting.

Evan guessed they could read the story on his face the second he walked in. James was sitting at a table on the verandah with both Alice and Manon keeping him company. Evan slumped into the one remaining chair and ordered ale. No one said anything until it appeared.

"Sir James has left, has he?" asked James.

"He has, but we stay." With a sigh, Evan briefed them on the conversation. As he spoke he watched their reactions with detached interest. James remained impassive, but the tense appearance of the two women disappeared. They didn't smile, though.

"It's all right, Evan," said James, once Evan had finished. "It's good to be considered valuable. I don't know if we'll ever get back on a ship, but being considered valuable at least gives us hope for the future."

Evan grunted and pulled out the letter from Captain Nelson. "Well, we shall see. There's this, too, from Captain Nelson."

James sat forward with interest, but grew a questioning look on his face as he looked at Evan.

Evan shrugged and put the letter on the table in front of them. "The Captain has been beached. He's been put on half pay and the only thing he's in command of now is his own little estate. He's written to all of his patrons to no avail. It sounds like he's been passed over for postings that rightfully should have gone to him and he isn't happy about it. But he seems confident this will change. He says they know of his ability and he still thinks the situation in France will mean employment for us all."

James stared at the letter on the table before looking up at Evan once again and nodding. Turning, James smiled and reached over to put his hand on

Manon's arm. "Well, as you say, we shall see. And in the meantime, here we are."

Manon smiled for the first time and leaned over to give James a kiss. As she did Alice reached for Evan's hand, although her smile was hesitant. "Evan? I know you are disappointed not to get a ship, but I can't say I feel that way. I'm glad you aren't going anywhere."

"Alice," said Evan, as he allowed a smile to come to his own face. "You know a ship is what I've wanted, and a part of me will continue wanting this. But there's a much bigger part of me that wants to stay here with you. So if they keep telling me my duty is to do just that, who am I to argue?"

Evan looked over at James and laughed as James grinned, his arm around Manon. Alice's smile was no longer hesitant as she came over to stand beside Evan with a tear running down her face, pulling him into a close hug that enveloped his head into her ample breasts.

"Yes, James and I know our duty," said Evan as he stared at the bounty enfolding him before looking up at Alice with a grin. She looked back in mock exasperation and pulled him even closer.

The End

Author Notes

As with *Dockyard Dog*, the first novel in this series, actual historical events and the behaviour of people involved serve as the framework for *The Sugar Revolution*.

The Marquis de Lafayette is one of these people, and a most interesting one at that. In the course of my research into the larger historical context I couldn't help coming across him, in much the same way as it would be impossible to miss learning about Horatio Nelson while researching this era. Everything you read about the Marquis in this book is true, including his involvement with the slave James Armistead, although the dinner inspiring the fictional de Bellecourt family never happened. But the Marquis's desire for reform and efforts to bring together the Society of Thirty served as inspiration for *The Sugar Revolution*, because while reading about him it prompted me to think about what might have happened had he made earlier, less organized attempts to change the direction French society was going in.

I found it curious to come across different perspectives on this man. Some reflect a man deserving of enormous respect, while others depict a vain, unscrupulous, glory seeker. I am certain there are people out there far better qualified than I to pronounce with authority which perspective best fits the Marquis. But if he really was a man with a sense of self-importance the size of France, he certainly wasn't alone. He would be in the company of more than a few well-known military and political leaders throughout history.

I think the Marquis was clearly a man who saw change was needed. These were harsh times for the vast majority of people and they were not confined to France, a point I have sought to portray in this novel. Based on the facts I see he attempted to steer a course for the French ship of state through the middle of dangerous waters on either side while new, radical thinking was fermenting everywhere. The Marquis supported change enough to help write The Declaration of the Rights of Man and of the Citizen in 1789, a defining document of the French Revolution. But with the coming of the Revolution people with extreme points of view also came to the fore and, over time, took charge. Despite continuing to promote middle of the road thinking the Marquis would end up in prison for a time.

I could not help considering as I wrote this novel how people with extreme points of view impact our world today, much as they did over two hundred years ago. I think the world needs people with balanced perspectives like the Marquis as much now as it did back then. Were he alive today I believe the Marquis and I could sit over a nice dinner, complete with a bottle of lovely French wine, and enjoy a great conversation. This would include applause from me for his work supporting the cause of liberty for my American friends and for helping write the Declaration of the Rights of Man and of the Citizen.

And then, once again, there is Horatio Nelson. Sent home and put on half pay for several years? A man with the skill and aggressive, driving ambition of Nelson relegated to managing his own little estate and nothing more is almost beyond belief. I suspect I am not alone in seeing a little irony in the eventual hero of the Battle of Trafalgar first being reduced to managing what was in essence a farm. But Prince William Henry was a real person who behaved as bad as described herein and his conflict with Lieutenant Isaac Schomberg was all too real. Nelson's simple faith that he would be rewarded for supporting the Prince regardless of what he did was a serious mistake. Senior officers had to be attuned to political implications of everything they were involved in and Nelson failed to see the embarrassing ramifications stemming from his handling of the matter.

Once on the beach Nelson's options at this point would have been few. A significant portion of the English economy was still very much agrarian at this time, despite the growing impact of The Industrial Revolution. Thus, what an English gentleman in his late twenties with a new wife to support, who knew only the life of the sea, could have done otherwise would indeed have been limited.

Nelson may have pretended he threw himself into the business of being a gentleman farmer and professed happiness during the years before the next conflict brought him a ship, but this is belied by his constant efforts to press for a new posting during the five years he was on the beach. I think he was a caged beast on the inside, lusting to be back at sea as much as my characters Evan and James.

So what does the future hold for Evan and his friend James? Now that both Alice and Manon have had a taste of excitement and have been to sea, will they want more? What will the onset of the French Revolution mean for the Caribbean? And will Nelson reappear in their lives once again? Evan and James may well be right they have not seen the last of Nelson.

To find some answers you'll just have to keep reading. *The Sugar Sacrifice*, the third book in this series, is coming soon.

58942961R00178

Made in the USA
Charleston, SC
24 July 2016